Butter, Sugar, Magic

*Baking Up a Magical Midlife,
Book 1*

by Jessica Rosenberg

Published by Blue Octopus Press

www.BlueOctopusPress.com

(831) 471-7028

Library of Congress Control Number:

Library of Congress Cataloging-in-Publication
Data

Rosenberg, Jessica

Butter, Sugar, Magic / Jessica Rosenberg

Cover design by Karen Dimmick/Arcane Covers

I dedicate this book (and all the ones that follow) to my husband and my children for being the best beta readers and cheerleaders imaginable. Sorry for all the late dinners.

"Reach as high as you can, and then reach a little higher. There you will find magic and possibility. And maybe even cookies."

~ Marc Johns
(marcjohns.com)

ONE

Aurie tossed her tablet onto the seat and groaned. If we'd been in the car so long even the appeal of electronics had faded, we'd been in the car too long. I stretched my neck and tried to figure out how many hours I'd been at the wheel. Definitely too many was the only answer that came to mind.

"Want to find us a place to crash for the night?" I glanced at her via the rearview mirror. She was at that tender age where she could look like a sullen teen one moment and a mischievous kid the next, though these days, I was seeing way more sullen than silly.

"Pool and breakfast?" she asked as she grabbed the phone I handed back to her.

"Pool, for sure. I could use a dip after dinner."

Putting her in charge of hotel bookings and restaurant research had been a stroke of genius. Mostly because it gave her something to focus on other than finding new ways to complain about our unexpected road trip.

"Bonus points if it's near a pizza joint."

"Mmmm, pizza. We haven't had that in a while."

I snorted. We'd had some for dinner the night before.

Guilt over pulling her away from all the summer fun she'd been planning with her friends was only a fraction of the emotional tornado I'd been riding since Max, her father and my husband of almost twelve years, decided out of the blue he was moving out and we had ten days to decide what we wanted to keep before the house went on the market.

To say his declaration had come out of left field was the understatement of the year. I was still reeling from the double-gut punch of losing my home and any semblance of stability. I'd managed to convince him it was insane to force us to move out until the divorce was finalized, but thanks to his golf club cronies, it hadn't taken nearly as long as I had secretly been hoping. Definitely not long enough for me to figure out our next steps.

Max had never let me work. He liked having me at home where I could take care of our baby and be ready to entertain friends or colleagues at a moment's notice. It might not have been the life I'd dreamt of as a child, but I had always felt safe.

As for Max, he'd had nothing to complain about. He had the right job, the right home, a cute kid, and a pleasant enough wife who went out of her way to help him maintain the illusion of status that mattered so much to him and his parents. We weren't lovebird happy, but never in a million years would I have guessed he'd risk damaging his image with something as sordid as a divorce.

When I remembered the prenup clause awarding me half of everything without contest if we broke up would go into effect soon and caught wind of a rumor of a hot new partner at his accounting firm, suddenly, our breakup didn't seem all that surprising anymore.

Whatever the reason, the truth of the matter was that I was a newly middle-aged single mom with zero real life experience and no earthly clue how I was going to care for my pre-teen daughter.

"Maybe she left you an old chamber pot." Aurie's latest guess kept my thoughts from falling into their usual downward spiral.

The call from the anxious-sounding attorney in Massachusetts couldn't have come at a better time. I'd only needed to hear the words "great aunt" and "will" to jump at the chance to drive up to collect whatever she'd left me and put off figuring out our future for a few more days. We had a destination and something to do for the next week. That was more than enough for me, even if I still wasn't sure how I felt about the whole secret great aunt thing.

"Maybe it's an old, haunted Ouija board!" I replied in a spooky whisper that made Aurie giggle.

The silly 'guess what the mysterious great aunt left us' game was the only thing making Aurie laugh, and I counted every giggle as a win. The guesses were getting increasingly ridiculous. My favorite had been a replica of her cat knit from his own hair.

"Hey, Mom?" A little tremor betrayed the anxiety underlying her words. "What are we doing after the lawyer meeting?"

"I told you. After the appointment, we can do whatever you want."

"Can we go home?"

"Everything except that." I did my best to inject a little excitement into my tone. "Onward and upward!"

It hadn't been my intention to be vague about what came after the lawyer's office. I just didn't know what to say. Despite pondering my options over endless stretches of highway, nothing could change the fact that I had no marketable skills. Or the fact that we couldn't afford to live in our old neighborhood on the measly amount of alimony and child support the court had awarded us. *Note to self: Never divorce another man who golfs with the judge.*

I'd shared with her the broad strokes of the breakup, doing my best to make it sound like it wouldn't upend her life, but I was pretty sure she didn't buy it any more than she was buying my "grand adventure" bit, no matter how much ice cream I fed her.

She wanted to be eating ice cream with her friends, *thank you very much*. We'd only been gone a few days, but to hear her, she hadn't seen them in a decade and nothing about our "fun girls' trip up the coast" would trump Becky Edward's big annual birthday slumber party.

"Then I don't care where we go." She shrugged half-heartedly and turned to look out the window.

My heart sank. Why did it feel like nothing short of a magical intervention would get us out of this mess?

TWO

A urie wasn't any more chipper in the morning, though a cinnamon roll from the cute coffee shop around the corner from the lawyer's office was improving her attitude. The double-shot mocha with extra whip in my hand was having a similar effect on me.

The hotel Aurie selected had been comfortable enough, but I still hadn't slept a wink. Too many thoughts, too many unknowns, all of them clamoring for attention. During the day, I could keep moving fast enough to outrun them. But once I lay down, they all crowded around me, leaving me breathless from the weight of everything waiting to go wrong.

I'd finally managed to make a list of potential ways I could support the two of us before I fell asleep. It hadn't been a long list. I could either get a job as a waitress in some quaint little town where rent wouldn't be astronomical, or I could beg my way into a kitchen job at a bakery or restaurant. I had no professional experience, but it wasn't unfathomable my passion for baking might sway some soft-hearted owner. While I was at it, I might as well pretend the owner was secretly a billionaire whose broken heart would be mended by my out-of-this-world brownies.

All joking aside, that was the extent of my list. I had zero secretarial skills, and my quirky degree in food history had seemed fun when I thought I'd have Max to take care of me forever. Now it was laughable. And it wasn't going to earn me enough money to convince Max he'd never be able to take Aurie away from me. Not that he'd even hinted he might be leaning in that direction, but, knowing him, he'd wait for me to be at my lowest before swooping in and demanding sole custody.

I shoved down my rising panic and ushered Aurie into the office ahead of me. The reception area was exactly what I would have expected from a law firm. Stuffy, austere, and unwelcoming. The prim receptionist looked right at home.

"Can I help you?"

I gave myself points for not matching her snooty tone.

"We're here to see Preston Lathrop?" My attempt to win her over with a large smile missed by a mile. The receptionist's dour expression morphed to include a raised eyebrow. Catching a glimpse of the firm's name above her head, I finished lamely. "Junior. Preston Lathrop Junior. He's expecting me."

With a deep sigh, she punched a few keys on her computer. As if she'd conjured him out of thin air, a slim, nervous-looking little man wearing a three-piece suit popped out from a room located a few feet down the hall.

"Mrs. Browne? I'm so glad you're here. Can I get you anything, cup of coffee? Water?" He wrung his hands and smiled nervously at me.

I waggled my paper cup in his direction. "I'm all set." I turned to the receptionist. "Would you mind terribly if my daughter stayed out here with you while we talk?"

"Is she going to make a mess?" The woman's lip curled down in distaste.

"She's a child, not a puppy." I rolled my eyes at her and did my best not to look at the cinnamon roll clutched in Aurie's hand.

The receptionist looked down her nose at Aurie and I got the sense she wasn't convinced I was right.

"Please, please sit." He gestured toward a chair that looked only a hair more comfortable than the ones in the lobby, lowering himself into one that looked equally uncomfortable. I winced for him as he leaned back.

"Thank you." I sat gingerly on the edge of the seat, shifting until I found a tolerable position.

The silence stretched out awkwardly until we both started speaking at once. I waved at him to start.

"Yes, yes. Well, Mrs. Browne."

"It's actually Ms. Berry."

"Oh?" Mr. Lathrop looked flustered for a moment and frowned down at his papers as though they'd misled him.

"Recently divorced. Very recently. A friend suggested it might be a good idea to reclaim my maiden name, normalize things as fast as possible, you know?" The look on his face slowed me down. "Sorry, I ramble when I'm nervous."

"No need to be nervous." His anxious smile almost made me snicker. "I promise I don't bite."

I laughed politely and waited for him to continue.

"I'm sorry if this situation is a little unnerving, Ms.... Berry. Berry? Are you sure? Shouldn't it be Blackwell?" He looked down at his papers again, clearly expecting different information than he'd found there moments before.

"No. When my dad...my mom took back her maiden name and had mine changed as well. So, Berry. Not Blackwell. Because who wants the name of a man who doesn't want them?" My half smile didn't make the comment any less awkward.

"Yes, right, quite so." Mr. Lathrop let me gloss over the situation with my dad without letting more than a twitch of interest cross his face. "Uh..." The conversation had gone so far off the rails he seemed at a loss as to what to say next. The papers on his desk didn't help him any more than they had earlier.

"You said you have some papers for me to sign?" I prompted. Relief relaxed his face.

"Yes! Yes! The papers. As I mentioned over the phone, your great aunt Mrs. Blackwell has left you everything in her estate other than a few knickknacks bequeathed to friends."

"I'm sorry, what?" My eyes threatened to bug out of my head.

Mr. Lathrop looked at me blankly.

"When you called, you never actually told me what I had inherited. I assumed it was some little family heirloom." I couldn't have heard him correctly.

"Oh, my goodness." Mr. Lathrop looked horrified. He glanced at the door a few times as though expecting someone, presumably Mr. Lathrop Senior, to barge in and give him hell for making such a rookie gaffe. "Oh my..." He looked down at the papers and back at me a few times, opening and closing his mouth like a fish.

"Could you maybe repeat what you said?"

BUTTER, SUGAR, MAGIC COPY

Looking relieved to be given some direction, Mr. Lathrop cleared his voice and read from the document. "'As the sole heir to the Blackwell estate, Cassandra Blackwell—'"

"Berry," I interrupted.

"Yes, yes, quite so. I'll have to make a note of that on the papers before we sign them. As I was saying, 'Cassandra Berry shall become the sole proprietor of the Blackwell family bakery and building as well as most of the Blackwell Trust.'"

"Holy shit." The words popped out of my mouth before I could stop them. "Did you really say *bakery*?"

Mr. Lathrop nodded nervously.

"And I'm sorry, but do you have a sense of what exactly 'everything' covers." I cringed. "I'm sorry. I couldn't think of a way to say that without sounding greedy or entitled."

"No, no, please. I'm sorry for not being more forthcoming." His smile wavered slightly, but he plowed on bravely. "Right, so, Mrs. Blackwell owned a bakery downtown. Well, really, the whole building, which comprises the apartment above the bakery and well, the bakery, as I mentioned. Your great aunt also had some modest savings which are also part of your inheritance."

"So we're clear, you're really saying 'bakery'? I want to make sure I'm not hearing things."

Mr. Lathrop glanced down at the paper as if he hadn't just read the words out loud. "Yes, bakery. A bakery in a small town with a fully furnished apartment above it."

Words completely failed me.

THREE

You will never believe what just happened at that lawyer meeting.

My hands shook as I typed the text. The thing that had just happened in that office didn't happen in real life. Mysterious great aunts didn't suddenly up and die and leave you entire buildings. Especially not buildings containing a bakery. I could count on Stacey to let me know if I had officially lost my mind. Because it truly was starting to feel like I had.

> **Was that today? What did the old lady leave you?**

> **I think I might be going crazy.**

> **What else is new?**

Brace yourself.
It seems I just inherited a bakery.

And I met a billionaire who's whisking me
off to Tahiti.

Stacey! I'm not even joking a little.
A building. A bakery. And some money.

What are you drinking?
I want some.

I'm not drinking. It's 10am.

Hasn't stopped you before.

OK. Fine. Maybe. But I am not drunk
Or mentally altered in any way.
Though I might be dreaming.
Am I dreaming?

I don't know. Are you? Am I? Pinch yourself.

Ouch. Must be awake.

Back up a couple steps.
Did you really inherit a bakery? Or are you shitting me?

Uh...I think I really inherited a bakery.

Holy shit. This is HUGE.
I need more details.
Can I call you? This seems like a bigger conversation.

Can't talk. Haven't told Aurie anything yet.

ARG. Give me the broad strokes.

Long story short.
My father's aunt died. I'm her only heir.
She left me a bakery and the apartment above it.

Was she really a baker? That's...uncanny.

Right!?

And she was rich?

No. But the lawyer says the building could be worth something.

Seriously? How much are we talking?

Not sure. But...

But?

A bakery.

It all sounds a little too good to be true.
We're sure this isn't an elaborate scam?

Was I being scammed? Her question dimmed the little flame of hope that had flickered to life in my chest while the lawyer had detailed everything my mysterious great aunt had left me.

I don't think so. Fuck. What if?
I mean, I have nothing, what good would scamming do anyone?
And how can giving me a building and a bakery be a scam?

Let's not panic until we have all the facts.
Have you seen the place yet?

No. Now I'm imagining that it's in ruins or something.

Wait, can Max claim any of it?

Lawyer says no.
It's all mine. Whatever "it" is.
The great aunt included a clause in her will.

He is so not going to like that.

No. He is not.

"Mom. Can we go?" Aurie's whine pulled me away from my phone. Her final shred of patience had vanished along with the last smear of cinnamon roll frosting. She was kicking the car's tires, gearing up for a Class-A meltdown. I could see it written all over her face.

"I, ah," I choked out around the ball of fear lodged in my throat. Chatting with Stacey hadn't settled me at all. If anything, it had confused me even more.

I'd gone from feeling numb and paralyzed about our future to holding a tiny nugget of glimmering hope and now I was settling in some sort of terror-filled, in-between state. I didn't want to hope this was going to turn out to be the answer to all of our problems, but I couldn't keep myself from feeling I had somehow lucked into being handed the dream I'd secretly harbored my entire life.

Part of me didn't want to know, didn't want the illusion to burst when I said anything about it out loud. If it was a dream, I wanted to stay in it a little bit longer. Plus, I had Aurie's emotional well-being to consider. After everything she'd been through this month, the last thing she needed was another disappointment.

Sure, Cassie, *let's pretend that's the real reason you aren't going to say anything.*

"Yep, we're all done here. We just have to check out one tiny thing, but it's on the way to Boston. So, it won't take us too far out of our way. That's cool, right? Hey, did I ever tell you about the famous duck pond in Boston?"

She rolled her eyes hard at me. Right, eleven-year-olds don't care about ducks.

"Does this have something to do with what great aunt what's-her-face left you?"

"It does!" I said brightly before quickly changing the subject. No use getting her worked up over something that might turn out to be nothing. "This next town is on the water. We can go to the beach if you want."

She looked skeptical. "Can we have a beach picnic?"

"Sure! Hey, I bet we can even get lobster rolls!"

"What's a lobster roll?" She made a disgusted face.

I laughed and pulled her into a side hug. "You're going to love them. I promise."

FOUR

"**W**hat are you looking at, Mom? We already had breakfast. Plus, it's closed," Aurie said, glancing up from her tablet.

I was too mesmerized by the bakery in front of me to answer. I rolled down the window to get a clearer look. Not a ruin. Not a hole in the wall. Not something made up to get me to hand over my personal information or however identity thieves operate. Just the most perfect bakery I could ever have imagined, smack dab in the middle of the most adorable downtown I'd ever seen.

La Baguette Magique!

The name was painted in a swirly font on a huge glass window framed in a pretty periwinkle blue. A loaf of French bread shooting sparks from the tip was stenciled under the name. Max would have hated everything about the place. The fantasy-loving child in me adored it. It was literally the bakery of my dreams, as in, I was pretty sure I had actually dreamed of this exact bakery at some point. And, if the lawyer was to be believed, it was mine. All mine. *My* pretty little bakery in the heart of a pretty little town.

"Aurie, pinch me."

She looked up from her game, scowl at the ready. "What?"

"Never mind." Shaking her head at the general absurdity of grown-ups, she went back to her screen.

Pinching my own arm did nothing to dispel the mirage in front of me.

When the lawyer said bakery, I heard Max snort dismissively in my head. *Foodservice! Ha! Total time and money suck.* I knew he was right. There was no way to get rich slinging coffee and croissants. Well, okay, a few people had, but they were making it near impossible for anyone else to do the same.

I tried to rein in my galloping imagination. It was all too easy to see myself in there, selling pastries and bread, chatting with regulars, loving every minute of it. But it simply wasn't a rational choice. Running a bakery wasn't a realistic career option for a single mom. And Aurie's dad lived a zillion miles from here. Not to mention the fact I knew exactly nothing about running a business of any kind, let alone something foodservice related.

I glanced down at Aurie. It had been a long two days and I absolutely had to deliver on my promise of lunch and fun, but first, I needed to set foot in the bakery. Just to see.

I mean, it was the responsible thing to do, right? We had nowhere to go after we explored Boston. The lawyer had mentioned a fully furnished move-in-ready apartment. If this place was livable, it would be smart to use it as our home base until I figured out what came next.

The rationale was flimsy at best, but I clung to it for dear life. I just wanted to see it. Walk around. Imagine myself living there. Indulge my inner child a little longer. After the last few weeks, I owed myself this tiny fleck of joy.

Despite my resolve, I didn't get out of the car immediately, instead letting my eyes drift lovingly over the store's façade, (*cheesy*) taking in the intricate baguettes carved into the molding around the window (*absurd*). The phantom scent of warm bread toying with my nose (*You've really lost it now, Cassandra*).

Shut up, Max! I hissed at the relentless voice. *I know running a bakery is a foolish endeavor. I know that huge shop window is just waiting for a kid to shatter it with a stray ball. I know I don't*

*know the first thing about managing a business. I
know I'm useless when it comes to long-term plans.
Just get out of my head and let me dream for one
freaking second!*

I let out a long slow breath and, miraculously,
the voice faded away. My eyes drifted around the
outside of the bakery. Cheesy, absurd, and utterly
adorable. The whole thing called to something
deep in my soul and I couldn't stop a goofy smile
from spreading across my face.

"What is wrong with you? You've been acting
weird all morning." Aurie peered at me suspiciously.
"I thought we were going to the beach. Is this place
where we're getting the lobster rolls? Because, in
case you hadn't noticed, it's closed."

"No," I chuckled. "We'll find lunch closer to the
water. There's something we have to do first."

"Why is that woman looking at us?" Aurie pointed
and I quickly pushed her hand down as I turned to
look where she was gesturing.

As if looking at her had been enough of an
invitation, the eccentric looking woman peeping
out at us from the doorway of the brightly colored
storefront next door to the bakery started making
her way toward the car. We extricated ourselves
from our seatbelts and got out as she got near
enough for me to notice she was middle aged, like

me, and was beaming at us like she recognized long lost friends.

"You're Cassandra, right?" Her obvious excitement at seeing me was almost as disconcerting as the fact that she knew my name.

"Uh, no, I mean, yes, I am Cassandra, but I usually go by Cassie." I gave her a puzzled look. "How...how did you know?"

She ignored my question. "I thought it might be you. The bakery is going to be so excited you've arrived. I *love* how it turned out!"

"The bakery is going to be excited?" Aurie leaned around me to get a closer look at the delighted woman.

"Oh, for sure! Without a doubt, sweetheart." Her laugh was almost musical. "It's been waiting a long time to meet you."

I heard Aurie open her mouth and breathed a little sigh of relief when she closed it again without saying anything. I couldn't think of any way to explain what this woman was saying, and I couldn't think of how to extricate ourselves from this exchange, but there was no doubt engaging her wasn't going to help our cause.

"Don't let me hold you up. Just wanted to introduce myself. I'm Harriet, though I go by Hattie for the most part. I own the pet shop." Now that she mentioned it, the items displayed in the window were clearly animal related, but her shop looked more like Ali Baba's cavern of treasures than a pet shop. A hanging sign above the door read "*A Familiar Place*," which made no sense. Maybe it had some bizarre family meaning. "I'm thrilled you're both here. I have a good feeling about you guys. I'm right there if you need anything, but I know the bakery will take good care of you."

Her gaze shifted from me to Aurie and, after giving her an intense once over, she winked. "I have a feeling I'll be seeing you sooner rather than later, young lady. I'm looking forward to it." She leaned over absentmindedly to rub the head of the fat orange cat winding itself around her ankles. He was so focused on my face he didn't acknowledge her pat. To say it was unsettling was putting it mildly. "Persimmon is thrilled you're here, too." How she deduced that from his bored expression was beyond me. "He likes meeting new friends."

The cat sniffed in disdain. Without so much as a glance backwards, he stalked proudly to the bakery entrance. Once he realized we weren't rushing to open the door, he let out an annoyed yowl and started grooming his nether regions. Hattie laughed at him.

"Don't mind him, he's just a cranky old man," she called over her shoulder on her way back to her store. I gaped at her as she walked away. She vanished into the store and popped right back out.

"You don't need the key!" she called over.

"I'm sorry, what?"

"The bakery knows who belongs." She winked at me and ducked back into the store.

I blinked in her direction. Maybe I really was dreaming. It was certainly starting to feel like it. Ignoring her comment, I fumbled for the key I'd shoved into my purse the instant the lawyer had handed it to me.

Aurie, fully focused on the orange tabby now sunning himself in front of the door, missed the entire exchange. How I'd managed to already forget about him was beyond me.

"Uh, excuse me? No one ever said anything about a cat!" I called toward Hattie's store, but she didn't pop her head back out.

I had two options, ride this fever dream to its conclusion or force myself to wake up. Awake, I'd have to face the shambles of my life. Asleep, I could visit a charming bakery and pretend everything was miraculously working out in my favor.

I stepped over the cat and grabbed the door handle.

The door opened with a *snick* before I'd even finished putting in the key. I yanked my hand back. I hadn't turned the key. Or the handle. The door shouldn't have opened. I glanced down at Aurie. The cat stared back at me with a bored look. For an instant, it even looked like he rolled his eyes at me. When I didn't move, he flicked his tail in annoyance and pushed the door open with his head.

"Mom! The cat went in!" Aurie scrambled to her feet and darted through the door.

The little nudge pushing me forward made sense in this dream reality. But the way the ground vibrated under my feet when I hesitated at the threshold was definitely weird. I reached out a hand and grasped the doorjamb to keep my balance and the building seemed to sigh with contentment when I touched it. I swallowed a startled cry.

It's a dream, Cassie. Weird stuff happens in dreams.

Doing my best to ignore the way my neck was tingling, I stepped into the bakery.

FIVE

For a dream, it all felt incredibly real. The cool wrought iron of the door handle felt solid under my hand and the lingering scent of bread and coffee made my mouth water. Had anything ever felt so real in a dream before? I couldn't remember. Either way, it had to be a dream. *Reality could never be this perfect*, I thought as I gaped at the interior of the bakery.

I blinked a few times, but everything stayed exactly as it was. Black and white checkered tile floor, French gray marble bistro tables and chairs, a gleaming counter begging to be piled high with pastries and cookies. There was even an ornate old-fashioned cash register partially blocking the view of wooden racks that would look amazing filled with golden bread loaves.

Utterly impractical. Who wants to clean those out every day? Max scoffed in my head.

Me. I would, I replied, easily imagining myself sweeping up breadcrumbs with the cute little broom I could see leaning next to the racks. My eyes continued their exploration. The sight of a refrigerated case for cakes and cream-filled pastries made my heart thump. And, oh, was that an espresso machine next to the bread rack? My mouth watered.

I was still taking in all of the details of the space around me when Aurie popped out of a set of swinging doors, clutching the cat to her chest. He was struggling in her arms, determined to get down. She released him and with a grace that belied his roundness, the orange feline thumped to the ground and strutted away, his tail sticking straight up in the air.

"You are going to freak when you see this kitchen, Mom. Come see!" Any trace of the disinterest she'd shown when I parked the car had vanished, leaving in its place unbridled, little-kid excitement.

In my hurry to follow her back through the swinging doors, I didn't notice the cat had settled himself right in front of me until I almost stepped on him. My feet went in opposite directions, and I crashed to the ground. The disdainful look on his face as I sat up and rubbed my knee was exactly the reason I'd never liked cats.

Aurie rushed back into the room. "What happened? Are you okay?"

"I'm not dreaming, am I?"

She frowned at me. "Did you hit your head when you fell?"

"No, it's just...never mind. Help me up, will you?" The solidity of the tiles when I'd crash landed on them had jarred me back to reality. This was no dream. Those tiles had been hard and cold. And the light streaming through the store window was warming my skin in a very tangible way. So, unless I was in something more like a coma than a dream, this bakery was real. And it was mine. I just couldn't bring myself to wrap my head around it.

"Wait, *this* is what the great aunt left you?" Aurie looked around with a dubious frown before giving me a look that made it quite clear she thought I'd finally lost it. A hint of distrust appeared in her eyes, and honestly, after the last month, I couldn't exactly fault her. I'd been doling out life-altering pronouncements like I was a Pez dispenser.

After I hobbled through the bakery kitchen, which, Aurie had been right, nearly made me pee my pants with excitement, the cat had meowed loudly at a door hiding the stairs leading up to the apartment. We followed him up to explore what I was hoping would be our digs for a few days.

Like the bakery below, the apartment looked plucked straight from my head. It even had a sweet little window seat overlooking the cutest back yard in the small kitchen's breakfast nook. Though, for a moment, I could have sworn the window seat had only appeared after I'd thought the space was perfect for one, so maybe I really did need to get my head examined.

The apartment was bigger than I'd expected. Way bigger than the downstairs somehow. Three rooms, one of which featured twin beds each covered in gauzy canopies, perfect for giggly girl sleepovers. To Aurie's delight, we found Persimmon curled up tight on one of the beds, purring so loud we could hear him from the doorway.

The rooms were all cozy and adorable, but the way my heart stuttered at the sight of the kitchen confirmed I was really and truly awake. This room hadn't been designed from my dreams; it was better than anything I could have imagined.

The large room—big enough for both cooking and entertaining—was decorated in an explosion of cottage-core chic that gave my heart a pang. I'd always wanted to decorate my home like this. Max would have rather been caught in a scandalous, homo-erotic three-way affair than let our "friends" think we were country bumpkins. Standing in the sunny kitchen with sweet flower wallpaper and blousy curtains, I already felt more at home in this apartment than I had ever felt in the house I'd spent countless hours decorating to his taste.

"Okay, here's the deal." I glanced over at Aurie to assess her mood. Wary, but listening. I could work with that. "According to the lawyer I saw this morning, this place belonged to my Great Aunt Beatrice. She died unexpectedly a few months ago, and, since we're her only living relatives, she left it all to us. So, by ours, I mean we own this place." I braced myself for an outburst.

"So...not a weird taxidermied squirrel?"

I shook my head no.

"I don't get it."

I took a deep breath. "I had a great aunt. She died. She left us this entire building. The end."

"No, I get that part. I mean, kinda. I don't get why it matters."

Ah, the wonders of growing up without ever having to think about money.

"Well, right now it matters because we don't have anywhere else to live."

She frowned at me, her face the picture of confusion.

"Yes, we do."

"No, babe, we really don't. Remember? I explained to you we had to sell the house?"

She rolled her eyes. "Duh." Fair, she hadn't exactly taken the speed packing well. "But we can't live here. We live in Georgia. We've always lived in Georgia. My friends live in Georgia. Dad lives in Georgia!"

Her voice got more and more shrill as her eyes got bigger and bigger and the worst part was I knew exactly how she felt. My mother had moved us a few times during my childhood and I had always hated feeling powerless every time she announced we were leaving. The words to make this right eluded me as my own emotions welled up. I reached out a hand that she batted away with a glower.

"We are here on vacation! You promised! You said we were coming here to see some stupid ducks and eat gross lobster rolls. You never said anything about living here!"

Tears gathered in the corners of her eyes, and she rubbed them away angrily.

"I know! I know. But I said all that before we found out about this place. And isn't it nice? Isn't it so much nicer than a nasty motel?" I could hear myself begging and I hated it. The apartment and the bakery had enchanted me so fast I'd let myself forget the cold hard facts of our situation. I'd let the dream win for a little too long. Watching Aurie's heart break was the bucket of cold water I needed.

"So, we're, like, going to live here? Like, forever? That's it? You've decided?" The anger in her voice had quickly given way to disgust.

"No! No! Sweetheart. I didn't say that! I said we should stay here right now. Maybe we can spend the summer here. We can discuss our long-term plan together, later." I mentally squared my shoulders and turned a deaf ear to the voice in my head screaming, 'YES, YES, YES! MINE, MINE, MINE!' and shot her the most reassuring smile I could muster. My dreams didn't matter. Aurie mattered. She was my number one priority. She had to be.

"Whatever. You're going to make the decision anyway." She shrugged, doing her best to act like she didn't actually care, but I saw her blink back more tears. My heart crawled higher up my throat. "Can I go outside?"

"Sure! That's a great idea!" My voice came out too high, and my heart twinged when she visibly recoiled. "If you decide to climb that tree, try not to fall out!" She didn't even sneer in response, and I winced. The last few weeks had weakened the trust between us. I'd thrown her curveball after curveball, and I didn't blame her one bit for her attitude. It was going to take a lot more than duck ponds and lobster rolls to fix this.

I leaned against the wall and let out a sigh. When Max had dropped his bombshell, a pit had formed in my gut I'd been forced to ignore as I dealt with the immediate fallout of losing my home and suddenly finding myself faced with financial insecurity. I'd done my best to not spend every waking hour obsessing about how I was going to keep us fed and warm, but the fear that had been keeping me up at night had been getting more and more intense. To have a solution fall out of the sky like this... I didn't even know what to think.

But I did know for the first time in weeks I no longer felt the need to avoid my thoughts. Nothing urgent called to me other than maybe checking to see if the beds had sheets on them. I took a deep breath and let it out slowly, savoring how much easier breathing had suddenly become.

Just a few weeks. Just to get my bearings and figure out a solid life plan to keep us housed, fed, and happy.

The apartment was truly incredible. Ridiculously amazing. Warm, welcoming, cozy. And I couldn't keep from grinning even thinking about the state-of-the-art professional bakery kitchen below.

The floor vibrated slightly under my feet like it had when we had first come in. As far as I knew, Massachusetts wasn't prone to earthquakes. Could it be some kind of machinery in the basement? I was going to have to check because I couldn't think of anything else that would make the building feel like it was purring contentedly. Hattie's words echoed in my head.

Get a grip, Cassie. The bakery isn't happy we're here.

OMG, Stacey. This place...

I fired off the text from the cozy window seat. I'd been right, this was a perfect spot for it. I could sit here and watch Aurie play in the garden. Right now, she was perched in a tree engrossed in what looked like an intense staring contest with a squirrel. Maybe it was telling her how awesome living in New England could be. One could only hope.

That bad?

No. That good. It's incredible.
So much better than I could have ever hoped.

Seriously?

Seriously. I almost wish it weren't so awesome.

What? Why not?

Kid. Max. Georgia…you know.
Life. Responsible adulting. All that.

Gimme a break.

None of this feels real.

I keep telling you, if it's too good to be true,
it probably isn't.

No, it's real. I have the papers.
It just feels like I'm dreaming.

I'm really happy for you.
Sounds like you're finally getting the break
you deserve.

I smiled and put my phone back in my pocket. Stacey and I had been friends since we'd met at a new mom support group, tired, stressed, and desperate for a little relief from the grind of new motherhood. The other moms had all been perfectly decked out, uptight, and crazy intimidating, but I'd spotted the one other woman with dried spit up on her shoulder the instant I walked in the door. While the other moms gossiped over the sad snacks supplied by the organizer, we snuck out to get coffee. We've been inseparable ever since. Luckily, our daughters had also developed a tight bond.

I'd never missed anyone more than I missed her right then and there. Being close to Stacey? Definitely another plus in the go-back-to-Georgia column.

SIX

T he fancy espresso machine located behind
the bakery counter hissed and gurgled at me
before spitting out three drops of tar-colored water
and a glop of wet coffee grounds. Cajoling, yelling,
cussing, caressing, and even watching half a dozen
videos on how to make it work did nothing to
help me produce a hot, tasty latte as a reward
for my efforts. I was so focused on the blasted
machine, when somebody said hello right behind
me, I almost threw my sadly still-empty mug at
them.

"Oh, I am so sorry! I didn't mean to give you
a heart attack. I was stopping by to welcome you
to Portney and introduce myself." The friendly
looking woman didn't seem at all fazed by the fact
I'd almost committed ceramic assault on her. She
stood there in her light- blue dress that looked fresh
from the pages of a 1990s L.L. Bean catalog and

smiled at me. I half expected her to also be wearing bobby socks.

On me, the dress would have looked boxy and ridiculous. On her, it looked sweet and a little old-fashioned. Not that my jeans, t-shirt, and plaid button-down outfit was anything to brag about. Max preferred me in pressed slacks and monochromatic cashmere twinsets. Throwing every single one of those sweater-sets into the Goodwill bin had been the highlight of my move.

Realizing I was staring, I pulled my eyes from her dress and met her smile with one of my own.

"Hi. Sorry! I wasn't expecting anyone to stop by. As you can see," I gestured to the empty counter in front of me, "we aren't exactly open yet." The *yet* surprised me as much as it delighted her.

"So, you *are* going to open?" She clasped her hands in front of her chest and gave a little happy squeal. "I miss the smells that used to float out of here in the morning."

"Uh, I'm not sure why I said that." I bit my lip and ran my eyes over the bakery. "I..."

After a long afternoon at the beach, during which Aurie and I had struck a tentative truce and agreed to enjoy ourselves for a few days, we'd picked up some Chinese food to eat in front of the TV. She'd almost fallen asleep mid-bite, and I tucked her into one of the twin beds before pouring myself a generous glass of wine and calling Stacey. We chatted long into the night, and by the time I drained my second glass, she'd almost managed to convince me I'd be an idiot to pass up an opportunity like this. I argued Aurie needed to be close to her dad and her friends and I could easily sell this place and maybe open a similar place down south, but she'd shot down each reasonable point I presented.

Her primary argument was that it was okay for me to pursue my dreams and Aurie would be better off in the wrong town with a happy, fulfilled mom than she would be in the right town with a bored, miserable one.

That had made perfect sense when I was slightly buzzed. Now that I was dealing with a sleepless night, a mild hangover, and a super high-tech coffee machine that wouldn't play nice, I was solidly back on the staying-in-Portney-isn't-an-option side of the fence.

At least I thought I'd been. The reasons I absolutely could not run a bakery while raising Aurie on my own were clear-cut and obvious. Selling this building would net me enough money to go back to Georgia, rent a reasonably small place, and find some kind of secretarial job to pay the bills. I could learn to type and file. How hard could it be?

My heart didn't seem to be listening to any of it. I could see myself here, welcoming customers and selling them pastries and bread and watching them enjoy cups of coffee with friends. I didn't have the first clue about ordering supplies or keeping track of expenses or any of the other things running a bakery would probably entail. And despite all that, the yearning in my soul was so intense, it was almost making my body vibrate with need.

"Well, I'll keep my fingers crossed, Cassandra. Portney wouldn't be the same without a Blackwell baker!"

I blinked at her, wondering if I'd know how she knew my name if I was caffeinated.

"Oh, I am so sorry, how rude of me. I totally forgot to introduce myself! I'm Juliette Matthews, owner of the bookshop down the street." She stuck her hand out over the counter and I shook it limply.

"A bookstore in this day and age?" The question popped out before I could stop it. I definitely wouldn't have been as rude if I'd had even a tiny sip of coffee. She waved off my embarrassed grimace with a smile.

"I know, it's crazy, but I believe every small town needs a bookstore, and..." she lowered her voice and leaned in, "it's not like Amazon carries the kinds of books the locals are into, right?"

"Uh..." I found myself blinking at her again without knowing what to say. Amazon carried everything. What on earth could the people around here be into that they didn't stock?

"In any case, I love what you've done with the place, and I can't wait to taste what you bake. Good luck with that beast," she said, nodding at the machine now making odd noises behind me. "I'm right down the street if you need anything!"

She breezed out the door with a cheery wave. I turned back to the machine, determined to make it work so I could somehow process our bizarre exchange.

Forty minutes later, largely thanks to the magic of the internet and the fact I never know when to quit, I was finally nursing a sorry excuse for a latte. It was by far the worst cup of coffee I'd ever made, but large helpings of cream and sugar had made it nearly palatable.

Once the espresso machine and I had come to a tentative truce, I turned my attention to preparing some breakfast for Aurie. The kitchen in the apartment would have been more than sufficient to make a few pancakes, but given this might be the only time in my life I'd get to cook in a state-of-the-art commercial kitchen like this one, I couldn't bring myself to pass up the opportunity.

Much to my surprise, the storeroom was fully stocked with high-end flour, sugar, all sorts of chocolate, and thankfully, top-of-the-line coffee beans. A further search revealed a modest walk-in fridge packed with butter, eggs, heavy cream, and milk. I had no clue how any of the stuff was still fresh, but I was grateful enough not to question my good fortune.

After days of eating mediocre motel waffles, I figured she'd be thrilled to eat something homemade. Though if she didn't wake up soon, it was possible I'd eat the entirety of the Dutch baby happily baking in my gleaming commercial oven. It wouldn't be the end of the world if I did; she was also a fan of the chocolate chip muffins I had whipped up.

"I don't know the first thing about running a bakery," I had argued to Stacey the night before. She'd brushed me off, pointing out people opened coffee shops and bakeries every other day so it couldn't be all that hard. Again, that had made perfect sense to buzzed Cassie. Now, with the sun shining through the pretty storefront window, lighting up this not-so-hypothetical bakery, her cavalier take on it was almost funny. And yet, the longer I spent in this kitchen, the more I was tempted to try.

Presumably, the hardest part of opening a bakery was decorating and outfitting a place, but this one was already perfect as it was. So, if I started slow, only made a few pastries and cakes, or pies, until I could work up to a full menu. I'd never baked in any sort of large capacity before, but how hard could it be to scale up my favorite recipes. Great Aunt Bea had left us just enough money to bankroll a few trial months. The most challenging part would be figuring out the coffee thing—I glared at the espresso machine—and convincing Aurie trying something out didn't mean I was committing for the long term.

Lured by the tantalizing scent of the Dutch baby, Aurie stumbled into the kitchen, rubbing her eyes sleepily.

"Hey, babe! There are still a few minutes on the timer, so how about you run back upstairs and brush your teeth and put on some real clothes."

She scowled at me. "But I like my jammies."

"I know, love, and your emoji jammies are adorbs, but I was thinking we could eat at one of the bistro tables in the bakery, and I'm not sure you want people walking by to see them."

I preempted her protest by shooing her back to the stairs, but she managed to make her displeasure known by stomping up each step as loudly as possible.

She was never going to buy it. Guilt tore through my burgeoning hope and threw me right back where I had started.

A tap on the door interrupted my spiral into how I was selfish to put my wants before her needs and how terrible a mother I was. The friendly face framed with loose auburn curls peering at me through the glass was a welcome distraction.

I opened the door and graced my visitor with an apologetic smile. "I'm sorry, but we're not open yet." I gestured vaguely at the empty store behind me. There was that *yet* again. It was determined to sneak itself in.

"Of course not. That would be crazy. You arrived less than twenty-four hours ago! I'm just here to welcome you to town. I'm Crystal Watkins. I was your great aunt's…" this time she was the one who gestured at the shop behind me.

"Her…?" I replied, my brain completely failing to fill in her blank.

"Oh, you know, coffee girl, salesgirl, waitress. You name it, I probably did it." She chuckled. "Did you find everything you needed in the pantry and fridge? Your great aunt made me promise I'd stock everything before you arrived."

My heart did a happy somersault. "Stop right there. I didn't hear a word after you said coffee. Are you telling me you know how to work that *thing*?" I pointed to the machine and glared at it in disgust.

"Well, not that one exactly. Bea had an older model, but they all pretty much function the same way." She pushed past me and made her way to the back of the shop. I felt weirdly protective as she started to fiddle with the knobs on the machine, but reason prevailed. If she could figure the monstrosity out, she was welcome to play with it however she desired.

"Please, show me. I'll be your friend forever."

She let out an infectious peal of laughter. "By the way, I really like what you've done with the place!"

"I have no idea why everyone keeps saying that. It was like this when we arrived yesterday."

She turned to me, her head cocked to the side and her lips pursed into a contemplative expression. One eyebrow crept skyward as she looked me up and down. "Huh. Interesting. Let me make us some coffee. Then we can talk."

SEVEN

"So..." Crystal started, seating herself across from me at the little table. She set down an espresso that had only taken her a twist of a wrist and pull of a lever to create. It would have been more irritating if she hadn't placed a gorgeous, frothy latte in front of me. "Just how much do you know about your great aunt?"

Her smile was open and genuine, but the glint in her eyes made her question seem more loaded than it sounded.

"Uh, nothing, actually. I didn't even know she existed until a few days ago."

"So, your dad never..." She raised one eyebrow suggestively.

"My dad ran out on my mom and me when I was a toddler. Haven't seen him since." Over the years I'd edited the story down to two short sentences. It barely hurt to say them out loud.

Crystal nodded knowingly and took a small sip of her coffee. I winced in sympathy. Straight espresso. Bad ass. I took a comforting swig of my own overly sweetened drink and sighed with pleasure. I loved the feeling of sugar coursing all the way through my body with the caffeine hot on its heels. Though, as each sip cleared my head a bit, the weirdness of the morning started to crystalize, leaving me more than a little off kilter.

"Why do you ask?" I leaned back as nonchalantly as possible, so I wouldn't look as unsettled as I felt.

Crystal drained her coffee and leaned back in her own chair leaving her hands on the table to play with a little packet of sugar. "It's a long story and it's not really mine to tell but given your great aunt is no longer with us and there really isn't anyone else, I might as well be the one."

"That doesn't sound mysterious at all."

Crystal smiled at my humorous attempt to lighten the conversation and asked if I'd noticed anything strange since I'd arrived.

"Uh..."

"Trust me, nothing you can say will surprise me." She made a little out-with-it gesture with her hands.

"Well, there was the window seat..." I trailed off, feeling ridiculous even saying it.

"What about the window seat?" Crystal leaned forward a little.

"It's stupid, but I could have sworn there wasn't one in the kitchen until I thought there should be one." I snorted a laugh at my own ridiculousness.

"What else?" she asked, her tone dead serious.

I hesitated and glanced around the shop, plucked directly from my dreams, all the way down to the drawer pulls and light fixtures. Everything was exactly what I would have picked out if I'd been decorating a bakery. It was an incredible coincidence, but there was no way that was what she meant.

I thought some more and something I'd forgotten surfaced.

"When I first checked out all the bedrooms, I only saw queen beds, but after my daughter checked them out, one of the rooms had twin beds in it."

Crystal nodded knowingly. "Perfect for sleepovers. Anything else?"

Maybe it wasn't coincidence? More weirded out than I'd ever been, I took a deep breath and continued.

"Well, there's this place." I gestured all around me with a little shrug.

"What about this place?"

"Well, for starters, it's perfect. Exactly the shop I once dreamed I'd have. And everyone keeps telling me they like what I did with the place. But I had no hand in decorating it." The words came out in a rush, and I looked away so I wouldn't see the ridicule I was sure was plastered all over her face.

Crystal opened her mouth, but I beat her to the punch.

"Oh, and the apartment upstairs is way bigger than it should be compared to the square footage down here. And..." Crystal interrupted me with a laugh and a wave of her hands.

"Enough, enough. I get the gist. It all makes perfect sense."

"It does?" I looked at her dubiously.

"Absolutely. But it's a lot to swallow. I'm not sure how you're going to take it."

The unsettled feeling that had been brewing intensified, and I crossed my arms protectively across my chest. Crystal winced slightly when she noticed my frown.

"Let me start by asking you this. What do you know about magic?"

An unexpected laugh burst out of me.

"Good one." Crystal stayed silent and lifted an eyebrow invitingly. "Fine, well, let's see. I've obviously read the *Harry Potter* series and my fair share of paranormal fiction, fiction being the operative word."

Crystal's eyebrow inched a little higher and she shot me a small, mysterious smile. Her eyes twinkled with mischief. She wiggled her fingers and drew my attention to her hands as a tiny glowing ball of fire appeared above her open palms.

"Holy sh..." I leapt out of my seat knocking my chair to the ground in my haste to back away from the table, glancing quickly at the door to make sure Aurie hadn't come back into the room without me noticing.

"You! I! That! Fire!" Four sentences tried to make it out of my mouth at the same time and got completely stuck in the process, making me sound like a demented toddler. Instead of trying again, I pointed repeatedly at her hands as though she might have somehow not seen the flaming ball hovering over the bistro table. The most important of the four sentences burst free. "Fire!" I looked around frantically as if maybe I'd see a fire extinguisher lying around.

With a twist of her hands, the little ball of fire vanished without leaving even a wisp of smoke behind as proof I hadn't imagined the whole thing.

"What. The. Fuck? Excuse my language. Wait, no, don't excuse my language. Swearing is a perfectly reasonable reaction when a total stranger lights her hands on fire in front of you."

Suddenly, every single reason I'd had to sell this place and race back to Georgia seemed beyond reasonable. Instinct screamed at me to run from the shop and keep running until every bizarre thing about this place was far, far behind me, but Aurie was in the apartment above us, and no matter how freaked out I was, there was no way I was leaving her behind.

Without taking my eyes off her hands, I squatted down to pick up my chair and set it down about three feet away from the table. And there I hesitated. Did I run upstairs to protect Aurie? Grab the chair and use it to protect myself as I ousted Crystal? Or was I radically overreacting? Maybe I'd imagined the whole thing, hallucinated through my coffee high? I stood behind the chair like an idiot, too shaken to come any closer.

"Take a deep breath. You're okay," Crystal said gently. My eyes rolled wildly in response. I almost laughed when the most logical reason behind all of this popped into my head.

"What did you put in my coffee?" I demanded, glancing from the cup sitting safely on the table, nice and far away, to her hands.

"It's not the coffee." Her smile was gentle. "I promise. I only put the usual stuff in there. Coffee, chocolate, milk, sugar, and maybe a smidge of magic."

"Magic isn't real," I said, glaring. "It's a thing writers make up to entertain their readers. Science is real. Magic isn't."

In response, she flicked her fingers and this time three orbs made of swirling rainbows danced above her hand.

"It's a trick. You've got a flashlight tucked into your sleeve or something." I focused my gaze on her eyes and made a concerted effort to not look at her bare arms.

Crystal stood up and took two steps away from the table, leaving the colorful orbs dancing over her coffee cup. She brandished her arms and waved her hands at the table like an old-school magician's assistant. "Ta-dah. No tricks, no strings, no flashlights." She moved back to her seat and wiggled her fingers around the balls of light. They vanished with a little pop.

"Magic *is* real. It's part of the air we breathe. It permeates everything in our world. If it helps, think of it as an element not yet explained by science." Her gentle smiles were starting to irritate me. "Certain people, witches, have the ability to manipulate the magic all around us. You're one of them. Or, rather, one of us."

I kept my eyes stuck on Crystal, jaw hanging open like the hanger bay of a cargo plane and didn't reply. Luckily, the sound of Aurie stampeding down the stairs kept me from having to find an adequate response to Crystal's insane claim.

"Mom! Mom! Mom! Guess what?" Aurie barreled through the swinging doors, clutching a fat book to her chest. "The bookshelf in my room has all my favorite books! Isn't that cool?" Her eyes were wide with delight as she bounced on her toes with excitement. "There are even a couple I haven't had a chance to read yet!"

"That is cool!" I beamed back at her and shot a side glance at Crystal who managed to say "I told you so" with just a half shrug.

Still thinking about her books, Aurie didn't notice. "What's for breakfast?"

"Well, coffee is my specialty. But I make a mean hot chocolate." Crystal beamed at Aurie. "Would you like one?"

Panic snapped me out of my torpor, and I glanced at Aurie. She was staring at the stranger with suspicious eyes, her brown corkscrew hair its usual just-got-out-of-bed mess. The sun hit her few reddish strands in a way that made her whole head look like it was on fire. My heart lurched in my chest. She took a step forward out of the sunbeam and the glow disappeared, but twin images of fires danced in my head.

"I think I'm going to be sick."

My stomach roiled and the coffee I'd just drunk threatened to come up for a visit. I gripped the back of the chair and focused on taking slow breaths in and out.

What had I gotten myself into? What had I gotten Aurie into? The vision of Crystal creating fire out of thin air replayed itself over and over again in my head as I tried to fit what was happening into terms I could comprehend.

Was I still dreaming? Everything since we'd arrived in Massachusetts had felt like a dream. Was I lying in a hospital bed, comatose after a hit on the head? That would explain so many things. But if this was a dream or a coma or whatever, it was amazingly real. I only got out of bed this morning because I had to pee. And everyone knows it's near impossible to pee in a dream. Right? Plus, things don't smell in dreams but that hot cocoa smells divine. The scent tickled my nose and, surprisingly, settled my stomach enough for me to stop worrying about making it to a sink before everything came back up.

I sat back down in my chair with a groan. It felt silly to be sitting so far from the table, but I couldn't bring myself to move it closer, not even when Aurie, completely oblivious to my distress, grabbed a chair from a neighboring table and scooped up the cat who had been fast asleep on it. She slumped down into the chair and snuggled him closely. He stared me down while rubbing his head lovingly on her chin.

Breakfast chaos unfolded around me as I sat in a daze. Crystal behaved as if she hadn't just casually destroyed my perception of reality. Aurie devoured her hot chocolate and the Dutch baby I finally pulled out of the oven while she listened with rapt attention as Crystal told her stories about the community. It was all so... normal. Like I'd imagined the whole thing. I would have chalked it up to an overcaffeinated and under-rested brain hiccup if, in the middle of a story, Crystal hadn't looked over and waggled her eyebrows and fingers at me.

Her gesture reignited my urge to run, and I was halfway out of my seat when I realized that despite the terror I had felt when she'd created fire out of thin air, I didn't actually want to run. I mean, my brain was still roaring at me, but my gut had settled down completely. I sipped my coffee, nibbled on a slice of Dutch baby, and asked myself why it felt like Crystal had told me something I already knew and had simply forgotten.

As unsettled as I was, part of me felt at home here. For some unexplained reason, my soul felt at peace in this bakery.

Aurie pulled me back to the present with a snort-laugh that made hot chocolate go up her nose. I was about to chuckle when she caught my eye and glared. With a grimace, I swallowed it back down. We were still on very thin ice, and it wouldn't take much to derail breakfast.

Crystal caught my eye and got us back on track by launching into a story about kids at the local middle school getting into trouble for freeing the crickets from the science lab the day they were supposed to be dissected. Even I cracked up at the visual of the science teacher hopping down the hallway as he tried to recapture the bugs.

"He never caught them all. They chirped all the way through the eighth-grade graduation. It was hysterical!"

"I wonder if they'll still be there in the fall," Aurie asked with a giggle. "That would be hilarious."

A tiny tendril of hope unfurled in my heart. Maybe, just maybe...

"Speaking of animals," Crystal said to Aurie, "have you been next door yet?"

"To the pet shop?" Aurie asked, "Nuh uh. We were too busy yesterday. Can I go now, Mom? *Please?*"

I hesitated and Crystal jumped in. "I'll take her over, show her around. I'm sure Hattie will be thrilled." My knee jerk response was to say no. There was no way I was letting Aurie go anywhere with a stranger, especially one who made fire appear out of thin air. My eyes nearly bugged out at the thought.

"It's okay, Cassie. I would never ever let any harm come to Aurie." Nothing but genuine sincerity shone out of Crystal's face.

Max's voice telling me never ever to trust anyone with our baby echoed deep inside my head, leaving my stomach in knots. My rational brain suggested it was sheer insanity. And yet, it was hearing Max's voice in my head that was making me uncomfortable, not the thought of letting Aurie go with Crystal.

"Please, Mom? I'm only going next door. I bet if you yell my name, I'll be able to hear you. Plus, Persimmon can come with me. He'll make sure I'm safe. Right, P?"

The idea of a cat bodyguard was the most ludicrous thing I'd heard yet that morning, but when I glanced at the orange tabby who'd been grooming himself by the bakery door during the breakfast hubbub, he looked me dead in the eye and nodded solemnly.

If this is a coma, they're giving me the really good drugs, because I swear that cat just agreed to supervise my daughter.

EIGHT

B aking had been my solace ever since I'd been old enough to turn on the oven. Losing myself in butter and sugar helped me clear my head and settle my emotions. Today was no exception.

Crystal returned from the pet shop—*sans* Aurie—to find me elbow deep in a mound of dough, gently patting biscuits into shape. The quiche I had prepared right after they departed for the pet shop hadn't been quite enough to make me feel in control again, so I'd turned to a recipe I knew always helped. It didn't hurt the biscuits were going to be amazing slathered with fresh butter and raw honey.

"She's a cute kid." She pulled a stool close to the counter where I was working and sighed happily at the yummy smells swirling around the room.

"When she wants to be." I grimaced. "These last few days..." I rolled my eyes and sighed.

Crystal chuckled and snagged a piece of the biscuit dough. "So...are we good? I know I blindsided you."

I wanted to say no, I almost wanted to kick her out of the kitchen, but much like it felt right for me to be here, it felt right for her to be there with me. I shrugged.

"I don't really know what I think. I should probably be afraid of you, or pissed at you, and maybe I'm just numb because I've been through too much these last few weeks, but I'm not any of those things."

Crystal made a sympathetic face and snagged another piece of dough.

"You're going to give yourself a stomachache."

She laughed and stuck the dough in her mouth.

"So, if we're past angry and scared, do you have any questions for me?"

"I actually came up with a couple while I was baking."

"Fabulous. Let me grab us some coffee, and I'll see if I can answer them."

I only hesitated for a moment when she returned with two steaming cups. Just long enough to take a sip and sigh with pleasure.

"Okay, in no particular order. Does everyone in Portney have magical powers? How does that work? Why isn't it pure mayhem out there? And you said magic is basically just another element, but what do we really know about it? Is it dangerous?"

"Whoa! Whoa!" Crystal held up her hands as though she could physically stop the flow of my questions. "Take a breath."

"Sorry. I'm not going to come to grips with any of this until I understand it. Facts will help me get there faster."

She didn't need to know I'd been curious enough about having magical powers I'd tried to waggle my own fingers. Nothing had happened other than flour flying everywhere.

"Fair enough. I'll try to be as factual as possible."

"Thank you." I felt a little buzz in my stomach, and I was surprised to realize it was anticipation. "I'm curious. And weirded out. And I still think there's a possibility you're crazy and somehow pranking me. But also, yes, I'm curious. But you have to understand. I grew up in a world where the slightest bit of whimsy was frowned upon. You should have heard the outrage the day I dyed a blue streak into my hair when I was fifteen."

"That's okay. You'll get there. But try to not set anything on fire on the way."

I glanced at my hands with a horrified look that prompted peals of laughter.

"Kidding! Kidding! You'll be fine. That doesn't usually happen."

"Usually? That is..." I blinked, not sure how I wanted to finish that thought. "Stacey is going to freak," I said, and then stopped. "Wait, is magic a *secret*?" I whispered the last question, eyes darting around the empty kitchen as though people might have snuck in while I wasn't looking.

"Not really, no." Crystal said with a shrug. "We're just careful about who we tell. There's no rule about secrecy. Just, you know, pick your audience carefully. Better to be safe than sorry."

I nodded thoughtfully. We were in Massachusetts. If history was any indication, humanity wasn't exactly kind to witches.

"No rules about secrecy? Does that mean there are other rules?" With my luck, I'd break a dozen without even trying. It had taken me years to learn all the "rules" about country club living. Wait, what was I even thinking? Me? A witch?

"Nothing major and definitely nothing for you to worry about right now."

I let out a breath I hadn't realized I'd been holding and started rummaging around the kitchen for the pastry brush I was sure had to be somewhere. So far, the kitchen had yielded everything I'd needed within moments of me wondering where I might find it. I found the brush and busied myself coating the biscuits with melted butter.

"Let's start with the fun stuff. I think it's fair to assume you're a kitchen witch." Crystal's eyebrow twitched up as she gestured to the gleaming biscuits ready to go into the oven. "Magical affinities are usually hereditary and Blackwell witches tend to be kitchen witches, but I wasn't 100% sure until I tasted that muffin this morning. Simply amazing."

"That's not magic. Just good baking." I pursed my lips and frowned at her, suddenly defensive of my work. Baking was the one thing Max had never tainted with his negativity. I was good in the kitchen, and I was proud of it.

"Don't get your panties in a twist. I'm not saying you're not a good cook." Crystal rolled her eyes at me. "But you know how people joke love is the secret ingredient that makes things taste extra good. In your case, it's magic. Kitchen witches have a knack when it comes to combining ingredients, when cooking or making potions."

"Potions?" I deadpanned, eyebrow raised, letting the comment about magic slide for now.

"Yes, potions." She laughed. "Why do you think my coffee's so good?"

I eyed the coffee cooling near my elbow. "You're a kitchen witch too?"

"Yep! As are all the women in my family."

"Not the men?"

"Usually, men are carriers of witchy genes and can't access the magic themselves. Major point of contention for many." She shrugged in a what-are-you-going-to-do way.

"Okay," I said, disconcerted at how reasonable this all sounded. "So, you and I are kitchen witches," I quirked an eyebrow in her direction before pausing to slide the biscuits into the oven, "are there other kinds of witches?"

"Lots! Take Aurie for instance."

"Aurie?" I spun back to face her.

"I'd put money on her being an animal witch. Which is interesting because the kitchen witch gene is usually strong in the Blackwell line." She eyed me thoughtfully. "Your mom, maybe?"

I couldn't stop myself from barking out a laugh. As if my always proper, always perfectly turned-out mother could possibly be something as whimsical as a witch. An animal witch at that.

"You sure?" Crystal asked, this time with her right eyebrow raised suggestively.

"I'm sure." But even as I said it, the endless parade of animals that had been part of my life as I grew up traipsed through my mind. All the strays and injured animals that always managed to end up on our doorstep. I hesitated. "Animals did follow her home, but if my mother has witch whatever in her blood, she definitely doesn't—" I corrected myself, "didn't know. Or at least she never said."

"Huh." Crystal said, letting my slipup slide without comment. "How are you with animals? And how's Aurie in the kitchen?"

I thought back.

"Well, I don't particularly like animals, and frankly, Aurie has never shown any interest in anything cooking related." I shrugged.

"Huh," Crystal said again. "Well, sometimes magic does strange things."

"Can we back up a step? What does being a witch even mean?" I asked Crystal, pulling the biscuits out of the oven. She considered the question as we broke open a couple to slather them with butter and honey.

"You said you read *Harry Potter*, right?" Crystal asked me with a totally serious look on her face.

"I mean, duh, who hasn't?"

At the look on my face, Crystal's poker face slipped, and she started giggling. "I'm kidding. Magic is nothing like that. No wands. No Diagon Alley. And no flying around on brooms."

"Oh." That part was a little sad. Aurie would have gotten a kick out of broom flying.

"Contrary to paranormal lore, witches are human like everyone else." Crystal put down her biscuit. "We're simply humans born with the ability to tap into the elemental world around us. We can all tap into all the elements to a certain extent, but we have different elemental affinities and strengths.

"Kitchen, garden, and animal witches are drawn to the earth. Healers are air and spirit witches. Weather witches are water and fire witches. Though, there are very few of those left. They were hunted to near extinction during the time of the Salem witch trials." A dark look crossed her face.

"Salem, huh?" We were less than fifty miles away from the infamous town.

"Yeah." Crystal replied with a loaded sigh.

"Are there witches everywhere, or is it primarily a New England thing? Wait, you never said, is everyone in Portney a witch?"

"Not everyone in Portney is a witch, but everyone in town either comes from a witching family or is aware of the witching community. Our town is a little unique in that sense. Witches don't all live in witch towns. Families scattered during the great witch hunts. Most moved away and were too scared to pass the lore and traditions down to their children.

"Blood stays true, but without training and knowledge, the abilities fade generation to generation until all that remains are little quirks."

"Like my mother and animals."

"Quite possibly. It would explain a lot."

"If everyone moved away to hide, how did Portney come to be?"

"A few witches chose to stay close to their ancestral lands despite the risk. Our magic is stronger here. It's easier to connect to the elements and the spirit world."

"Connect to the spirit world?" My eyebrows shot up. She'd had me until that moment, but apparently, communing with spirits was where my suspension of disbelief hit a wall.

"I know, it's a lot." She patted me kindly on the arm. "It won't seem strange forever. I promise."

I shot her a dubious look and didn't reply.

"Hey, listen, I have to run home, but would you like me to come back in the morning and show you how the espresso machine works?"

I wanted nothing more than to hole up in my room for days and try to process all the information she'd just thrown at me, but the promise of coffee was just too good to pass up.

"That would be nice, thank you."

She let herself out while I stared at my biscuits. Light. Fluffy and flakey. Bursting with buttery goodness. It wasn't like my entire self-worth was wrapped up my ability to cook, but I'd never been much good at anything else. Of all the things Crystal had just revealed, the fact that I might have been cheating with magic all along was the hardest to swallow.

NINE

When Aurie came back from the pet shop, nearly levitating with excitement and bursting with stories about bunnies, I did my best to shove everything Crystal had told me out of my mind. The poor kid was still processing the divorce and the move. Magic seemed like one thing too many. Also, I had no idea how I would even start to tell her. I mean...

Hey baby! I'm a witch! And so are you. And my mother. But not my dad because men can't be witches. But he did pass us his witch genes. Pass the salad, please.

It was all too easy to picture the look on her face...and how fast she'd call her dad to tell him I'd completely lost it and could he please come get her.

I let her do most of the talking as I watched her carefully to see if I could see any hints of magic in her.

"Mom? MOM? Are you even listening?" Aurie's whine cut through my thoughts, and I realized I'd stopped paying attention and had no clue what she'd asked. "I *said*, is it okay if I go back to *A Familiar Place* after lunch?"

"Go where?" I blinked at her blankly, and she rolled her eyes in response.

"The pet store?" She gave me a look that clearly spelled out how lame she thought I was being.

"Oh. Right. The pet store. I, uh, are you sure Hattie is okay with that?"

"I *just* told you. She needs my help cleaning out the birthing pens. She has a dog who's going to have puppies any day. Did you know she also runs the pet rescue for the town?" And with that, she was off and running again, speaking a mile a minute about how awesome Hattie was and how she was already in love with half the rescue dogs.

I groaned. We were so getting a dog. At least dogs were marginally better than bunnies.

The instant she was out the door, I grabbed my phone to text Stacey.

I think we're getting a dog.

Oh, yeah? Are we happy about this?

I dunno how the cat is going to take it.

What cat?

The one that came with the bakery.

The bakery came with a cat?
Are you okay? You're not making any sense.

Sorry. It's been a day.

What happened?

Uh. It's a long story.

You know me. I like a good story.

Of course, I knew that. She was a photojournalist. A good one too. She freelanced for a few agencies that sent her all over the world to shoot whatever they thought would sell. When she was on location, her ex watched their daughter, Shane, who didn't seem to mind bouncing from house to house. The mere thought was exhausting. I couldn't fathom how we would manage if Max changed his mind about custody.

I know, but this one is a little much for text.
But I swear I'm okay. Just processing.

Well, whatever it is, I'm here for you.
You know that, right?

I know.

I'm serious! Whatever you need, I'm there.
You can count on me.

The best part about my friendship with Stacey was I knew she wasn't just saying it. As someone who'd never experienced that kind of love and loyalty before, it still stunned me at times.

I know. I love you, too.

When can we talk so you can catch me up?

The thought of telling her made my blood run cold. Sure, she loved the Cassie she'd known in Georgia. Boring, predictable Cassie who could always be counted on for a cup of tea and a sweet treat. But would that change when she discovered there might be more to me than met the eye?

Soon. I promise. But right now, I've got to run.

Well, I love you. And I know whatever you're
dealing with, you've got it.
But I want to know everything.
I need to live vicariously through you.
Because, you know, you're the only heiress I
know.

TEN

T he quiet angst that settled in my gut after I put
down my phone lingered. Stacey and I had
been through so much together I couldn't fathom
she'd react badly to discovering I was descended
from witches—was a witch myself—but I couldn't
quite tune out the uneasy little voice in my head.
Between the divorce and the sudden departure, I
was already a lot to handle. What if this was the
thing that made our long-distance friendship seem
not worthwhile?

To drown out the voice, I browsed the internet for
recipes, but everything I came across only gave me
inspiration for recipes of my own. A week earlier,
I would have chalked that up to years of baking
experience. Now, I couldn't help thinking maybe
there was something witchy about it. It didn't sit
well with me. If I was brutally honest, I'd held off
from telling Stacey anything in case she judged me

for secretly boosting my baking with magic this whole time.

Ugh, Cassie, you are ridiculous. What does Stacey care about how you cook as long as you keep serving her delicious treats? What does it matter?

I shoved that thought and the not-so-positive retort my brain supplied aside and turned my attention to making the best snickerdoodles the world had ever tasted. Perfect for days when you're craving cinnamon rolls and don't have time to let the dough rise. The end result was an adorable swirly cookie I couldn't wait to top with cream cheese icing.

My phone rang as I finished glazing the last cookie.

I hesitated before picking it up. I was impressed Stacey had held off as long as she had before calling, but the thought of answering the phone was still making my heart pound and my hands feel clammy.

Oh, buck up, Cassie. Be honest with yourself. You don't want to tell her because that makes this whole debacle real, and you're scared shitless about what that means.

The truth hit me like a wrecking ball. Until I told Stacey, I could keep pretending this was some sort of temporary insanity that would end the moment I got back into my car and hit the road again with Aurie. Telling Stacey took this out of fantasy land

and brought it into the real world where things were scary, and people could be judgmental. I'd spent a lifetime trying not to stand out so people would accept me. After this, there was no blending in.

But the thought of going back to a world where I pretended to be someone I wasn't made my stomach turn. It clearly hadn't worked for me. Time to try something new.

Go big or go home. And even if I could, I wouldn't want to go home anyway.

I took a deep breath and hit accept.

"Perfect timing! I just finished making myself a snack." I smiled into the phone, ignoring the butterflies whirling in my stomach. "Want to have tea with me?"

"Tea sounds lovely. Sadly, I cannot partake. I'm sitting in traffic, and I thought 'who better to spend the next half hour with than my BFF?'"

"Ah, big city traffic, how I do not miss thee."

"Rub it in why don't you?"

I laughed in reply and then promptly scalded myself on my tea. *Karma.*

"I know you're not ready to tell me what's going on, but you sounded seriously out of sorts earlier. I just wanted to make sure you're okay." The love and compassion in her voice settled the panicked butterflies. I was insane if I thought she would think of me differently after I told her.

"I'm fine. I promise." I firmed up my shoulders. "This has been different than I'd expected, that's all."

"I thought you said the place was great?"

"Oh, it is! It's amazing. But it comes with some unexpected strings. No, that's not right, not strings. It just it came with a few unexpected surprises."

"Good surprises?"

I hesitated. "Surprising surprises."

"Uh-huh. That's, ah, clear as mud, my friend."

"I know! I'm sorry. I don't even know where to start."

"AHA! I knew there was something! Is it a guy? I bet it's a guy. Is he hot?" Delight bubbled through the phone line.

"It's not a guy!" As I opened my mouth to tell her, I realized I couldn't. The words refused to come out. "Arg. I'm sorry, I'm still not ready to share."

I needed to process everything I'd learned and figure out how it would affect our lives before I could share it with anyone, even Stacey. Plus, the part of me that prided herself on the ability to mix flour, eggs, and sugar expertly wasn't ready to have people assume the results were delicious because of magic rather than talent.

Visions of Samantha from *Bewitched* twitching her nose to serve up dinner flashed through my head. I'd always thought she was a cheater. I didn't want anyone to think that of me.

"Gaaaaarrrrggggggg," Stacey replied before leaning onto the horn and yelling, "just *goooooo*, you mothereffer. Did you get your license in a cereal box?"

"Enjoying your drive, are you?" I said when she'd stopped yelling and started mumbling to herself.

"I don't think anyone around here knows how to drive. It makes me insane. Anyway, you were saying?"

"Ha. Still not ready to talk about it."

"It was worth a try," she replied with a chuckle. She took a deep breath and continued. "As your best friend, it is my duty to tell you I understand and will patiently wait until you are ready to spill. As a person with zero patience, I'll just say I hope that time comes soon. Very, very soon."

"I appreciate both sentiments. I promise you'll be the first to know when I'm ready to share. I just need more time to process."

"Is it about Max?" she growled into the phone, and I could all too easily imagine the murderous look on her face.

"No, for once, my mixed up, confused feelings have nothing to do with Max."

The silence on the other end of the line told me exactly what she thought of that.

"Well, okay, it's his fault we had to leave Georgia, and it's his fault I don't yet know what I'm going to do with my life, and it's his fault I'm worried about Aurie and her emotional well-being. But none of that is what's currently preoccupying me. The thing I'm not ready to talk about is blissfully unrelated to Max."

That alone predisposed me to think about this turn of events in a favorable light. Something untainted by Max and his negativity? Unimaginable.

"Hey," I said cheerfully in a blatant attempt to change the subject. "Want to help me brainstorm bakery items I could make if I were to stay? I have to discuss all of this with Max. Making a list of all the pastries he'd never ever allow to cross his lips is going to strengthen my resolve to make this work."

"Now we're talking. Cinnamon rolls for sure. Mmmm." I looked at my plate and smiled. "How are you at croissants? Almond croissants are my fave, and isn't Max allergic to nuts? Might keep him away."

ELEVEN

I 'd called Max a million times over the years, but I'd never dreaded hearing him pick up more.

"I'm busy, Cassandra. Is this an emergency?" *No "hello." No "how are you?" No "haven't heard from you in a while. Is everything okay?"* I almost cussed him out and hung up, but I reminded myself why I was calling in the first place and bit my tongue.

I opened and shut my mouth a few times, unsure of how to start.

"Cassandra. I'm serious. I have things to do. What is it?" The sound of his keyboard made me grit my teeth. He always read his emails when he was on the phone. It had annoyed me when we were married, now it was downright pissing me off.

I hadn't talked to him since we'd finalized the divorce. He hadn't once texted to see how Aurie was doing or asked about her since we'd left town. Until right this second, it had made me sad on her behalf, today it was pushing me one step closer to a decision about staying in Massachusetts.

"Hey, sorry." I winced. *What did I have to be sorry about?* "I needed to let you know something."

"What?" Distraction or annoyance made his tone extra snappish.

"Long story short, a great aunt I didn't know about passed away last month."

"Oh, yeah? Wealthy?" For the first time since he'd picked up the phone, I had his full attention.

"No, not wealthy." I made my tone as casual as possible. This building and the little nest egg it came with wasn't what he'd consider serious wealth, but Max was a bloodhound when it came to money. The last thing I wanted was for him to come nosing around what Preston Lathrop Junior had assured me was entirely mine. "But she did leave me her bakery."

"A bakery?" he scoffed. "What's that going to net us when you sell it?"

"First of all, there is no us anymore, but more importantly, I'm not selling. I want to stay here and run it." As I said the words, the truth in them sank in and took root. I wanted to make a life for us here in this quirky town filled with strange people. That it was so far from Max was just the cherry on top.

I could feel his disdain radiating through the phone. "Absurd. There's no money to be made running a bakery. And what about Aurora in all of this?"

"How much money I make is none of your business. As for Aurie, who's doing well by the way, thanks for asking. The bakery comes with a modest apartment. We'll live there and Aurie can go to the local middle school."

I hadn't checked the place out yet, but he certainly didn't need to know that.

Max didn't reply, and I couldn't quite tell if it was because he'd gotten distracted by an email or because he was considering what I was saying.

"Max? Do you understand? I'm asking if you're okay with me moving to Massachusetts with Aurie."

"Massachusetts? You didn't say anything about New England." He pulled himself from whatever had distracted him.

"Sorry, I should have said. The bakery is in a small town near Boston."

Whatever interest my mention of Massachusetts had sparked was gone by the time he spoke again.

"Whatever. It's not like it's going to last. No way in hell you can make a living wage from cake. I'll bet good money you'll be back in Georgia in less than three months begging me to help you get back on your feet."

I dug my nails into my palm and forced myself to stay calm. What he thought no longer mattered. I didn't need his support, and I certainly didn't need his approval.

"Pastries, but that's not the point." My mouth hadn't gotten the memo my brain was distributing. "So, just to clarify, you're okay not seeing her every fourth weekend?"

"Yeah, yeah, whatever. I was going to call you anyway to cancel next weekend. Going sailing with some buddies."

I bit my tongue and took a deep breath. The fact that he didn't care was going to make my life easier. It hurt and it made me livid on Aurie's behalf, but in the long run it was for the best. Though telling her we weren't going back wasn't going to be easy.

"Ah, shit." Max's disdain had suddenly turned to annoyance. "My mom is going to flip if Aurora doesn't start prepping for cotillion. She said something about etiquette class and dance class the other day. I'll have her call you to figure it out."

Before I could even open my mouth to protest, the phone went dead in my hand. If he thought I was answering any calls from my ex-mother-in-law, he was sorely mistaken. Never having to deal with her again was one of the silver linings of our divorce.

TWELVE

M y eyes snapped open, and I groaned. It was still pitch black and there was no reason for me to be awake, especially considering how hard it had been for me to fall asleep in the first place.

One of these days, I'd be able to go to sleep without first listing all the ways my life was an out of control train wreck, but it hadn't been last night. My dreams had been filled with massive black cauldrons filled with bubbling green ooze I was trying to serve to horrified customers. Actually, being awake was a bit of a blessing. That last dream had been particularly disturbing. I shook off the vision of Aurie grinning up at me from inside the bubbling goo and turned over, pummeling my pillow into submission.

I was drifting off again when a loud creak coming from somewhere downstairs made my eyes fly open. My heart stilled before lurching into high gear. I was alone in the house with Aurie. If someone was downstairs, there was no one else to go investigate.

Damn you, Max. Damn you to hell and back again.

I lay as still as possible and listened. The silence was deafening.

It's nothing, Cassie. It's an old building. Old buildings creak. Maybe it's the damn cat. Aren't cats nocturnal? Or is that a myth?

Aurie had been fast asleep with Persimmon curled up on her belly when I had checked on her earlier. I'd considered putting him outside for the night, but the look on his face had made it quite clear it was in my best interest to leave him right where he was. Maybe he'd gotten up and was exploring the downstairs kitchen.

CREAK.

Persimmon wasn't a small cat, but he wasn't that big. Was he?

It took almost superhuman effort not to pull the covers over my head and pretend everything was just fine. With my heart in my throat, I slipped out of bed and grabbed my robe. It was ridiculous to pretend the flimsy material offered any sort of protection, but I still felt safer wearing it.

It's just the dumb cat, Cassie. You don't need your dumb robe to protect you.

Oh yeah? You sure? Because you definitely closed the door to the stairs and, while he's hardly a normal cat, he probably still can't open doors.

Fantastic, Cassie, now you're talking to yourself and answering yourself. I'm starting to really worry about you.

An extra loud creak followed by the sound of something metallic clattering to the ground silenced all the voices in my head. I froze with one hand on the doorjamb.

The noise was definitely coming from downstairs. And I could no longer pretend it was a normal house noise. The glow of my phone on the nightstand revealed a poker leaning against the fireplace.

My ears on high alert, brandishing the poker in front of me like a sword, I eased myself down the stairs. I kept my back glued to the wall, as I carefully rolled my feet onto each step so they wouldn't make a sound. At the bottom of the stairs I paused, staying hidden in the stairwell's shadows. I cocked an ear and listened.

A soft rustling sound drifted over from part of the kitchen I couldn't see. What was over in that corner? I'd been so engrossed in my baking I hadn't explored anything beyond the pantry and walk-in fridge. Was it a desk? Maybe some shelves? I couldn't remember.

My heart was pounding so hard it was all I could hear, so I forced myself to think of peaceful, soothing things like melted chocolate drizzled on warm cake. Wrong choice. My heart sped up. I cast around for a better option. My soft pillow waiting for me upstairs and the endless stretch of highway between Virginia and Maryland did the trick. I'd almost fallen asleep twice while driving it the week before.

Now my heart had stopped dancing the samba, I focused on the rustling sound again. When it stopped, my heart gave a loud thud and started racing again. The kitchen was silent long enough I had almost convinced myself I had made up the whole thing when the beam of a flashlight danced across the ceiling right in front of me.

Oh my god. There really is someone in there.

There was someone in my brand-new kitchen. In the middle of the night. While my baby slept upstairs. Mama rage smothered my fear and fueled the courage I'd been lacking.

"I'm warning you, I've got the police on the line," I bellowed as I leapt into the kitchen, brandishing my poker high in the air with my right hand and waving my phone menacingly with my left.

A slight person dressed in black from head to toe jerked in surprise and dropped something before making a mad dash to the wide open back door, toppling over the desk chair in their frantic run.

By the time I made it to the door all I saw was someone passing over the top of the wall at the far end of the yard. The tree limb reaching over the wall was still quivering. I stood there, clutching my robe, gasping for breath, as my entire body shook from a mix of adrenaline and terror. When we'd lived in a big city, the risk of break-ins or attacks had been constant enough to keep me alert. The quaintness of this small town had lulled me into a false sense of safety.

I went back inside, locked the door, and tucked the desk chair under it for good measure. Then I sheepishly dialed 911.

Trained by big-city police response times, I was startled when the quiet knock at the bakery entrance came barely a few minutes after I called. For a moment, I had the irrational thought it was the intruder coming back to finish the job. It didn't take me long to realize this tall, broad-shouldered stranger holding what looked like a sheriff's hat looked nothing like the person who had run off into the dark. The glint of a badge on his chest calmed my racing pulse. Almost dizzy with relief, I let out the breath I'd been holding.

The door to the bakery unlocked itself the instant I put my hand on it, which meant the building clearly thought the stranger on the other side was trustworthy. But I still stared him down until he pulled out his badge and showed it to me through the glass.

"Sorry," I pulled the door open and ushered him in. "I'm super jittery."

"Rightfully so. Good call asking for a badge before letting in anyone wearing a law enforcement uniform."

His eyes twinkled and I couldn't tell if he was serious or poking a little fun at me. The twinkle was joined by a dimple when he smiled and held out his hand.

"Deputy Sheriff Griffin, at your service."

"Deputy Sheriff? Was the actual sheriff too busy to come?" I slapped my hand over my mouth and stood there in stunned silence. The deputy looked down at me, completely unfazed by my rudeness. If anything, the way the corner of his lip twitched made it clear he was doing his best not to laugh. "Oh my god. I am so sorry! I have no idea where that came from. I'm just so..." I waved my hands helplessly and opened the door wider so he could come inside.

"Please, don't worry about it. It's late and you've had a shock. I won't hold it against you. And yes, the sheriff was...otherwise engaged." I quirked my eyebrow in his direction at the hitch in his voice. In response, the deputy grinned at me.

That the deputy who had shown up to rescue me from an unwanted intruder was a handsome man in his mid-forties with a smile that made my insides feel funny was utterly irrelevant to the situation. It wasn't his fault he was tall, filled out his uniform nicely, and had hair I had the sudden urge to reach up and touch, and dammit, I was staring and suddenly felt underdressed in my pajamas and robe.

"Uh, uh," I stammered. "It happened in the kitchen. Back there." I pointed toward the back, and he led the way. We both pretended I wasn't blushing.

The sight of the door with the small desk chair jammed under the handle brought me crashing back to reality. A person had broken into the building while my daughter and I slept upstairs. To my utter mortification, a strangled sob worked its way up my throat. The deputy, who had been examining the door to look for signs of forced entry, glanced back at me with a worried frown.

"It's okay. I'm okay." I forced my lip to stop quivering and shot him what I hoped mildly resembled a confident smile. "Can I make you a cup of tea? I think I need a cup of tea." The babbling probably wasn't helping convince him I was fine.

"Let's not touch anything in here," he said with a kind smile. "At least not until I give it a once over."

"Oh, right. I'm so sorry. Of course." Feeling like an idiot, I slid onto one of the counter stools and closed my eyes. The fear I'd experienced in the moment had been visceral and intense. Under the harsh overhead lights of the kitchen it settled into a more subtle tightness around my chest. It was going to take me a long while to feel safe in this kitchen again.

"Do you have any idea what they might have been looking for?"

My eyes flew back open. He'd moved away from the door and was standing on the other side of the counter, looking around the room with questioning eyes.

I glanced at the desk in the corner of the room. "I think they were going through the desk or the bookshelf, but I have no idea what they could have been looking for."

I didn't think my uninvited visitor had taken anything. Not that I would have known, seeing as I hadn't even registered the desk in the room, let alone what was on or in it until someone tried to steal something from it. The only thing that looked out of place was the cup of pens that had been knocked over on the desk. That must have been what I thought the person had dropped.

The deputy looked over the desk and the contents of the shelves above it, lips pursed in concentration and nodding every so often. When he turned back and shrugged, I shrugged back. We both knew there hadn't been anything noteworthy for him to find.

If you knew that, why did you bother calling him?

"It doesn't look like anything has been disturbed. Whatever they were looking for, you probably interrupted them before they could start looking seriously."

"Oh." I'd been so focused on the fact they hadn't found anything I hadn't considered the fact there might have been something to find after all.

"I think you're safe for now, but you might want to have someone come in and add an extra lock or two to the door. Maybe install some motion sensor lights out there." He gestured at the back yard.

"Yes, right. That sounds like a good idea." I nodded, my head bouncing up and down like a bobblehead, and tried not to let him see I'd broken into a cold sweat at the thought of him leaving.

He looked concerned despite my stellar bit of acting. "Is there anyone you can call who could come spend the rest of the night with you?"

Sadness washed over me. I had never felt as alone as I did right then. "Ah, no, I'm... ah, new to town." I felt dumb even saying it. Every single person I'd met so far had known pretty much everything about me. There was no way he didn't also know who I was and why I was in town.

"Right. Yes. Of course." This time, he looked sheepish, and a hint of red colored the tip of his ear. "I think you're going to be fine. You scared them off for now. But I'll leave you my cell number. You can call me anytime." He looked up from the card he'd pulled out of his pocket and caught my raised eyebrow. "I mean, in case anyone else tries to break in or anything." He grimaced and thrust the card in my direction.

I snagged it out of his hand with a smirk and ushered him back out to the front of the store, a giggle threatening to worm its way out of my throat.

The urge to laugh faded the instant he tipped his hat at me from the other side of the door. He waited until I had made a show of locking the door and securing the deadbolt before walking away, and it took every ounce of self-control I possessed to stop myself from calling him back. I might have if the cat hadn't chosen that moment to show up and start winding himself around my ankles.

"Right, you're right," I murmured to the large cat. "Who needs that guy? We're totally safe without him."

I scooped up Persimmon, and, after double checking the doors were all firmly locked, headed back up to bed.

As I slipped into my now-cold sheets, my mind replayed the whole event. Crystal had explained that the building had the ability to adapt itself to my needs and desires. I'd seen it in action when it had unlocked the door for the deputy.

But, in that case, why had it allowed the intruder to come in? Was it possible that other people had similar powers over the place? The thought chilled me to my core, and I scrambled back out of bed to grab the poker I'd returned to its spot next to the fireplace. I tucked it into bed with me and did my best to go back to sleep.

THIRTEEN

The day before, I'd been irritated at the birds welcoming the dawn with their loud chirping. This morning I was grateful for their chatter because it meant I could finally get out of bed. Every time I'd been on the verge of drifting off, I'd woken up with a jerk, convinced someone was breaking in again.

My eyes were gritty, and I was moving at about the same speed as the old ladies at my mother's memory care facility when I faced my nemesis, the fancy shmancy coffee machine. It acted like it couldn't have cared less I hadn't slept a wink after having the fright of my life and gave no quarter, staring me down with its steely, emotionless face. I was in the process of telling it I was going to replace it with a Mr. Coffee machine if it didn't start cooperating when the shop door opened. I jumped a mile in the air, every single muscle in my back protesting loudly.

"Maybe coffee is the last thing you need today?" Crystal chuckled.

"*Noooo*," I wailed, turning around to greet her. "Coffee. Now, please. I'm begging. Must have coffee and the machine won't give me any. It's mean." I turned back to glare at it again, but it was utterly unmoved by my despair.

"Not to be rude, since we hardly know each other and all, but you kinda look like shit. You okay?"

"Thanks for that. I'm okay," I said, sinking into a chair at the table I was rapidly starting to think of as mine. "Long night without much sleep."

"Were you up worrying about the stuff we discussed yesterday?" Crystal asked, placing a perfect mocha latte in front of me. She slipped into the seat across from mine and took a sip of her own.

"No. I mean, yes, for a while that stuff was going through my mind, but there was an unrelated incident in the middle of the night."

"Does it have something to do with your late night visit from the delightful Deputy Sheriff Griffin?" Crystal asked, with a mischievous look in her eye. I gaped at her. How on earth did she know he'd been here? Crystal laughed at my expression. "Small town. You get used to it."

"It's really not a big deal," I said, wrapping my hands around the warm mug and groaning with delight. "There was a weird noise in the bakery kitchen last night. When I came down to investigate, I found someone rifling through the desk. They ran out the back door before I could see who it was or stop them."

"Are you serious?" Crystal's jaw dropped and her eyes bugged out. "That is a huge deal!" I winced and shushed her. If Aurie woke up and demanded breakfast, I might just start crying. When no tell-tale noises drifted down from above, she continued in a slightly lower tone of voice.

"There was someone in your kitchen and you came down to investigate? Alone? Are you insane?" The hissed words were no less impassioned than her shout had been a moment earlier.

I shrugged. "I thought it was the cat getting up to no good." I didn't tell her I'd kept going down the stairs even when I'd realized there was no way it could have been the cat. She seemed upset enough as it was. "I had a fireplace poker. I wasn't in any danger." My stomach twisted painfully in response to my lie, but I somehow managed to hide it from Crystal, masking my wince with an annoyed scowl. In the light of day, her outrage seemed somewhat justified. If any of my friends had investigated a suspicious noise like that, I would have been out of my mind.

"Sure. Because it's a well known thing pokers are a great defense against flying bullets," she said, rolling her eyes at me.

"Oh." Shame heated my face. "I hadn't thought of that."

Crystal rolled her eyes again and threw her hands up in the air in defeat.

"Anyway," I pressed on, not meeting her gaze. "I don't know if they took anything. I didn't get a chance to look through the desk or the shelves above it before the break-in, so I have no idea if anything is missing." I glanced at Crystal out of the corner of my eye and was surprised to see anger flashing in her eyes.

"What?" I asked.

"Nothing," Crystal answered tersely.

"Clearly it's not nothing," I replied. She'd gone from concerned and compassionate to cold and furious so fast it had almost given me whiplash. "Why are you mad at me? Because I wasn't careful? I'm a grown-ass woman. I can take care of myself."

Irritation flared and kept on growing, pushing out the fear still lingering in my gut. Maybe coming down to face danger with nothing more than an iron poker hadn't been the smartest thing to do, but I'd also called the cops. I wasn't entirely stupid.

She looked equally irritated for a moment and then she let out a puff of breath. "I'm not mad at you, just at the situation. Your great aunt had a..." She glanced at the ceiling and back down at me. "A cookbook of sorts. A special one." She stressed the word special and gave me a pointed look.

"A special cookbook?" I frowned. Of all the things she could have said, this was the last thing I'd expected to hear. "What are you talking about? Did it contain secret family recipes she didn't want anyone to get their hands on?"

Crystal forced a smile through her pinched lips. "Something like that." She stood up abruptly and pushed her chair back. "I have to go check on something."

I watched her rush out of the bakery, my frown deepening. *That was weird, even for this town.* Maybe I'd misread Crystal and our friendship wasn't as destined as I'd assumed.

An unexpected wave of grief washed over me, bringing tears to my eyes. Everyone I'd met so far in Portney had been so sweet and welcoming. I'd been lulled into assuming most of them would become friends. It wasn't hard to imagine myself laughing over a bottle of wine with Hattie, Crystal, even Juliette. But that weird outburst had highlighted how little I knew them. They were polite, friendly, but strangers, nonetheless. Not that they knew me either. If I packed up our things right now and vanished, we'd be nothing more than a brief "Hey, remember when?" story before the week was out.

It was all so depressing.

Choking back tears, I grabbed my phone and fired off a text to Stacey.

I miss you.

A moment later a reply popped up.

Have you been abducted?
Is this a cry for help?
Should I call the FBI?

Very funny.

Well, it's not like you to be so maudlin this early in the morning.

Oh, shit. I'm sorry.
I didn't even realize how early it was.
Did I wake you?

Nah. I'm out running. What's eating you?

Just homesick, I guess.

For Max and the mausoleum?

I laughed. She wasn't wrong. Our house had been more museum than home.

Nah. Just missing my snarky, smart-ass friend.

Oh, yeah? Do I know her?
Think she might need a new friend now that
you're gone?
I have an opening.

Isn't running supposed to make you tired or something? Dull your wit?

Never! Sharpens it.

Fantastic.

Are you going to tell me what's really going on?

I sighed. "I'm a witch" didn't seem like the kind of thing that would go over very well via text even if I said it using emojis. And "I'm lonely and I have no friends" seemed overly pathetic and needy.

Are you almost done with your run?

Could be. Call me.
I'll try not to huff and puff too much into the
phone.
Wouldn't want you to think I've turned into
a creeper.

I put down my phone with a laugh, made myself a cup of tea (since I'd already drained my latte and had no idea how to coax another out of the damn coffee machine), and sat down to call her.

"Spill," Stacey said, in lieu of a greeting when she answered. "You've got ten minutes until I have to get in the shower."

"Please tell me you're not lounging on your couch all sweaty and gross."

"Fine. I won't. What do you care anyway? It's not your couch."

"I sit on that couch, thank you very much."

"Not any more you don't." Our friendly banter ground to a halt.

"We don't know that for sure," I mumbled.

"Yeah, yeah," Stacey said, and I could all too easily imagine her waving away my sad little protest. "Anyway, spill, what's eating you?"

I groaned. I had to tell her. I knew it. Our relationship couldn't weather a secret of this magnitude. But it didn't make any of the fear go away.

"That bad?"

"I just, I don't know where to start," I replied, dropping my head onto the table. I desperately wanted to tell Stacey. Wait. No. I desperately wanted Stacey to already know, to already have gone through the whole "You're insane, this isn't possible, I think we should call the people in the white coats so they can take you away for a little grippy-sock vacation" thing and have accepted what I was about to say as just a quirky fact of my life so we could get to the part where she gave me advice. Try as I might, I couldn't think of another time in our relationship when she hadn't known what was going on in my life.

"You know, I find the beginning is usually a good place to start," she said, her voice so nonchalant I knew she was forcing herself to stay calm so she wouldn't spook me.

"Okay. Fine. I'm just going to dive in. I've learned some weird things about my family since I arrived. For instance, I'm... I'm a witch descended from a long line of witches."

The silence on the other end of the line was deafening, so I almost didn't hear Stacey's reply.

"As in, you come from a long line of Wiccans?"

"No, as in, I come from a long line of witches."

"Have you been hitting the early morning hooch?"

"I know. It sounds insane. *I* sound insane. But I swear it's true. Magic is real. Witches are real. It's blowing my mind and while I know it's a lot to swallow, I kinda need you to get on board so I have someone to freak out with."

Stacey didn't say anything for the longest time until she asked me to hold on a second. I heard her put her phone down and move around her apartment for a moment. She couldn't have been gone for more than a minute, but it felt like a thousand. I was on the verge of hyperventilating when she finally picked up her phone.

"Sorry. I needed to reschedule something. I didn't want to feel rushed. Okay. Start at the very beginning and tell me everything."

The breath I'd been holding squeezed out of me with a hiss, and I almost sobbed in relief. I filled Stacey in, starting from the moment we'd arrived in Portney and things had gotten weird pretty much immediately. The quieter she got, the faster I talked and in no time, the whole story was out.

"That's it? That's the whole story?" I couldn't read her tone and it was freaking me out.

"Yeah, that's it. That's the whole story."

"And you're 100% sure you're not high, drunk, or suffering from a head injury?"

The doubts that had plagued me the day before came flooding back.

"I don't know! How would I know if I was in a coma?"

"Do you smell antiseptic? I read a story once about a girl who was comatose, and she remembers all the hospital smells."

I sniffed the air tentatively. "No, just vanilla and lemon."

"Oh? What are you baking? Wait, never mind. Tell me later. Shit, Cassie, that's one heck of a story."

"I KNOW!" I wailed.

"She really floated balls of fire in the air?"

"Yes!"

"Was it cool? It sounds cool."

"So cool. Abso-fucking-lutely terrifying, but so very, very cool."

"And you can do that?" Something akin to awe suffused her voice.

"No. Yes. Maybe. Not yet. I don't really know what I can and can't do or even how to find out. It's all so freaking terrifying and what with the break-in and all, I haven't had much time to think about everything."

"I'm sorry, back up a second. You didn't say anything about a break-in! What is going on up there? I thought it was a sleepy little town."

I gulped. I hadn't meant to mention my late-night intruder. "Sorry. I forgot to include that piece in the story. It wasn't a big deal. Someone broke in, I chased them out with a fireplace poker, a cute deputy sheriff stopped by, and that's pretty much the whole story."

"Oh, we are so coming back to that whole bit, especially the cute deputy piece, but first I have a few more questions about this witch thing. Wait, you are saying witch, not bitch, right?"

"Very funny."

"Okay, okay, but in all seriousness, how are you with all this? I mean, other than terrified."

I stopped to think about it for a second.

"I don't really know. Scared. Mad. Frustrated. A little excited. Overwhelmed mostly," I sighed.

"Why mad and frustrated?"

"Mad at my dad for leaving me to grow up without knowing any of this. Frustrated, ugh, this one is embarrassing."

"Try me."

I heaved a big sigh and mumbled, "I'm worried people are going to think my baking is only good because I use magic."

"What? I couldn't hear you."

I repeated myself louder and she laughed.

"That's ridiculous and you know it." I still wasn't convinced, but I let it go for now.

"If you say so."

"Can I ask you something? We've been friends a good long while, right?"

"Yeah," I replied, not sure where she was going with this.

"So, pray tell, if you're a witch, how is it I've never seen you do anything witchy?"

Her question stopped my thoughts in their tracks.

"I'm not sure. Maybe you have, every time you eat something I bake."

"Nuh-uh. I've eaten a LOT of things you've made and, as yummy as it all was, there was nothing supernatural about your baking."

"Thank you! That's what I've been saying!"

"Though..." Stacey paused. "The muffins you made right before you left..." her voice sounded wistful, as though she'd never eat another muffin in her life, "made me feel calm and happy and like everything was right with the world." She let out a sad little sigh and I made a mental note to ask her what was going on with her. "That wasn't totally normal."

"Well, yeah, chocolate will do that to a girl," I snapped.

"And your carrot cake. It made me feel like I could take on the whole world and nothing could stop me."

"Wait, when did I make you carrot cake?" I asked. The last few months had been a blur, so even though I had a vague recollection of grating carrots one day, I couldn't remember what had inspired me to bake a cake I didn't enjoy much.

"Remember? It was right after Max dropped his bombshell? I was feeling down because *Time* magazine rejected my photo series on urban warriors, and I said something about carrot cake being the ultimate comfort food. You came over that night and surprised me with one. I couldn't believe it, not with everything you were going through."

"Oh yeah!" The following weeks had blown that memory right out of my head.

"Other than being ridiculously good, which isn't surprising since you baked it, that cake totally changed how I was feeling. I went from thinking I should hang up my camera and take up macramé, to picking up the phone to give the photo editor of *Time* a piece of my mind."

"You what?" I laughed, imagining all too well how that conversation had gone down.

"Okay, not exactly. But I did call to pitch him the story again. He said he was impressed by my passion and optioned the photo series. Cassie, I have never, ever argued with a rejection before, and I've certainly never cold called an editor. What if it was your cake?"

"That's ridiculous," I replied. "Cake is cake." But even as I spoke, the memory of that afternoon came into focus. I'd been so angry at Max. Furious he would take the life we'd painstakingly built together and toss it like yesterday's trash. The rage had been building up in me all day, making me feel hot and twitchy, and I'd decided baking would help settle me so I could figure out what to do.

I'd forced all thoughts of Max and my future out of my head and focused on my friend and her struggles instead. The whole time I'd been grating carrots and stirring everything together, I'd been thinking about Stacey and how talented she was and how I wished she had enough confidence in her work to stand up for herself when people dismissed her without taking the time to look at her photos. Baking hadn't made my skin stop tingling, but it had settled something else in my soul.

"There's no way. It's absurd." I shook my head vehemently. "Bananas. Crystal is clearly a little woo touched and she's putting ideas in our heads."

"There's really only one way to know, isn't there," Stacey said, with an impish tone. "Bake something. See what happens."

"I already have scones in the oven. Also, that's ridiculous. And, even if I did somehow magically imbue the carrot cake with some... what would you even call what I did to the cake?"

"I dunno," Stacey said. "Magically imbuing it with feelings? Impulses? Motivation? Encouragement? Intent?"

"Alrighty, put down the thesaurus. Anyway, none of those feel quite right. Whatever. Moving on. Even if I did somehow magically imbue the carrot cake with whatever filled you with enough confidence to call that guy, I have no idea how I did it or even if I could do it again."

Stacey hummed thoughtfully. "What were you thinking about when you made the chocolate chip muffins?"

The morning I'd made the muffins, I'd been standing in my mostly packed up kitchen, thinking about how baking was the only thing that made me feel like *me* in a house that always felt foreign and uncomfortable. While mixing the ingredients for the muffins, I'd pushed the stress aside and focused on what made things feel like home while letting myself imagine life was going to work out just fine if I simply let the universe take care of everything. I had felt so full of peace and hope when I'd finally pushed the muffins into the oven.

By the time I was done describing the experience to Stacey she was whispering "yes, yes, yes!" into the phone. "That's it! That's exactly how eating them made me feel! Which is crazy because that is SO not how I was feeling when I took the first bite!"

"You ready to talk about that yet?" I asked. She'd been gracious enough to let me decide when I was ready to talk about my big secret, I figured extending the same courtesy would be nice.

After a quiet beat, she replied, "It's such a banal story, I almost don't want to tell you at all." She got quiet again, and I instantly knew.

"Aw, babe. Dylan?"

The sigh she heaved was a clear enough answer.

"What did he do this time?" The calm in my voice completely masked the rage bubbling inside me. Stacey's ex was the biggest asshole I'd ever met. He jerked her around constantly, making her dance at the end of his line in a way that made me think violent thoughts. Every single time Stacey started getting her feet under her or started to make serious headway in life, he'd show up, charm the pants off her—literally—then drop her like a hot potato as soon as she was well and truly back under his thumb.

"The usual," Stacey sighed sadly. "I just, I dunno. I thought it would be different this time."

"Of course, you did." I tried to keep the irritation out of my voice. Honest, I really did. But some must have leaked through because Stacey huffed.

"That's why I didn't want to tell you. I know you think I'm a loser for falling for his schtick every time." Her voice was filled with so much sadness I wanted to kick both myself and Dylan at the same time.

"Hon, I do not think you're a loser." I placed extra emphasis on the word not. "I think Dylan is an asshole. A very, very charismatic asshole who is very, very good at getting what he wants." We'd had this conversation a zillion times. I was convinced Dylan was constantly playing her. She was convinced he was a misunderstood genius who had trouble expressing his true feelings. *Gag.* "I just love you so much and I hate to see you get hurt over and over again like this."

"I know," she sighed. "But he's Shane's dad..."

I stifled a groan. This was her second favorite excuse for why she let Dylan get away with treating her like shit.

"Yep. He sure is," I said, with as gentle a smile as I could muster, hoping she could feel it through the phone. Maybe one day Stacey would hear what I was constantly telling her. Just because Dylan had fathered Shane didn't give him the right to bulldoze his way through their lives whenever he wanted. Today was clearly not the day.

Her silence made it clear she knew exactly what I was thinking and was grateful I had opted to keep it to myself.

"It'll be okay. I just need a little time to get him out of my system again," she said with fake cheer. "Won't take long this time, I'm sure."

"Totally," I replied with a smile. "And if you need a place to crash while you figure it out, you could always come here. I think we have room."

"You *think* you have room?"

"Oh yeah, that's another thing I forgot to mention, but I think I'll save it for another time," I replied. I'd given her a lot to process. The magical house could wait.

FOURTEEN

Talking to Stacey on the phone was lovely, but it didn't hold a candle to chatting with her over a cup of tea. Hearing her voice had made me crave the chocolate-orange scones she always requested. They wouldn't be fresh when they arrived, but even slightly stale, I was sure she'd appreciate the treats.

At the very least, I knew she'd appreciate a little delivery of love. She certainly wouldn't be receiving any from Dylan.

I'd hated the guy the instant I'd met him. His smarmy smile and slimy charm had instantly rubbed me the wrong way. Stacey and I hadn't known each other long when the four of us had gone on our first double date, and the evening would have put an end to our budding friendship if we hadn't wordlessly agreed never to couple date again.

There wasn't a single Dylan story that painted him in good light. He'd once told Stacey he was taking her out for a special night and had come home trashed at two in the morning instead, claiming that after-work drinks had gotten out of hand. Another time, he'd laughed at a new haircut she adored and told her she looked like an aging spinster. But the icing on his jerk cake was the story about the time he'd missed all the calls and texts informing him Stacey was in labor because he'd turned off his phone to watch a game. He'd missed the birth of his child and somehow managed to make Stacey feel like she was the one to blame.

It all infuriated me, but I couldn't say anything without making her jump to his defense. Poor Dylan, no one understood him. Poor Dylan, he had a terrible childhood. Poor Dylan...*Ugh*.

My greatest wish was that Stacey would one day see Dylan for who he was, and she would finally, once and for all, realize she deserved someone who thought she was made of pure sunlight and should be showered in diamonds, not snide, judgmental comments that left her self-esteem in tatters.

I punctuated that last thought by banging the mixing bowl hard on the counter to dump out the scone batter. The noise made me jump and I realized how worked up I'd become thinking about Stacey and her on-again-off-again relationship with Dylan. I took a deep breath to calm myself and forced my shoulders to climb down from their position next to my ears. If I kneaded this dough too much, the scones would come out hard as rocks.

The aroma of the orange zest tickled my nose and soothed me. Three deep breaths later, I was calm enough to work the dough the way it deserved to be treated. My poor scones shouldn't have to bear the brunt of years of pent-up frustration over a situation I couldn't control.

I slid the baking sheet into the hot oven with a sigh. Might as well wish teleportation were real or I could make things appear out of thin air with a snap of my fingers while I was at it. But maybe... I glanced down at my hands. There was no way, was there?

Crystal swore up and down I was a witch, and I could manipulate magic, but so far, I hadn't seen any proof of that. The only magic I'd seen were the fireballs she'd created.

I held my breath and stared hard at my fingers. A snap. That's how they did it on TV, right? A snap and poof––magic happened. With my face screwed up so tightly I could barely see, I held my hand out as far as possible as I cautiously snapped my fingers.

The tiny sound that emerged wasn't accompanied by a spark or anything resembling magic. I tensed again and snapped a little harder. Nothing.

Feeling like an absolute idiot, I put the tip of my finger on my nose and waggled it. Nothing. Maybe

I needed to think about something specific for it to work.

I closed my eyes tightly and visualized a mocha latte appearing in front of me as I snapped my fingers again. No such luck. When I opened my eyes, there was no coffee of any kind anywhere. With a forced chuckle, I shrugged and went to work on the dishes in the sink.

"Something funny?" Crystal asked as she came through the swinging doors.

My jaw dropped when I turned from the sink to say hi.

"Mocha latte?" She held up a steaming mug and frowned at the look on my face. "What?"

I looked down at my fingers and back up at the cup she held in her left hand. "I, uh, I snapped my fingers."

"Uh, good for you? Has that been challenging for you in the past?" She looked utterly baffled.

"No, I mean, I thought about a mocha latte and snapped my fingers and you walked in with one. Is that a witchy powers thing?"

At first only a small chuckle escaped. Pretty soon, Crystal was laughing so hard she had to place my latte on the counter so she wouldn't spill it. She held her stomach as laughter bubbled out of her. Every time she managed to catch her breath, she'd look up at me, glance at the latte, and start laughing all over again.

"Very funny," I said, grabbing the mug. No need for it to get cold while she had her moment. "Make fun of the newbie witch. How am I supposed to know what's possible or not?"

Crystal took a deep breath and tried to settle herself. "No, no, you're absolutely right. No way for you to know." She giggled again. "But..." she snapped her fingers and laughed again. "Wouldn't that be nice?"

I harrumphed at her. "Yes! It would!"

"Bummer it's not possible. Sorry to say, but magic can't create things out of thin air." She laughed at my disappointed face and hoisted herself onto a counter stool. "Okay, basic facts. Whatever you've seen on TV is most likely not true. You can't snap your fingers or wiggle your nose to make things appear. And, as I mentioned yesterday, you can't fly on a broom." I grimaced. She absolutely did not need to know how bummed I was about that. How cool would that have been? "Let's see, what else? Oh! There are no magical closets that transport you to other realms. And I've never heard of any potions that actually use eye of newt or frog toes or bat's drool. How would you even go about collecting bat drool? Absurd."

"So, no cauldrons?" I asked, pretending to be disappointed. "I kinda had my heart set on a nice shiny black one."

"Oh, no, those are totally real." Crystal said, dead seriously.

"You're shitting me."

"But only because it makes sense to keep your potions away from your regular cooking things and everyone knows cast iron is the best for heat distribution."

"Well, duh." I felt a little dumb for not thinking of that. "Do all witches have the same powers? Wait, are they even called powers? Abilities? Skills?"

"Abilities is a good word. Affinities works too. And everyone has different ones. Kinda. It's complicated."

"So, how do I discover what I can do?" Visions of making things fly through the air danced through my head.

"Well, your powers are only just starting to appear. You'll figure it out as they mature."

"And why is that exactly?"

"Why what?"

"Why are my powers only appearing now? Is that a witch thing? Only coming into your powers in middle age?"

"Nah, that has everything to do with your upbringing. If powers aren't nurtured and encouraged when they first appear during childhood, they can go dormant. Occasionally, a huge shock can trigger them later on in life, but it's pretty rare."

"A huge shock like...?"

"Divorce. Sickness. Accident. Grief. Something that makes all your emotions go haywire."

"Ah." Well, that made sense.

"Any other burning questions?" She peered at me over her mug. She looked like she knew exactly what I wanted to ask, so I decided to throw her a curveball.

"Yeah. How'd you know Deputy Griffin came by in the middle of the night?" I raised my eyebrow and stared at her.

"Oh, Sam and I go way back," she shrugged. "Small town and all that."

"Good to know." Note to self, nothing is secret in small towns. "Are you guys like...an item?

Crystal laughed again. "Oh, no. He's not my type at all. We're just friends. He texted me after he left last night. Wanted to see if I'd come by this morning to check on you."

"That was nice of him!" Or creepy. Possibly both. Hard to tell at this point.

"Well, we're generally a nice bunch."

"Generally?"

"What can I say, every town has its witches."

FIFTEEN

The scones came out of the oven looking as tasty as they smelled. I almost couldn't wait to let the orange drizzle dry before I tore into one.

After the magical reality versus fiction crash course, Crystal had finally given me a quick coffee machine tutorial before dashing off. She'd left me to face the beast on my own, and I was still screwing up my courage when Aurie ran into the kitchen, lured by the smell of warm goodness. She paused in front of the cooling scones with a calculating look on her face.

"You know, Mom, I bet Hattie would love these scones. We should walk over and bring her some." She batted her eyelashes in an attempt at an endearing expression that only made her look like she had something in her eye.

"Oh, really, you think that do you?" I replied, with both eyebrows raised in mock surprise.

"Totally. She was telling me yesterday how much she loves chocolate and orange together."

"I'm sure you totally had that conversation." One eyebrow climbed a little higher, this time in disbelief.

"Mom, please?" Aurie wheedled, her face the picture of innocence.

Resistance being futile in the face of a pet store with actual live animals less than fifty feet away, I shook my head and piled a plate high with scones. If I couldn't keep Aurie away from the place, the least I could do was butter up the owner with some, well, butter.

Holding my breath, I pulled a passable double shot of espresso into a to-go mug. After heaving a sigh of relief the machine had cooperated, I topped it off with a mound of foamed milk. I sprinkled the cappuccino with a dash of cinnamon, popped a lid on it, and stuck a few packets of sugar into my pocket before picking up my own half-finished cup and gesturing to Aurie to grab the scones.

"I'm only going next door. Don't let anyone in," I whispered to the bakery after we stepped out. As ridiculous as I felt saying it, it was nothing compared to how absurd it was I felt the building acquiesce.

The door to *A Familiar Place* was wide open, so Aurie's squeals of excitement reached me long before I crossed the threshold, but even when

I entered, the source of the joy wasn't readily apparent.

My original take of the place hadn't been far off. It was Ali Baba's cavern of pet treasures. Everywhere I looked there were either animals or accessories, all of it organized in some haphazard way beyond my comprehension. I had to hand it to Hattie though. It may have been chaotic, but it wasn't unpleasantly so.

I soaked it all in, from the hamster cage perched on top of large bags of dog food to the colorful, chirping birds hopping around on the rafters. Beady yellow eyes gleamed at me from within a stack of what looked like pet beds high up on a shelf. To the left of the entrance was an ornate little pond filled with fat golden fish. Some kind of lizard was sunning itself under a heat lamp positioned over a big rock next to the pond.

I was trying to decide whether the pond was magically real or simply well-made when a loud voice announced my arrival with an ear-splitting screech.

"Visitor! We have a visitor!"

The ungodly noise was coming from the gorgeous parrot hanging upside down in a tree growing right in the middle of the store. He preened when he noticed me eyeballing him and took up his chant again until Hattie popped out of seemingly nowhere. She shushed the parrot and grinned widely at me, the scone in her hand missing a huge bite.

"You have a tree and a pond in your store." My mouth was hanging open in wonderment, but I didn't think I could close it. Never in my life had I been so transported by walking into a store. "This place is..."

"Magical?" Her eyes twinkled with delight.

"Well, yeah." I laughed. The hot cup in my hand reminded me I had brought Hattie something to go with the scones. "I brought you a cup of coffee. I wasn't sure what your drink of choice might be, so I went simple. Cappuccino. I have sugar in my pocket if you'd like." I handed over the cup and took a swig of my own coffee to settle myself. As if more caffeine was going to help me at this point. "This place is truly amazing." The longer I looked, the more marvels popped out at me.

"So are these scones," she replied with a laugh, taking another bite, and nodding her thanks for the coffee which she took gratefully.

"Mom! Mom! Come see!" Aurie's voice called to me from behind the tree and I looked at Hattie for direction. She nodded encouragingly before taking a sip of her coffee and grinning appreciatively.

"It was a long night. This coffee is very welcome, thank you."

"Long night?"

"You'll see." She smiled mysteriously and led me to the back of the store.

The image that greeted me when I rounded the tree wasn't immediately clear. A little squeal drew my eyes to a pile of small squirmy bodies in a plastic toddler pool lined with a cozy, tattered quilt. Aurie was kneeling by the pool watching the action with rapt attention and not a small amount of longing on her face. A tired looking mama was lying against the side of the pool, occasionally nudging the puppies that wormed their way too far from the pack and whimpered piteously.

"Mom! Look! Newborn puppies! They're not even a day old yet! Can we have one? Please, please, please? I promise I'll take care of it. You won't have to do *anything*!" As Aurie looked at me with eyes as big as saucers, one of the tiny puppies bumped up against the hand she was holding open on the blanket.

We all watched in wonder as it somehow heaved itself onto her palm and curled up, letting out a little mewl of contentment. She looked down at it with awe and carefully lifted her hand to her chest. It nestled against her as she crooned and rocked it gently before she turned to me, her mouth a perfect 'O' of awe and delight.

Hattie chuckled. "Seems like this little one's familiar has found her."

"Familiar?" Aurie and I both asked at the same time.

Hattie beamed at us both. "Oh, this is so fun! A witch's familiar is an animal that has a special connection to her. Not all witches have familiars, but it's very common for animal witches to have one." She winked knowingly at Aurie who made a point of not looking in my direction. "Don't worry, this one won't be ready to go home with Aurie for a while. You'll have time to come to grips with it." She nudged me with her elbow and chuckled. "I know it's a lot to take in. Don't worry about a thing. We've got your back. You'll catch up soon enough."

"Aurie? You know about all this stuff?" How had she not said a word?

Aurie shrugged looking down at the puppies. "Yeah, Hattie told me, it's no big."

Really, kid? If it's no big, why are your shoulders so tense? The puppy wriggled in her hand and Aurie's shoulders relaxed as she let out a delighted giggle.

"Look how cute she is, Mom." She held up the tiny pup and I had to agree. Its tiny pink nose just begged to be booped.

Everyone seemed so sure I'd adapt and find my place in this community, but every day brought new, increasingly unsettling surprises that left me feeling more and more out of place.

Hattie held up her coffee and scone. "Let's go have a sit. You can ask me whatever you want. I'll do my best to answer." She gestured to a little table nestled in a corner of the room under a couple hanging bird cages.

"Are you sure that's safe?" I asked, gesturing to the puppy pool as I settled myself in one of the chairs. "They look fragile."

"Totally sure. It's good for them to be handled a lot even now. Socialization is important. And Aurie is a natural. I have complete faith in her."

"You do?" I tried to erase the dubious frown forming on my face.

Hattie laughed as if I'd told a great joke. "Absolutely."

"If you say so." I was willing to give Hattie the benefit of the doubt. After all, she knew animals better than I did. But just in case, I kept a wary eye on Aurie.

I couldn't quite make out how many puppies were squirming around their tired looking mama, but I could see Aurie's puppy hadn't strayed far from her hand. *Aurie's puppy*. My life had officially gone off the rails.

"So, tell me, what has Crystal shared with you about witches so far?"

"I'm one, Aurie is one. It's hereditary. Only women are witches, so my father wasn't one, but passed down his witch genes to us. The rest is a bit fuzzy. Crystal said something about magic being all around us, but I'm not clear on where it comes from. Or on how it manifests differently from one witch to another. Can I learn to control it? What will Aurie's magic look like? What do animal witches do?" Visions of my daughter controlling zoo animals to do her bidding suddenly made me gulp. "Can we hurt people?" The last question came out as a whisper, and I realized that out of all of them, it was the question I needed answered the most.

"Well, in a word, yes. Magic can be used to harm people." When my face blanched, she hurried to finish her thought, "But most witches don't dabble in the kind of magic that can hurt others. Not intentionally at least. Let me back up a little." She smiled warmly and my racing heart slowed to a fast trot.

As though she knew I needed more help relaxing, she leaned forward and scooped up a squirming pup and plopped it unceremoniously onto my lap. I snatched the tiny dog up as it was about to roll off and pulled it close to my chest. The newborn squeaked and snuggled into my neck before relaxing into sleep with a little whuffle sound.

I tried to glare at Hattie to let her know I was onto her game, but it was hard to be mad with something so sweet and innocent in my arms. She laughed at the conflicted emotions warring across my face.

"I'll find you books that go into more detail, if you'd like, but here's the gist of it. As Crystal told you, magic is everywhere." She waved her hand around her vaguely. "It's all around us. It's the force holding the universe together. It keeps nature in balance." She glanced at me to see if I was with her. I nodded uncertainly. "Most mundanes, if they are in tune with themselves and with the world around them, can somewhat feel the flow of magic, but they can't impact it or influence it."

"Let me guess. People with magic can?"

"Yes, exactly. Much like a person can dip into a river and pull out water to drink or use, witches can dip into the flow of magic and use the magic they pull out. Untrained witches do it instinctively." She nodded at Aurie, who was gently soothing the squealing puppies fighting over their mother's teats. With a light touch of her hand on their back, they settled down and relaxed. "Trained witches can access the magic intentionally and shape it to their will."

"That sounds..." *Terrifying. Horrific. Atrocious. Potentially lethal to everyone in the vicinity.*

"I know, it sounds scary. But there are rules. Rules that have been in place since the beginning of time. Rules that keep witches from doing harm and keep magic safe for all."

"Rules are good," I said with a nervous grin. "Are there many?"

"Only three. But they're rules, not guidelines. Rules." She cut me a very serious look. "Rule number one. There's a price for everything. Big magic equals big price. Little magic, little price. The price doesn't look the same in every case. Most of the time, it's energy. Occasionally, it might be more." I was a little grateful she didn't elaborate.

"Rule number two is actually the rule of thirds. Everything you put out into the world magically comes back to you threefold. People think we tell newbies this to keep them in check, but take my word for it, it's a real thing." She visibly shuddered. I grimaced sympathetically.

"So, in short, magic isn't something to be trifled with," I said. I was already scared of what I could do with my baking, but now I was downright terrified.

"No, definitely nothing to be trifled with, but it's not all bad." She laughed at my skeptical look. "The witching community is one of the most diverse and amazing collections of people you'll ever meet. Strong, capable women with massive hearts. Which leads us to rule number three. Sharing is caring."

After the dire solemnity of the first two rules, the last one made me laugh out loud. Hattie chuckled as well. "Fine, that last one is more of a guideline than a strict rule. Witches have different affinities. As you probably deduced, I'm an animal witch. You're a kitchen witch."

"Crystal told me as much. She also mentioned garden witches, healers, hedge witches and..." I blanked for a moment, then it came back to me, "weather witches."

Hattie nodded at me, looking a little impressed. "Yes, all those and a few other rare types you'll probably never encounter. Did she explain about how we all have affinity with the different elements?"

"Yes," I nodded, "Water, air, fire, earth."

"Exactly. While we all have some access to all the elements, we each have our own affinities. So, a kitchen witch might have some garden abilities, and a hedge witch might have some healer abilities. But an animal witch will never control the weather or be able to commune with spirits."

I nodded again. Amazingly, that made a certain sort of sense.

"So, we share. We rely on each other. We're a community."

"Sharing is caring," I parroted.

"Exactly. Think of yourself as part of a whole. A spoke in a wheel that only turns properly if everyone does their part. We believe magical abilities were divided the way they were to make sure no one ever gets too much power on their own. Obviously, it's not a foolproof system. There are witches with more innate power than others, and sometimes that goes to their head." Her eyes narrowed, and I wondered about the things I didn't yet know. "But for the most part, it's a good system."

I watched Aurie playing with the puppies for a moment.

"It sounds to me like the rules are in place to protect the witches and the community more than anything," I said, something about it all poking at the back of my brain.

Hattie nodded and waited for me to continue.

"What about protecting the people who can be affected by magic?"

Hattie shrugged. "Occasionally, there's collateral damage, but it's rare. Intent is what powers our magic, so, if our hearts are in the right place, people don't usually get hurt."

"Usually." My heart sank. "But we don't really know, do we?"

"Well, no. No more than a therapist really knows if their advice is going help their client or a doctor

133

knows if a medication's side effect isn't going to make things worse."

"Then why risk it? It doesn't seem to me like it's worth it."

"Oh, honey." She reached over and patted my shoulder. "Trust me, it's worth it. Magic is amazing. You'll see. But we don't have a choice. Witches have a duty to use magic."

"A duty?" I looked at her skeptically.

"We're kind of like magical monitors. Every time we connect to the flow, or dip into it for some magic, we get a feel for how it's doing. Pulling magic in and out of the flow allows it to stay stable and healthy. We keep the flow in balance, which in turns keeps the world balanced."

"And if we didn't?"

She shrugged. "People seem determined to destroy our world. What we do negates a lot of what they do."

"But not all?"

She shook her head sadly. "No, not all. We do our best and we can only hope it'll be enough in the long run." She forced a smile onto her face. "Your job right now is to learn everything you can about your magic so you can raise your little witchling. The rest will fall into place later."

She gently took the tiny puppy from my arms where he was starting to squirm and nose around my neck. "This little one is hungry. Let's return him to his mother, and I'll show you around the rest of the store."

"That's okay," I replied. "I think I need to go process all of this. Do you mind if Aurie stays here a little longer?"

She smiled lovingly at my daughter who was giving the mama dog some very welcome ear scratches. "She's welcome to stay as long as she'd like. Always."

I stopped with my hand on the door and looked back. "Hattie?"

"Yeah?"

"Can I hurt people with what I bake?"

She turned and eyed me seriously. "That you're worried is what assures me you'll make a fine witch." She smiled.

Not reassured in the least, I grimaced and turned to leave.

"Cassie?" Her voice stopped me, and I turned back to look at her. "Have you found her grimoire yet? I'm sure you'll find all the answers you need in it."

"Grimoire?"

"Big ol' book. Leather bound. Probably somewhere in the kitchen. She never let it too far out of her sight. It contains all her spells and notes about magic."

135

SIXTEEN

"**F**ind anything good?"

The interruption surprised me so much I nearly jumped out of my skin. Guilt flooded me and it took a few deep breaths to get my racing heart under enough control to turn around and greet my unexpected visitor.

I hadn't been doing anything wrong. I was in my kitchen, technically looking through my things, but I couldn't shake the sensation I was snooping through my great aunt's belongings. Being caught in the act didn't help.

"Hi! Hi!" Sorry, I didn't hear you come in!" I winced. My voice was about three pitches too high. I knew the woman smiling awkwardly at me, could picture her standing in the bakery introducing herself, but my brain point blank refused to supply her name. Mortification made my face hot. "I'm so sorry, I know we've met, but I'm terrible with names."

"Hi. Juliette. I own the bookstore up the street." Her smile had a slight edge to it, but I couldn't tell if it was because she was offended or because she could tell something was off with how I was behaving. "I stopped by the day you arrived to introduce myself."

"Oh! Of course! Sorry, again."

"No worries." She smiled again, this time a little more warmly. "Sorry to barge in on you like this. I called a number of times from the front of the store, but no one answered. I heard you rustling around and thought it might be okay for me to come find you back here."

"Of course!" If people were going to keep coming in unannounced like this, I was going to have to invest in a bell for the bakery door. Being startled every time was starting to get embarrassing.

"I just wanted to drop off a little housewarming gift." She held out a rectangular gift beautifully wrapped in colorful paper.

"Oh! Thank you!" I reached out eagerly for the package. "That is so sweet. In case I didn't mention it when we first met, I love books."

"I could tell. Bookseller sixth sense." She tapped the side of her nose, her facial expression thawing a little more. The laugh that escaped when my eyes flew open brought her face to life. "It's not magic. I'm just good at my job. Anyway, open it!"

"I'm actually craving a cup of tea. Can I make you one, too?"

"Oh, yes please, that would be lovely," she said, easing herself onto one of the tall stools lining the counter.

I filled the kettle and turned it on before perching myself on the stool next to hers. The package was slim, but it felt substantial in my hands and a little thrill raced through me as I unwrapped it. My love for books knew no bounds. For a shy kid who moved around a lot, they'd offered a crucial lifeline.

The book I pulled from the wrapping looked like it had been self-published on a small-town press. The paper was new and shiny, but it looked like an old-timey pamphlet. The title, *A Short but Accurate History of Portney Witches* was splayed across an old-fashioned photo probably taken in the early 1900s. None of the women in the photo were familiar to me, but something about the old lady in the middle called to me. The mischievous twinkle in her eye and the twitch of her cheek made her stand out from the austere women surrounding her.

"I, uh, thank you. This is great!" I said, looking up from the photo to find Juliette looking at me intently.

"Do you recognize her?" She pointed at the book's cover.

"Recognize?" I looked down at the cover again. "The woman in the middle?" Juliette nodded, her expression carefully guarded. "Can't say I do, sorry." I tilted the book a little so the light would catch the old woman's face better, but other than a vague sense of familiarity, I couldn't place her.

"She was the matriarch of the Blackwell clan. Dottie Blackwell. Her given name was Dorothy, but no one ever called her that. I know a little about the position you're in. I thought you might be curious about where you came from." Juliette's mouth quirked up in a little half smile.

My heart sped up as I realized what I was holding. Juliette's eyes gleamed as if she knew exactly how much this gift meant to me.

"Thank you." My voice hitched on the words. I'd grown up knowing so little about my extended family, but I'd never stopped wondering, even going so far as to make up elaborate stories about the people my grandparents might have been. It was hard to believe I was holding the real story in my hands.

I couldn't stop myself from flipping through the booklet. The witches of Portney had apparently lived fruitful lives if the many family portraits were to be believed. I was peering at a photo of the Blackwell clan when I realized my visitor's attention was wandering.

"Oh, I am so sorry, I was being so rude." I regretfully let the booklet close and looked up at my guest.

Juliette's face spun back, but not so fast I didn't see her eye the kitchen bookshelves with more than idle curiosity.

"I've only just started going through the books," I said, tilting my head at the shelves. "It's an odd assortment of things." I laughed awkwardly and wondered if I was imagining the undercurrent of tension I was feeling.

"Oh?" Juliette said, with a studied nonchalance that piqued my interest.

"Pretty much everything from classic cookbooks to mass market paperbacks. The range is actually pretty impressive."

"Cookbooks?" Interest flared in her eyes. "How fun. Do you mind if I take a look?"

I shrugged and smiled blandly, which she took as an invitation. She sauntered over to the shelves while I pretended to go back to perusing my book. A quick glance in her direction revealed I'd been right to be suspicious. Instead of reading the spines, she was peering behind the books. The moment she tilted her head a little to the left, she looked enough like the person who'd broken into my kitchen to send a shudder down my back.

I narrowed my eyes and looked closer. It had been dark, and I'd been a little too freaked out to pay close attention, but their builds were similar. Juliette spun around and smiled at me when my breath hitched. The suspicious part of my brain noted the smile didn't quite reach her eyes.

"It really is an eclectic collection. If you decide there's stuff in here you don't want to keep, I'd be happy to sell them for you. In fact, I have a little free time today. I could help you sort through the books if you'd like!" Her excessive eagerness made me recoil a little. She dialed it back and waved at the books as though they were the reason she was excited. "I just, you know, old books."

"Oh, I know," I replied, forcing myself to smile back. "I can't wait to go through them all. I'll be sure to bring by anything I don't want to keep, though!"

I kept my bland smile on my face and watched her fish for an excuse to stay, but since we'd finished our tea and she had ostensibly fulfilled the purpose of her visit, she came up empty. With a longing look back at the shelves, Juliette said her goodbyes and headed out.

I'd been idly curious about the bookshelf before, not convinced in the least it would contain the book Hattie had mentioned. Now I was anxious to see what secrets I'd find tucked between the ordinary covers.

SEVENTEEN

Cassie! OMG! Scones!

Wow. They arrived fast. Are they stale?

No. They're perfect.
And I'm not sharing them with anyone.
Not even my beloved crotch fruit.

I take it she's home from her dad's?

Can't text.
Too busy stuffing face with glorious scone goodness.

Wish we could be enjoying those together.
I miss you.

I miss you too, but I said I'm not sharing, so you'd be out of luck.

You seriously think I sent you the whole batch? Got my own right here.

With a chuckle I popped a scone into the warming oven while I made myself a cup of coffee. As soon as my latte and my scone were ready, I tapped Stacey's video call icon. While I waited for her to pick up, I breathed in a deep and happy breath. The combined scent of chocolate, orange, and coffee was as soothing to my soul as a nice, hot bubble bath.

"Still can't talk. Too busy eating," Stacey garbled through a mouthful of scone.

"Then why did you answer, you nut?"

"You call. I answer. Them's the besties rules."

"Fair enough. Anyway, how's it going?"

"Well, I'm languishing over here, reduced to only getting stale leftovers instead of fresh baked goods right from your oven. If this keeps up, I might have to find a way to relocate us to whatever the heck backwards town you've moved to."

"A, that would be ridiculously amazing. And B, there's nothing backwards about this town. Quaint, maybe, but I haven't seen a single outhouse yet."

"Yet."

"I did see the library yesterday on my walk. You'd love it. So cute. Exactly the way a small-town library should look."

"Brick walls, whitewashed pillars?"

"Yes!" I gushed. "So cute. I can't wait to take Aurie. It was closed when I went by, but I bet the inside is just as amazing."

"I do love a quaint, old-timey library," Stacey said, scone crumbs falling out of the side of her mouth. "These are amazing, by the way. You've outdone yourself. Even slightly stale they're still better than anything I could ever buy around here." She moaned contentedly. "Hey, thanks for letting me vent the other day. I know all my Dylan stuff drives you a little batty."

I avoided answering by taking a bite of my own scone. She wasn't wrong. They were exceptionally good, even a couple days old. The orange flavor blended delightfully with the rich Madagascar chocolate, enhanced by the hint of nutmeg I'd thought to throw in at the last minute. I'd considered going with cinnamon, but something had pulled my hand toward the nutmeg instead. I didn't regret it in the least.

"Sometimes I think you're right, you know."

"I'm sorry, what? Can you repeat that so I can hit the record button?" I teased. I knew I was always right, but Stacey, for some strange reason, didn't consistently agree. Rude.

"I mean it," she said, smiling shyly like she wasn't sure how I would take what she was about to say. "About Dylan. I was trying to figure out how long he might be gone this time and if maybe I should cancel my weekend plans in case he comes home and wants to spend time with us. But then I thought about you and Aurie in an awesome new place that has so much potential, and I couldn't stop myself from thinking maybe you're right. Maybe I do need to tell him to get lost once and for all. I deserve better!"

The passion in her voice and the fire in her eyes made me sit up, a little stunned. Never in all the years we'd been having this conversation had she sounded so determined.

"Shane deserves better!" I held my breath. "How dare he keep wafting in and out of our lives like that? Does he think we're always going to be here waiting for him?"

I bit my lip to keep from pointing out she'd been doing exactly that for as long as I'd known her. We'd had conversations about Dylan a million times over the years, but hearing my words come out of her mouth was new. I'd always suspected she didn't believe a word I counseled even as she nodded yes and made little agreeable noises. I almost didn't dare believe what I was hearing.

"If my kid were being strung along like this by a guy, I'd be livid!" She stopped and gasped. "What am I saying?" My heart dipped a little and I checked my hope. "She IS being strung along! And I'm not only allowing it. I'm enabling it! What the heck is wrong with me?"

I kept my mouth shut, but Stacey didn't seem to need my input. She moved away from the phone and started pacing around the room. Her kitchen was big enough she kept moving in and out of the camera's frame. "Almost ten years he's been leaving and coming back when it suits him. Did you know every single time I've been asked out on a date, he somehow magically reappears?"

I nodded grimly. She'd mentioned it once or twice. Dylan had a sixth sense when it came to Stacey. As soon as it seemed like she might be getting ready to move on, he'd swoop back in and reclaim his place in her life. Then, as soon as she was well and truly ensnared once more, he'd fly off again.

"I could be with someone who actually cares about me right now! I could be happy instead of constantly wondering when he's coming back and if he's going to stay this time. *Eh-nough*. I am done!" She pounded her hand on something off camera and cussed under her breath. I bit back a laugh when she walked back into the frame, rubbing the side of her hand with a wince. Her tone dropped and she said the next sentence in a quietly determined voice looking me straight in the eye. "You're hearing it for the first time, Cassie. This girl is 100% moving on. Dylan is officially in my past."

She sat down with a thump, exhausted by her outburst, picked up her mug, and drained it in one gulp. I waited to see if she was done, fully expecting to see remorse come thundering across her face but only firm resolve set up camp. Resolve that looked a whole lot like relief.

I was about to open my mouth, but before I could say anything she continued.

"I'll still have to see him of course." I flinched, here it was. "Because Shane. He is her dad. But we're not going to live our lives waiting for him. That's over. I deserve better. She deserves better. I don't want her to grow up thinking it's okay to let a guy treat you like he's been treating us. I'm going to take a page from your book." She looked at me again, eyes ablaze. "New start. New life! Just us girls, amirite? Guys! Who needs 'em? We're plenty enough on our own!" She pumped her first victoriously in the air, raining scone crumbs down on her head.

Scone. Scone I had baked hoping she'd have this very kind of epiphany. Scone she'd been inhaling during this entire outburst. Ah. *Shit*.

The piece of scone I'd been holding made a moist little thud when it hit the table. It hadn't tasted strange or magical, either today or when they'd been fresh out of the oven. I didn't *feel* strange or magically influenced. Aurie and Hattie hadn't *seemed* affected by them. My heart did a little lurch in my chest, and I rolled my tongue around my teeth probing for crumbs to see if maybe they felt different. I'd already eaten half the scone, listening to Stacey, but surely I would have noticed if the scone tasted tingly or something.

"Did your scone taste tingly?" I asked Stacey, interrupting her.

She paused mid word. "What?" Her tongue did the same probing thing mine had done then she smushed an errant crumb on her plate with her finger and stuck it in her mouth. "No, it tastes..." she paused, "like a scone. A really good chocolate-orange scone. Why? Did you put something different in it? Wait..." Her eyes opened wide. "Are they magical?" The last bit came out in a bit of whispered awe. She sat up and narrowed her eyes. "What were you thinking about when you baked them?"

I squirmed in my seat and avoided meeting her gaze. "I didn't do it on purpose! I swear!"

"What. Did. You. Think. About. When. You. Baked. Them?" The hint of anger in her tone made me cringe.

I stared at my plate and mumbled. "I was thinking about how I wished you could see Dylan the way I do."

"I'm sorry, you were mumbling. Did you say you were thinking about me and Dylan while you were baking?"

I nodded sheepishly.

"And...?" she prompted.

"I wanted you to see that you deserve to be treated like the amazing human being you are." She didn't start yelling, so I continued. "It's been so long, Stacey. He treats you like shit. He makes you wait around for him, and it makes me so sad because you're incredible and you deserve to be with someone who sees that. I just want you to be happy."

"I am happy!" she protested. I stared at her without speaking. "Okay, right now I'm not all that happy. But it's temporary." I stared at her again. "I swear! And anyway, I'm done with him! He's gone. I'm over it. Okay, I'm not *over it* over it, but this time

I'm not letting him come back." She glowered at me and my skeptical look. "Listen, you don't know how hard it is."

"Right, because apparently my marriage was a fairytale. And yes, while I am fully aware I didn't realize it was all messed up until it ended, looking back, I can see how much better things should have been. You deserve that too." I softened my words with a gentle smile. "I know what Dylan is like when he turns on the charm. I know how much you have invested in him. I just wish..." I glanced at the remains of my scone, my stomach twisting in on itself. What if my magic had done irreparable damage? Who was I to mess with people's lives?

Stacey eyes followed my gaze and she reached out to grab the remains of her scone. She locked eyes with me and lifted it to her mouth, daring me to stop her.

"What are you doing? That thing might be full of magic!" I screamed, jumping up and shaking my phone as it if could dislodge the scone from her hand. She smirked and shoved the rest of the scone in her mouth.

Crumbs sprayed out as she spoke. "I've already eaten two. Whatever effect it's going to have on me is already happening." She gulped down the scone still lodged in her mouth. "I can't tell you how determined I am to cut Dylan loose once and for all.

Whether that's the scone or me being finally, really done, I don't know. But I'm not scared of you or whatever you cook up in your kitchen." She took another swig of coffee.

"Why are you so okay with all this?" I was freaking out inside, but she looked cool as a cucumber as she put the last bite of the scone in her mouth.

Stacey shrugged. "I wasn't at first. I freaked out hard when you first told me. I almost called Max to tell him he should have you committed."

I shuddered at the thought. He would have done it, too. Just to spite me.

"But the more I thought about it, the less it panicked me. There are plenty of things in this world I don't understand. I'm willing to keep an open mind. Plus, it's you. If you told me you were an alien from another planet, it would still be you. And I love you no matter what."

My heart melted. I wasn't sure what I'd done to earn that kind of loyalty and love, but I was glad to have them.

"Let me ask you something."

"Okay," I replied, bracing myself.

"Do *you* feel any different? Did your scone affect *you* in any way?"

I didn't feel any different. I ran through my thoughts quickly. My feelings about Dylan hadn't changed at all, nor had my feelings about Dylan and Stacey as a couple. Had my feelings for Max been influenced by the scone? Nah, I was still totally numb about the demise of my own relationship.

"No. I feel the same."

"And did anyone else eat these scones?" I nodded in reply, and she continued. "Did *they* act any different?"

I shook my head.

"That makes sense."

"It does?"

"Yeah, I've been thinking about your magic. I'm not the only one who ate those chocolate chip muffins you made, but I don't think anyone else was affected. And these scones only seem to be affecting me. I think the magic only works on the person you intend it for."

"That makes sense in a roundabout way. But what if..." I stopped. How powerful was this magic? Could I make anyone do anything I want? I gulped.

"I don't think you have ultimate power." Stacey said, rolling her eyes at my dramatic expression.

"You don't?" I wasn't even surprised she'd guessed what I was thinking.

"No. I think your magic only works if the person is already feeling a certain way and just needs a nudge. Like, I really wanted to stand up to that editor. And I've wanted to cut Dylan out of my life for so long, I just haven't felt strong enough to do so. I don't think you could persuade someone to do something they don't ultimately want to."

"How can we be sure?"

She shrugged. "You might want to check with that Diamond chick, but it seems logical to me."

Relief made me sag against my chair. "Oh, thank goodness. And her name is Crystal, not Diamond."

"Whatever," she said with a dismissive wave before letting out a little giggle. "You had visions of people jumping off bridges and committing crimes after eating your pastries, didn't you?"

"Something like that. I can't always control my thoughts. What if I thought something horrible while I was baking?" I shuddered. "Maybe I shouldn't risk it. Maybe it would be best if I didn't bake anymore."

Sadness washed over me, and I looked forlornly at the gorgeous bakery around me. Max might have thought I was an idiot doomed to failure because a bakery was a stupid investment, but if I failed because my baked goods harmed people, he'd be proven just as right in the end. I didn't want him to be right. But I also didn't want to hurt anyone.

"Now that, my friend, would be a crime against humanity." Anger flashed in Stacey's eyes. "Listen, let's not jump to any conclusions. Talk to Crystal. Maybe pop into the library and do a little research on your ancestors. See if anyone is connected to any suspicious deaths or tragedies. So far, all your magic has done is give me a few well-meaning nudges in the right direction."

"As far as we know." I looked at her glumly. The only thing guaranteed to pull me out of a funk like this was an afternoon of baking, but that didn't seem like a great idea at this point. I valiantly resisted the urge to stuff a scone into my face to smother my feelings and mustered a smidge of excitement as I said, "Guess what?"

"What?" Stacey replied, gamely letting me change the subject.

"Magic shelves." I flipped the camera around and showed her the endless stacks of books on the floor of the bakery kitchen.

"Where did all those books come from?" she asked.

I laughed. "The bookshelf." I panned the camera over the shelves above the little desk.

"That bookshelf?" Stacey asked, skepticism written all over her face.

She wasn't wrong to question my comment. The bookshelf in question was a little one, four shelves, deep enough for a book, two if they were small paperbacks. I was surrounded by dozens of books.

"I don't know what to tell you. I started pulling books off the shelves and they kept appearing."

"Magic shelves?" Stacey whispered reverently, her hand hovering over her open mouth. Her eyes widened and she looked at me, excitement splashed across her face. "Do you know the kind of money you could make if you could market those babies?"

I laughed. "Somehow I don't think that would be kosher with the witching community."

"Harumph. Figures." She frowned and glanced at the stacks of books on the floor. "Find anything good?"

"Not really. There's no rhyme or reason to it. There's literally everything from space-opera novels to some really ancient-looking cookbooks. I'm sorting through it, but there's so much variety I don't know where to start."

"Maybe you could...?" Stacey put her finger on her nose and wiggled it a little. I laughed.

"Yeah, no. Apparently that's not how magic works."

"Bummer."

"I know!" So far the whole magic thing had been a whole lot of stress and disappointment, nothing nearly as cool as I'd imagined. "I think I'm going to start sorting old from new and take it from there."

"Seems like as good a plan as any. I wish I were there to help."

"Ditto," I said, shooting a despairing glance at the piles of books at my feet. "I'm really looking for an old leather-bound diary."

"A diary?" Stacey asked. "Hoping to find some inside dirt on Great Aunt Bea?"

"Hardy har. No. Someone told me she kept one and I have a hunch it's important."

EIGHTEEN

Pulling all the books from the shelf took longer than expected. Eventually, I'd looked through each and every book and could say with 100% certainty Bea's book wasn't among the eclectic assortment of mass-market paperbacks, cookbooks, and herbalist reference guides.

The mass-market pile was by far the largest, and I made a mental note to add a bookshelf to the bakery to house them. Offering something to read to the customers might encourage them to stay longer. Then I made a second mental note to stop making plans about running a bakery until I had officially decided to run a bakery.

With a deep sigh, I got to work putting everything back on the shelf. If the grimoire wasn't here, I didn't have a clue about where I'd find it. I'd checked the bookshelf in Aurie's room and the one in mine and had come up empty, so, unless the grimoire was in a super-secret hiding place, it wasn't anywhere here.

Which begged the question, where was it?

I was debating which of my new acquaintances might be able to tell me where else to look when Aurie barreled through the door.

"Mom! If I don't get some lunch right now, I'm going to die."

"Wow. You must be really hungry." I laughed at her dramatic expression.

"So hungry. Feed me. Please."

A quick glance at the clock confirmed what my stomach had been yelling at me for a while. It had been more than a few hours since Stacey and I had virtually shared a scone. Sadly, despite being within arms reach of a packed pantry, I didn't have anything ready to serve Aurie. She was going to need a little more than a leftover scone.

I grimaced as I straightened up, my back protesting the way I'd been mistreating it all morning.

"How about...a hot dog?" Her eyes brightened at the suggestion, "or we could go get some lobster rolls to eat by the water!"

"But what if I don't like lobster rolls?" Aurie gave me a leery look.

"We can get you a hot dog AND a lobster roll," I said, ruffling her hair. "I'm sure we can find someone who'll want whichever you don't eat."

Less than twenty minutes later, lobster roll in hand, feet and butt planted in the sand, I looked at the glittering sea and took a deep breath. Aurie was already halfway done with her lobster roll and the happy sounds she was making told me the local treat had skyrocketed to the top of her favorite foods list.

"Now, this, I could get used to." Back in Georgia, we hadn't lived too far from the ocean, but somehow the beach hadn't been part of our regular haunts. Max loathed getting sandy or dirty and had a visceral aversion to crowds. Or rather, he thought sitting on a towel at the beach all day was reserved for "the lower classes." He believed the cabanas lining the country club pool were more fitting for "our station." I rolled my eyes and dug my toes deeper into the warm sand.

Sitting here on an almost deserted beach, looking out on a breathtaking view, the sun caressing my shoulders, I couldn't remember why Aurie and I had never gone without him.

I took a bite of my roll and let out a groan of my own. I hadn't tasted all the lobster rolls on the coast, but I was willing to take the "Best Lobster Rolls in

Massachusetts" poster on the Lobster Shack wall at face value.

"Definitely a plus in the Portney column." I wiggled my toes deeper into the sand and felt myself relax.

Lunch scarfed down, Aurie abandoned me to go splash around in the surf.

The normalcy of the situation washed over me, and I tried hard to let go of the fear that had gripped my stomach while talking to Stacey. She'd done her best to talk me down, but there was no way she could understand how terrifying it was to know something I baked could directly affect someone's life.

Baking to make people happy was one thing. Knowing my baking could influence their actions felt like a doozie of a responsibility. One that was seriously making me wonder if it would be reckless to open a bakery.

Aurie squealed as she jumped over a wave, and I suddenly remembered the moment a nurse had first placed her tiny body in my arms. She'd made a tiny peep and pursed her lips together before falling into a deep sleep, and I had been overwhelmed with the scope of the job I'd undertaken. I'd been clear on the basics of infant care, but it hadn't occurred to me until then that everything I did would shape her life one way or another. The sheer weight of the responsibility had made me dizzy.

The realization had quickly been overshadowed with basic infant care, but occasionally something happened to remind me how much my decisions and actions affected Aurie's life. As she'd grown, I'd come to realize that despite all that, she was very much her own person. I could guide her and try to impose my values by setting good examples, but ultimately, guiding was all it would ever be.

She burst into giggles when a wave caught her by surprise and knocked her off her feet. Some of the tension gripping my shoulders seeped away. Gentle nudges to push people in the right direction didn't seem immoral. I could learn to live with magic like that.

"Hey, babe, come over here for a second!" I called to Aurie before she could leap back into the water. "There's something I want to discuss with you." If there was a better time to bring it up than now, I couldn't think of it.

The wary look on Aurie's face as she approached was so reminiscent of her father's when I'd first met him it made my heart hitch. There was enough of me in her I sometimes conveniently forgot half her genes were his.

I hesitated. What if tearing Aurie from the life she knew in Georgia triggered the kind of cynicism that made Max always see the glass as half empty? Who was to say what part of his childhood had made him distrustful of everyone and everything?

Maybe she'd be better off if I took her home and rented out the bakery until she was ready to leave home in eight years or so.

And maybe she wouldn't.

I could feel myself coming alive in this quirky little town. Parts of me that had been ignored for way too long were stretching and tingling with excitement.

Surely a happy, fulfilled mom would be better for Aurie in the long run?

Trust your gut, Cassie.

I shoved aside the thought that maybe my gut was purely self-motivated and patted the clear spot on the towel next to me.

With a sigh, Aurie threw herself down onto her belly and started poking at the sand in front of her.

I took a deep breath and let it out slowly.

"Do you like it here?"

Aurie looked over at me, a whirlwind of emotions rioting on her face. She settled on leery.

"Why?"

The intense, grown-up look on her face, still rounded with lingering hints of baby fat, sent a laugh hurtling through my anxious stomach. My giggle lifted some of the worry on her face, and she didn't fight me when I reached over to pull her closer.

She giggled and wriggled on my lap as I peppered her forehead with butterfly kisses. When I stopped, she settled into my embrace and some of the tension between us eased, making it easier to continue.

"I like it here. I like the ocean and the way the air smells. I think the town is cute and the people are lovely. I even like the way the ground feels under my feet. I want to know how you feel."

"That's silly. Ground is ground." She squinted and thought before answering. "I like the pet shop. And that lobster roll was pretty good."

I laughed. Pretty good? She'd inhaled it in three bites and had asked for a second.

"You want to stay here, don't you, Mama?"

I hadn't realized how much I missed being called Mama until the word came out of her mouth. When had I become "Mom"?

"I do, baby. I really do. I think this place would be really good for both of us. But we're a team and teams make decisions together."

"I miss my friends and my school." She looked over at the ocean and continued quietly. "And Daddy. I miss Daddy."

I hugged her closer. "I know you do. It's hard to be so far from people we love." A pang of longing for Stacey's smile twisted my gut. "But we can talk to them, and video chat, and visiting is always fun."

Her minute nod was accompanied with an equally small shrug.

"What would you think about living here instead of going back to Georgia?"

I did my best to not tense up as I waited for a reply.

"Like, *live* live? All the time? Like I'd go to school here?" Aurie pulled away enough to look at my face. An uncertain scowl creased her forehead.

"Yeah. We could stay in the bakery apartment with Persimmon, and you could go to the school up the street." Her scowl deepened.

I backtracked hastily. "What if we made a deal to try it for a little while? You know, how I asked you to try ballet for a month before giving up on it."

"But I hated ballet."

I laughed. "You really, really did. But you toughed it out for the full month, right? So, we knew when you stopped going it was because you'd really tried it and it hadn't worked, not because you'd given up because it was scary at first."

Aurie's nod was slow and hesitant.

"So, if I really hate it here in a month, we can go home? And I wouldn't have to go to school here?"

I hesitated. This could royally backfire on me, but it seemed only fair for the deal to work both ways.

"How about this? Since this is bigger than a dance class, let's say that if you really hate it at the end of the summer, we'll talk about it again and find a solution that works for both of us."

Aurie stilled as she thought it over, and I held my breath as she inspected my face to gauge how sincere I was being.

"You pinky swear we can really leave if I'm miserable?"

My gut twisted painfully. Leaving here wouldn't be easy, but for Aurie...I'd do pretty much anything.

"I pinky swear if you are miserable, we will find a solution that makes us both happy. Fair?"

"And I get a puppy?"

I felt her teasing smirk more than saw it and laughed.

"And you get a puppy."

Aurie sat up in my lap and looked at me, eyes open wide.

"Are you serious?"

She didn't need to know I'd already agreed to take the puppy Hattie had identified as her familiar. Not that Hattie had made it seem like I had much of a choice in the matter. I didn't particularly want to deal with a puppy, but if that was what it took to make Aurie fall in love with Portney, I would happily deal with pee, poop, and all the other unsavory aspects of pet ownership.

"As serious as I am about my first cup of coffee in the morning."

Her eyes went even wider. "Whoa."

Her eyes twinkled with mirth and hope flared bright in my gut.

NINETEEN

As opening day grew closer, my nights grew increasingly shorter as I woke up earlier, partly to prepare myself for the brutally early mornings and partly because sleep eluded me more and more. I'd used the time to test out new recipes.

A nauseating mixture of excitement and terror fueled endless attempts to perfect my pastry game. My taste testers, Crystal, Hattie, Aurie, and anyone who wandered past the bakery during the day, assured me they'd never tasted anything better, but my imposter syndrome was running rampant.

It wasn't enough to make pastries my friends found tasty. They got them for free. Asking people to buy them was a different story, and I worried my baked goods weren't quite good enough.

Crystal thought I was insane for contemplating even for a minute people wouldn't want to fork over their hard-earned cash for something I'd baked.

The day before our soft opening, she finally ran out of patience with me.

"Cassie, you are a magical baker. A magical baker from a long line of magical bakers. What don't you get about that?" she'd exclaimed, exasperation making her roll her eyes.

"Uh...none of it?"

I still wasn't sold on the concept my magic made my food better. Or, rather, I was still offended at the thought of a magical assist. If other bakery owners could be successful without magic improving what they baked, then I should be able to as well.

Today, my baking would be put to the test. And even though I didn't technically need the bakery to do well, I wanted it so badly I could almost taste it. And hopefully it would be as delectable as my pastries.

For years, I'd wished I had something to look forward to in the morning other than baby play groups or PTA meetings. Now I had something amazing to get up for, I was petrified it would vanish into thin air and leave me face to face with the shambles of my life.

I slapped the dough hard against the counter and grinned. Max would have been horrified to come down in the morning to find the kitchen covered in flour and the remnants of a baking frenzy. To him, success looked like a wife and kid living in a pretty house in the suburbs. He wanted breakfast at seven and dinner at six and for the house to be impeccable when he got home from work.

He'd been handed a lucrative job selling insurance for his father's company. The work made him feel important and it gave him a reason to golf whenever he pleased.

Our relationship might have unfolded differently if he'd noticed his ideal life made me miserable, but years of waiting for him to see me as I actually was rather than how he wanted me to be had chipped away at any optimism I'd had as a blushing bride.

The one thing he did notice was how badly I played the role of good little wife. I'd hated the country club lifestyle he adored. I'd never gotten over feeling like I stuck out like a sore thumb amongst the perfectly turned-out wives who talked endlessly about their home renovation projects and their bridge games.

It hadn't helped that Aurie loathed frilly dresses and point blank refused to attend tea parties. The fights over that had been something else.

If I can't make this work...

I stopped that thought in its tracks. That woman didn't exist anymore and would never exist again. I was free to fill my days however I pleased. And even if the whole Portney bakery thing didn't work out, I would never again pretend to be someone I wasn't.

I chuckled as I slid the first batch of croissants into the proofing oven. At least Max and his parents had never had to contend with my magical powers. A vision of Darrin Stevens shooting daggers with his eyes at Samantha on the verge of twitching her nose in a room full of his colleagues played through my mind and I laughed even harder.

Thump!

The laugh froze in my throat.

Thud!

Whatever was making that noise in the backyard was big. Bigger than the raccoon who'd been digging through our trash. Holding my breath, I tiptoed to the door, grabbing my large rolling pin on the way. I would rather have had my trusty fireplace poker, but the rolling pin would have to do.

I'd been working quietly and hadn't turned on the harsh overhead lights. To someone wanting to break in, it might have looked like the place was empty.

The window in the top half of the back door revealed a dark figure perched on the brick wall enclosing the yard. Shadows from the tree hid the intruder from sight, but the tips of a tall ladder peeking over the top glowed in the moonlight.

Rage burst to life in my chest. This was not happening a second time.

"Stop right there!" I screamed as I yanked open the door. "I see you! Don't think I don't! I'm calling the cops!"

I fumbled for my phone in my apron pocket as the person froze on the verge of jumping into the tree leaning against the wall. The whites of their eyes flashed briefly in my direction as they scrambled for the ladder. I'd seen those eyes before, but where? And the shape of those shoulders...

"Stop! Don't you dare get down!" Keeping an eye trained on the intruder, I shakily dialed 9-1. Before I could dial the second one, the person made it to the ladder and started to clamber down. The sound of running footsteps faded until all I could hear was my own pounding heart.

Instinct propelled me forward. If I was fast, I could catch them, finish dialing 9-1-1, and put an end to this nonsense. It wasn't until I was at the base of the tree that reality snapped me to my senses. I was an out of shape 40-year-old woman. The person hightailing it away was clearly more fit than I'd ever be. Plus, they had a serious head start. Even if I could figure out how to climb the tree to get to the top of the fence, they'd be long gone before I ever made it to the ground on the other side.

I growled under my breath and stormed back to the kitchen, making sure to double lock the door behind me before shooting off a quick text to

Deputy Griffin, whose direct number Crystal had helpfully added to my contacts.

> Hi Deputy Griffin. This is Cassie Berry.
> Someone tried to break in again.

> Are you ok?

> Yeah. I scared them off before they could get in.

> Good. I'll be right there.

> No, no. You don't have to come.
> I don't think they're coming back.
> They know someone is awake.

> If you're sure…

I checked in with my gut. I was okay. Plus, I had a ton of work to do.

> I'm fine. I double-locked the door
> and I turned on the backyard lights.

> Text me again if you change your mind.
> I can be there in minutes.

I put my phone back in my pocket and turned my attention to the beeping cinnamon roll timer. By the time I'd pulled them out of the oven and started on the frosting, my breathing was almost back to normal.

What were they looking for? The thought nagged me as I slathered the rolls in a thick layer of buttercream frosting. *And why did they look strangely familiar? Did I know the intruder? Had I met them around town at some point?*

"I mean, come on house, you've been so helpful up to now. What am I missing?" I felt ridiculous talking to a building, but as if in response to my question, a light in the far corner of the kitchen pulsed brighter for a moment.

Sucking on the icing stuck to my finger, I glanced over and stood there, with my finger in my mouth, trying to make sense of what I saw. The wall behind the desk was decorated with gorgeous floor to ceiling panels I'd fallen in love with as soon as I'd set eyes on them. Some of the panels were carved with intricate, swirling patterns. The thing that had caught my eye was the pale green light seeping from the cracks around one of prettier ones. To add to the weirdness, I could have sworn the glowing panel was calling to me.

As nonchalantly as possible (ridiculous because I was the only one in the room and I certainly wasn't fooled), I washed my hands and dried them carefully before finally admitting to myself I could not keep ignoring a glowing panel that called to me.

I glanced back at the panel, secretly hoping I'd been having an exhaustion-induced hallucination. But the panel was still glowing, the light now pulsing softly like a heartbeat, perfectly in tune with the one in my chest. The rhythm of the light sped up at the same time as my heart.

Not for the first time since we'd moved in, I reminded myself I had a child asleep upstairs and running away screaming wasn't an option.

The light kept beating in time with my heart as I approached the wall. It didn't look any brighter up close, but the pull got stronger with every step I took. With no small amount of trepidation, I reached my hand forward to brush my fingers along the edge of the glowing panel. The wood was surprisingly warm, and I had the weird sensation that if I tried, I could push my hand right through it. Even as the thought crossed my mind, my fingers started pressing into the wood, as though something from the other side was tugging on them. I jerked back and shook my hand. Had I imagined that? A secret panel my hand could pass through?

The skin on the back of my neck prickled, but despite every ounce of self-preservation screaming at me to go back to my baking and pretend nothing witchy was happening in this corner of the room, I couldn't walk away, couldn't stop my hand from drifting back to the panel.

I didn't rest my hand on the panel again, though. Visions of being trapped with my hand on one side and my body on the other danced through my head as I felt around the outside of the panel. The light emanating from the cracks wasn't warm or tingly and didn't keep my fingers from dancing over the ornate carvings. The panel didn't budge when I slipped my nails into the crack and tugged. I tried pushing, sliding, and even punching, but it wasn't until I tried turning it that the panel clicked open.

Holy. Shit.

After glancing around me quickly to make sure I was still alone and the intruder hadn't snuck back over the wall to spy on me, I pulled the panel fully open.

My jaw dropped.

Books, as a rule, don't tend to glow, and this one was glowing so brightly, it was hard to see what it even looked like beyond big, old, and possibly leather bound.

I'd almost convinced myself it was safe to touch what I presumed was Aunt Bea's grimoire when a strident beeping from one of my kitchen timers startled me. I gave the book a longing look, but if

I left the croissants in the oven even a minute too long, they'd be ruined.

Just to be safe, in case someone came in before I had time to come back to the book, I clicked the panel shut again. The hollow feeling that formed in my chest when the grimoire was once again out of sight surprised me. As did the little voice in my head that hissed with frustration when I turned my back and made my way to the oven.

Get a grip, Cassie, it's a book. Behind a secret panel. It'll still be there when you're done with your work.

TWENTY

W hen the sun finally made its appearance, I was sliding tray after tray of pastries into their proper places in the display case. We still had a full half hour before the doors were scheduled to open, but it didn't feel like I'd be ready in time. Heck, it didn't feel like I'd ever be ready. What if no one came? Or, worse, what if they came and hated everything they ate?

I shoved down the ball of terror rising in my throat and focused on arranging a plate of samples to put next to the cash register. I was pondering whether a third cup of coffee would be one too many when Crystal breezed through the front door and offered to make me one.

"Though, maybe I'll make it a decaf. If you vibrate any harder you might vanish from sight."

The butterflies cavorting in my stomach made it hard to smile properly in response to her joke. With the sample plate ready and displayed, I meandered to the bistro tables to reorganize the sugar packets and creamers for the third time since I'd set them out.

A glance out the window confirmed there still wasn't anyone lined up outside waiting for us to open. Amazing how I could be simultaneously relieved and disappointed. A little gray cat stared at me from across the street, patiently waiting for Persimmon to come out. It would be waiting for a while. Last time I'd checked, the orange cat had been fast asleep on top of a heat vent in the apartment.

"Don't worry. They'll come." Crystal said from behind the counter. "People have been talking about the opening all over town. It's only six fifteen. We don't open for another fifteen minutes. Plus, I warned you that it's too early for this crowd. Bea didn't open until eight."

I'd based my hours on those kept by bakeries around where we'd lived, but I hadn't considered that a bustling city contained more people who started work early than a small town like this. If it was this quiet every morning, I was seriously going to have to reconsider our opening time.

"I know, I know. I'm just excited. And nervous." I attempted another smile as she placed a steaming cup on the immaculate table I was anxiously wiping down again.

"Sit down a second. I'll place our sign outside. We might as well relax while we wait for our first customer."

The sign in question was a chalkboard sandwich board for the sidewalk that featured some of our offerings along with a cheerful greeting. My hope was to have a funny new saying on it every day to lure people inside. Today's was

Drink coffee.
Do dumb things faster.

Aurie had rolled her eyes at me so hard I knew I had a winner. Crystal and I had called Stacey to brainstorm a whole list of sayings over a bottle of wine. The options had gotten sillier and sillier as the night wore on. My favorite was "*Pastries: Drool optional,*" but Aurie had vetoed it loudly with gagging sounds. Whatever, it wasn't like I was out there advertising *moist* pastries or anything. Though maybe that would bring people in if only to complain about the sign. Something to think about if things started out slow.

With the doors open and the sign on the sidewalk, everything suddenly felt very, very real. Unable to sit for a second longer, I popped up and walked over to the bookshelf to reorganize the books for the millionth time. Board books to keep littles entertained and best sellers from Juliette's store sat alongside magical-themed, cozy mysteries I'd found on Bea's bookshelf. Something told me that a town of witches probably got a kick out of fictionalized versions of their lives. I'd found that reading them made my new life feel a little less weird.

"Oh, I've read that one! The twist is great." The woman peering over my shoulder was around my mother's age but looked more spry and with it than my mother ever had. Her joyful energy washed over me and settled my nerves. This was why I'd wanted to do this so badly.

"Good morning!" I replied. My smile threatened to split my face in half. "Welcome to *La Baguette Magique!* You're our first official customer. Can we offer you a free hot drink to celebrate?"

"Free! I like you already!" The older lady's laugh was like a cascading waterfall. "What's the most expensive thing on the menu?"

"Miss Sadie! It's much too early for your shenanigans." Crystal's teasing tone belied the stern look on her face. "Don't think I don't know you're here this early because you wanted to be sure you'd be first." It didn't take long for her tough expression to be replaced by a wide grin. "Cassie, allow me to introduce Miss Sadie, one of your aunt's oldest friends and the self-proclaimed expert on all things Portney."

"That's right! If you need to know anything about this town, you come to me, you hear?" The twinkle in her eye promised some seriously entertaining tales, and I made a note to check in with her soon. Now that I was standing in her shoes, I was more curious than ever about my great aunt.

Before I handed over Miss Sadie's free coffee and a warm apple turnover, another customer entered the store.

"Am I first? Do I get free coffee?" Where Sadie had been all light and laughter, this elderly woman oozed negativity. The disdain on her face as she looked around made me wonder why she'd bothered coming in at all. And how had she even guessed we'd be giving away a free drink to the first customer? I'd come up with that on the spot.

"Good morning, Margie!" The forced cheer in Crystal's voice made me cringe. As unpleasant as this woman was, we couldn't afford to alienate any customer at this point. The sour look on the woman's face didn't change, and I let my shoulders unclench. "Miss Sadie beat you to the punch, but maybe we can make an exception for the town matriarch and offer the second visitor one as well. What do you think, Cassie?"

"Matriarch?" I asked, eyebrow raised as I stepped behind the counter.

The woman rolled her eyes dramatically as if this encounter was grating on her last nerve. "Just a fancy shmancy way of saying I'm the oldest witch in town. Wasn't until your great aunt passed." She turned down the corners of her lips as though Bea had put her out by dying, but a glint in her eyes belied the expression on her face.

"You? The oldest?" I couldn't help myself from blurting out. "That can't be possible." She wasn't young by any stretch of the imagination, but I would have placed her in her mid-to-late seventies, hardly old enough to be the oldest in town.

A hint of something that might have been a smile crossed the woman's eyes. "I'm ninety-six." A smug sniff accompanied her words as though she'd won some kind of competition. "Your great aunt was three months older than me."

"You are not," I gasped. No way this woman in brightly colored tennis shoes and an eye-searing orange and fuchsia velour tracksuit was over thirty years older than my mother.

"Sure am. Now, where's my free coffee? I'm not getting any younger over here." She cackled. "Make me one of those newfangled vanilla lotties, Crystal."

"It's a latte and you know it," Crystal said, throwing Margie an exasperated look.

"Of course, I know it," Margie scowled. "This one was expecting me to act old and I aim to please."

"Since when?" Crystal's murmured retort was so quiet Margie missed it. Probably a good thing.

"Ninety-six, really?" I couldn't drop it, or take my eyes off her. "What's your secret?"

"As if I'd tell a green witch any of my secrets." Margie scoffed and rolled her eyes at me. She grabbed for the drink Crystal handed to her and sniffed with her mouth turned down in a scornful scowl. "I get a free pastry with this too, right? This is hardly a filling breakfast."

Crystal's smile started to melt so I stepped in. "Of course." Miss Sadie opened her mouth to protest, but I cut her off. "You too, Miss Sadie! Have to reward our first two customers!" If anyone else walked in, we were going to sell out without ever making a dime.

I gestured to the pastry case and rattled off the various offerings. "I have a sample of my cinnamon rolls right here if you'd like a taste?" I pointed to the plate near the cash register.

Margie zeroed in on the samples, and I pretended not to notice when she grabbed three pieces. She popped them in her mouth one at a time in quick succession and nodded appreciatively as she munched.

"Not bad," she said, crumbs from her last bite falling out of her mouth. "I'll take one of those to go and one of your apple turnovers for here." Her unblinking gaze met mine as she waited for me say something about only offering one pastry. Instead, I smiled at her and did exactly as she asked. Today was not the day to pick a fight with the town matriarch. Today was a day for pastries and smiles. But I don't think anyone would have begrudged me the little thrill of victory I felt when my lack of reaction made her scowl even harder.

The steady stream of customers that followed kept us on our toes. It was like the whole town had turned out to see what the new bakery owner looked like and to judge the offerings for themselves. At some point, Aurie peeked her head through the swinging kitchen doors and ducked back out of sight, eyes as round as saucers. We ran out of pastries by eleven and were on track to run out of bread around lunch time. No one seemed to mind.

My first real taste of the town was both overwhelming me and blowing me away. The energy here was so different than it had been in Georgia. Or maybe it was that I'd been forced to live in a significantly more reserved circle of people. Everyone here was unapologetically and delightfully themselves.

When we completely ran out of food—we'd taken to slicing bread and toasting it for people to enjoy with their coffee—Crystal and I started tidying up. As soon as the final duo departed with loud promises to return bright and early the next morning, I closed the door and sagged against it, drained to the last drop.

"Well, that was..."

Crystal laughed. "Welcome to Portney."

"Is it going to be like that every day?" I asked her, aware my eyes were almost bugging out of my head. "Because, if so, we're going to need to hire some more help."

"Nah, I think that was first day excitement. People came to feed their curiosity."

"Thank goodness!" I let myself slide down the door until I was sitting on the ground. I had enjoyed every moment of the chaotic day, but the thought of now having to go bake twice what we'd just sold made me want to curl into a ball and cry. I lifted my head and smiled ruefully at Crystal. "Guess I didn't need to serve magical cinnamon rolls as the sample, eh?"

She gasped. "You didn't!"

I shrugged sheepishly. I had filled her in after witnessing the spelled scones in action, but she had yet to see the magic at work for herself. "It was unintentional, mostly. I was thinking about how much I wanted people to like my food when I was baking them. I think it worked a little too well. Though the spell didn't affect Margie, so maybe there is some truth to that whole 'won't make people do something out of character' thing."

TWENTY ONE

All day long, between greeting new customers and serving them, bussing tables, and generally managing the chaos, I was tortured by the knowledge that Great Aunt Bea's grimoire was a few feet away, waiting to reveal family secrets and stories I could only begin to imagine.

Once Crystal and I had somewhat recovered from our hysterics, I headed back into the kitchen, debating whether I should wait for her to leave before pulling the book out or if I could risk letting her see it. My gut told me Crystal was trustworthy, but my gut had been wrong more than once in the past and I was loath to trust it with something so precious.

A single glance told me something was wrong.

It wasn't so much that the panel wasn't glowing. Other than the few minutes earlier, it hadn't ever glowed in my presence. It was that the panel didn't look straight, like it had been opened and not closed properly.

I had closed it fully. I'd heard it click shut.

Mother trucker!

I knew what I would find even before the panel opened fully, or rather, what I wouldn't find. Disappointment still made my shoulders sag when the only thing that greeted me was an empty storage space. Nothing glowed or called to me.

"Come *on*, house! What is your deal?" I growled in the vague direction of the ceiling. "You're supposed to be on my side!" The house shuddered slightly under my feet, but I couldn't tell if it was shrugging or apologizing.

"What's wrong?" I'd been so focused on the empty compartment I hadn't heard Crystal come into the kitchen. Her voice startled me enough to make me jump and bump the panel door shut.

"It's nothing." I moved away from the wall. The gut instinct that had told me Crystal was trustworthy had given way to wariness. Countless people had been in and out of the bakery during the day, but Crystal had been the only one with access to the kitchen. If that didn't make her prime suspect number one, I don't know what would.

I headed to the stack of dishes piled high in the sink and hoped Crystal would allow herself to be distracted. "Hey, thanks again for everything you did today. I couldn't have done it without you. It was all a lot more intense than I anticipated."

She glanced toward the panel wall with a slight frown before replying with a smile. "Of course! It was my pleasure. I've missed being in the bakery." She frowned and glanced at the wall again. "You sure everything is okay?"

"Yeah, yeah." I replied, studiously not following her gaze.

"So, no one broke in and took something from Bea's secret hidey hole?" She smirked at me, her left eyebrow raised.

My heart leapt into my throat, and I narrowed my eyes at her. "How do you know about the hidden compartment?"

"She hardly kept it a secret. We used to laugh about it all the time. That's where she kept her private stash of chocolate."

"Who was she hiding chocolate from?" Was there a kid around that I didn't know about? Did Persimmon have a secret sweet tooth?

"No one. That's what was funny about it." Crystal gave me a strange look. "So, is something missing?"

Her concern seemed genuine enough, but I still hesitated. Crystal's frown reappeared when she noticed.

"Cassie, Bea and I were good friends. There were no secrets between us. You can trust me. I swear."

I opened my mouth and shut it again. My gut flip-flopped a couple times before stilling, which didn't help me decide one way or another, but another glance at Crystal's earnest face and the genuine concern in her eyes made me reconsider.

"I think it was Bea's grimoire, though I'm not entirely sure." I groaned. "I only had the panel open for a moment this morning before I had to get back to work. Call me crazy, but I thought an ancient glowing book needed more time and attention than I had at my disposal. I thought I'd have time this afternoon! I didn't expect it to get stolen!"

"It was glowing?" Crystal stared at me with wide eyes.

I sat down heavily on one of the kitchen stools and frowned.

"Yes, glowing green and pulsating. It was really weird."

"Wow. I've never seen it do that. And you're sure it's not there anymore?"

I didn't dignify her question with a reply other than a deadpan stare.

"Right, right. Big book. Small compartment. Obviously you're sure. Sorry." Crystal tapped her chin thoughtfully. "What doesn't make sense is why the building let someone other than you take it."

"Yeah house, what gives?" I scowled up at the ceiling. "I thought we were buds." The house, unsurprisingly, didn't reply.

"Maybe Aurie saw someone lurking around while we were busy."

My stomach twisted painfully at the thought. Aurie had been exposed to danger fewer times in a thriving metropolis than she had since we arrived here.

"She would have said something, right?" But, even as I said the words, I knew that wasn't a given, especially since the bakery had been slammed from the moment we'd opened, and I'd barely been able to say three words to her when she'd come through to grab something for breakfast. Now that I was thinking about it, I hadn't even been the one to get her food. My attention had been fully absorbed by new customers wanting to know "absolutely everything" about me. Even if she'd tried to tell me, I wouldn't have been able to listen.

I grabbed my phone and sent Aurie a quick text asking her if she'd noticed anything out of the ordinary that morning.

I didn't see anything,
but Keith says a human person climbed the
wall.

Keith?

Squirrel. Hangs out in the tree by the wall.

I'm sorry. What?

Don't be lame mom.

My kid was speaking to squirrels, and I was lame for questioning it? Really?

Lets put a pin in the speaking to squirrels thing. Can Keith describe the person he saw?

"I can't believe I asked my kid to ask a squirrel a question for me," I muttered, eyes on my screen.

"What?" Crystal raised an eyebrow questioningly.

"Wait, she's replying."

He says it looked like a human. About half a tree high.

Our tree?

Yeah.

Okay, so that made the person about my height. Probably not tall enough to be a grown man.

Anything else?

> **Yeah, he says the human tossed something big over the wall and its skin was loose.**

Loose? Ew. And tossed what, something like a book?

> **Mom, he's a squirrel. He doesn't know what a book is.**
> **I think he means the person had on loose clothing.**

Again, she was talking to squirrels, but I was the irrational one.

Right. Thank Keith for me.

> **He wants a treat.**

Of course, he does. Love you.

I stood up and went to the door to toss some leftover crumbs on the stoop. A fat gray squirrel scampered over and chirped at me before grabbing the two biggest crumbs in his little hands and dashing off again.

"Uh, thanks, Keith." I shook my head and headed back into the kitchen. "It's official. I'm either having the weirdest dream in the world, or my life has gone completely off the rails." Crystal just chuckled in response.

Thanks to Keith the squirrel, we knew that our thief was probably a woman wearing a flowing skirt or dress. In a town of eccentric witches, that narrowed it down to just about everyone.

"Except the older witches," Crystal said.

"How do you figure?" I asked.

"You said the person you saw was able to scale the wall somewhat easily, right? Keith also said they scaled the wall."

"Yeah, so?"

"So, they were probably on the more agile side."

"I dunno," I said, "Margie looks pretty spry and she's over ninety."

"Come on, there's I-wear-funky-sneakers-and-walk-a-lot spry and then there's climbing-over-walls-in-a-skirt spry."

"Fair enough. So, youngish witch, long and flowy clothing. Sound about right?" I glanced at Crystal to see if I had it right. She nodded. "So, how far does that narrow it down?"

"Um..." Crystal looked up at the ceiling and thought for a moment, "to about two thirds of the female population in town."

"Piece of cake," I said, rolling my eyes.

"Uh..." Crystal hesitated. "You think it's going to be easy to figure out who it was?"

"No, I think I want a piece of cake."

Crystal chuckled again. "Me too. You get the cake, I'll get the coffee."

"Deal." I rummaged around in the walk-in fridge for a cake I'd made the day before. I'd deemed it good enough to eat, but not good enough to sell. Given how people had been eating this morning, I probably should have brought it out. Not that I was unhappy I'd forgotten about it until now.

"I don't know that we're any closer than we were before we talked to Keith." I was doing my best not to fixate on the fact that our best eyewitness was little more than a rat with a fluffy tail. "Is there some magical way for us to find the missing book?"

"Grimoire," Crystal mumbled around a bite of cake. She thought for a moment and then shrugged. "I don't think so. Search spells are finicky. I don't think you got a good enough look at the grimoire for one to work, and I can't think of anything else that could help."

"Ugh, what a mess," I groaned. "I want to search for it right this second, but I have a zillion pastries to prepare for tomorrow or I'm going to have a lot of unhappy customers. Maybe something will come to me while I bake."

"If we had the grimoire, we'd be able to track it," Crystal grumbled.

"Yeah, well, if we had the damn thing, we wouldn't need to find it, would we?" I replied with a laugh.

TWENTY TWO

The events of the day tumbled around in my head as I mixed the ingredients for more chocolate-orange scones. The secret to light and fluffy scones is having a gentle hand while kneading. Luckily, my fingers knew what they were doing because I couldn't keep my mind on task. I didn't know enough about Portney, its inhabitants, or even about magic as a whole to get a good grip on the problem.

The concept of the grimoire as something to be coveted wasn't hard to grasp. It had been hidden for a reason, most likely because it was valuable in some way. But if that was the case, why had the building let a stranger get their hands on it? I'd been led to understand that, as the sole heir to Bea's estate, the building was supposed to consider *me* the rightful owner of everything it contained. It was also supposed to be attuned to *my* needs and safety.

I'd seen it in action. It had clearly deemed Crystal trustworthy since it had let her in that first day without checking in with me. But other people, like the produce guy, had been forced to knock to get in even though the door had been wide open when he'd stopped by. I hadn't been able to tell if the house had created an actual forcefield in the doorway or if it had somehow made the guy not want to cross the threshold, but I'd watched him almost take a step through the door and then stop and wait.

Assuming the person who had taken the grimoire was the same person who had broken in that first night and attempted to break in earlier this morning—wait, could I even make that assumption? What if it hadn't been the same person? My heart sank. I just didn't know enough. But that didn't stop my brain from trying to make sense of things. Assuming, for the sake of argument, that it was the same person, the building had let them in multiple times. Which meant that it either recognized or trusted them. If it wasn't the same person, then something was up with the building, and I didn't have the faintest idea about how to figure out what.

"Seriously, again, what gives?" I asked the ceiling, still not expecting an answer, so when one of the desk drawers slid open with a small squeal, it caught me completely off guard.

I didn't take my eye off the open drawer as I quickly washed the sticky dough off my hands. That drawer had definitely been empty when I'd gone through the desk.

"What else are you hiding from me?" I mumbled as I sidled up to the desk. This time, of course, there was no response of any kind.

Since the drawer had only popped out an inch or two, I tugged it open the rest of the way. At first glance, it still appeared empty, so I waved my hand around inside. My thumb brushed against the edge of a piece of paper stuck to the underside of the drawer above. It came loose with a gentle tug.

A little thrill of excitement fluttered through my chest as I pulled out the old photograph. A sad, tired lady looked up at me from a faded picnic blanket, a chubby baby perched on her lap. A cherubic looking boy of about five leaned against her, his hand resting on the baby's head. It was hard to tell if the baby was a girl or a boy, but it seemed like a happy little thing. On the other side of the woman stood a toddler, this one clearly a boy. The camera had caught him mid-scowl and I smiled. He was the spitting image of Aurie.

I flipped the photo over and tried to make out the faint purple script scrawled across the back. The first part looked like a date. Nineteen something. The last two numbers were too faded for me to make out clearly. Either a six or an eight. Under it I could almost make out a series of names. I squinted harder and did a little guessing. Elizabeth, George, Beatrice and the last one was either William or Winston. I couldn't tell.

Thanks to the book Juliette had brought me, I knew Elizabeth was Bea's mom, so it was safe to assume she was the adult in the photo and Bea was the baby on her lap. My grandfather's name had been George, but I'd never once heard of another sibling. Though, to be fair, until Mr. Lathrop had contacted me I hadn't known about any of them.

"So, I had a great uncle as well as a great aunt, eh?" I asked the building. True to form, it didn't reply. "I have no clue how this connects to the grimoire, but if you think it's relevant, I'll take your word for it." I still felt silly for talking to an inanimate structure, but I shook it off. If Aurie could talk to rodents, why couldn't I talk to my somewhat sentient home?

With the photo snug and safe in my apron pocket, I went back to my scones, adding this latest bit of information to the growing stack of seemingly unrelated facts I was amassing. At some point it had to all start coming together, right? Unless none of it was related, which was a distinct possibility. I groaned and plunged my hands back into the sticky dough as my phone pinged with a text notification.

How was day one?
Things are slow at the store today.
Hoping it's because everyone was at the
bakery.

Warmth filled my heart at the unexpected text, and I voice texted Juliette a quick reply letting her know how well the day had gone. Maybe I'd imagined the weirdness during our last interaction. She'd probably been preoccupied about her store, and I'd misinterpreted her fascination with Bea's books. A thought crossed my mind.

You probably know a lot of people in town.
Do you know how I can find Miss Sadie?

I felt a little thrill when her reply bounced back almost immediately. If you want information, you go to the people who've been around the longest. At the very least, Miss Sadie could confirm my grandfather, great aunt, and great uncle were the kids in the photo. With a little luck, she might also have some valuable information to impart.

TWENTY THREE

"Miss Sadie?" I spoke softly as I approached, not wanting to startle her out of her intense focus on a nearby tree. Juliette had told me I'd find Miss Sadie sitting in the small park near the town square and I'd given in to the impulse to delay the rest of my baking to pay her a quick visit.

The small park was darling, a little haven in the middle of the bustling town. I could see why an elderly lady might relish spending time soaking in nature here.

Without turning her head, she gestured for me to come closer. When I was within arm's reach, she pulled me down onto the bench next to her and pointed.

"Do you see it?"

I peered into the branches, but nothing jumped out at me.

"Uh..."

"There, on the top branch." I narrowed my eyes. A little brown bird tilted its head at us and let out a happy trill. "He's a generous one. He always comes to sing for me."

The delight in her eyes was authentic and it warmed something deep inside me to know there was no age limit to enjoying life's little pleasures.

"Are you..."

"An animal witch? No, though don't I wish! I come from a long line of kitchen witches like you."

"Ah."

"But that's not what it was you hunted me down to discuss, was it." She turned her piercing gaze on me. "You have a question about your family."

"You got me." I smiled. "I found a photo that made me realize how little I know about them. I was hoping I could take you up on your kind offer from this morning."

I pulled the photo out of my pocket and handed it over. A wistful look crossed her face as she gazed at it.

"Your great grandmother was a looker, wasn't she? I always admired her when I was a child. And that boy... such a troublemaker that one. But such a joy to be around. Even as a young child he was something to behold."

"George?"

"Oh, no, he was as serious and solemn as they come. William, he was a handful. Drove his parents around the bend on a regular basis."

"You knew them well, then?"

"Oh, no, not well. I was several years younger than your great aunt, but I was always an observant child and the Blackwell family fascinated me."

"So, Bea really had two brothers?"

"Oh, yes! George the oldest, and William, the scalawag."

I laughed. "I haven't heard that word in years."

Miss Sadie's eye twinkled. "He lit up the room, but he broke his parents' hearts over and over again. It was a real tragedy what happened to that family."

I opened my mouth to ask her to clarify, but she shook her head before I could get a word out. She reached over and patted my hand. "Something tells me you'll find the answers you seek at a certain bookshop in town."

"Juliette's shop?" I frowned. "Really?"

Miss Sadie cocked her head and nodded slowly. "Yes, I think that is exactly what needs to happen."

"But she..." I hesitated. How could I explain that, despite our little text exchange earlier, I still wasn't sure how I felt about the book shop owner. I flashed back to the moment I'd realized she had a similar shape to the intruder and shivered.

Miss Sadie shook her head and smiled at me kindly. "Things are rarely what they seem, dear." She gave my arm a final pat. "Now, help an old woman to her feet, please. I have places to be and things to do."

Without any actual assistance from me, she stood up and brushed imaginary dust from the front of her slacks before sashaying off. The woman had more pep in her step at her age than I'd ever had in mine.

I waited until she'd moved out of sight before getting to my own feet with much less grace than she'd demonstrated. In my defense, I'd been working harder than ever before and every single one of my back muscles had something to say about it.

Despite everything still awaiting me in my kitchen, I found myself detouring via Juliette's shop on my way back to the bakery.

My body ached and I was exhausted, but something in me was desperate to know more about my family. There was no logical reason to assume getting answers about my mysterious great uncle would help me find Bea's grimoire, but I couldn't let go of the thought that the two were connected.

Besides, I'd already done a lot of the prep for the next morning. I had three types of croissants (chocolate, almond, and ham and cheese) proofed and sitting in the fridge waiting for a second proofing in the morning. The puff pastry for the fruit Danishes and apple turnovers was also sitting in the fridge, ready to be assembled in the morning. A variety of breakfast cookies and muffins were ready to serve, and I was almost done with the last batch of biscotti.

That left me with plenty of time to enjoy a little walk through town and a chat with Juliette before I had to start working on the bread.

"You're going to kill yourself, you know," Juliette said, taking one look at my face when I let myself into her store. "You look done in. I don't think it's physically possible to run a bakery alone."

"I'm not doing it alone!" I replied, doing my best to school my face into something less tired looking. "I have Crystal."

"That's not what I mean, and I'm pretty sure you know it. Don't get me wrong, I'm glad you're not manning the coffee monster as well as everything else, but if you try to do all the baking after you've spent your whole day selling, you're going to last at most a week before you collapse."

Juliette's moods swung so fast and hard it was enough to give a person whiplash. I straightened up and tried not to let her see me wince at the spasm of pain that shot through my lower back. "I'm fine. Really."

"Sure thing." Juliette's smile hid a hint of something more than just neighborly concern. "And I can run a bookshop on my own while having a thriving social life and getting a degree in library science."

"You're doing all that?" My eyes nearly popped out of my head at the thought.

"No! That's my point! A person can only do so much!"

"Oh. Very funny." I gave in to the pain and rubbed my back with a groan. "It's only the first week. I'm going to figure out a system. It's all going to be okay. Wait, are you really thinking of getting a degree in library science?"

"No!" she laughed. "Are you insane? Running this shop takes all my waking hours as it is. If I ever went back to school, I'd have to hire serious help. And that is so not in the budget right now. If it were, you can bet your backside I'd hire someone in a heartbeat."

"But then it wouldn't be *your* shop anymore." Even saying the words sent an uncomfortable ripple through my stomach.

"What are you talking about? Does Amazon belong any less to Jeff Bezos because he has staff? The company belongs to the person who gives it a soul."

Something deep inside my chest unclenched as my worldview shifted. In my need to prove to Max I could be successful on my own, I'd forgotten I didn't actually need to do it alone.

Juliette smirked at the look on my face. "But I'm sure you didn't come here for life coaching advice. How else can I help?"

I hesitated. My gut was still sending me mixed signals about Juliette and my brain was having a conniption, but I badly wanted for her to not be involved in my grimoire and family mystery so we could be friends. I needed a friend way more than I needed answers.

She stared at me patiently, waiting for me to speak. The quiet calm in her eyes pushed me to decide. She was exactly the type of person I wanted on my side.

"I'm hoping you can help me with a little research project."

Her whole face lit up, and I shoved away my qualms. I pulled out the photo, held it out to her, and explained what I needed to know.

She took a moment to study the picture before pausing to think. "If the answers aren't in the book I brought you earlier, I probably don't have them here. But I can do a little digging and let you know what I find."

"Don't go to too much trouble, please. I know you have a lot on your plate as it is." She jerked her hand back when I reached out to take back the photo. My eyes flew open as shame flooded her face red. With an awkward chuckle, she held the photo out to me.

"Sorry. I don't know why I did that." Her blush deepened and she glanced away before looking back at me with a tremulous smile. "It's no trouble at all, really. I want to do this for you. I'll swing by later and share what I find."

Just as I was putting the last batch of bread dough into the proofing oven, Juliette tapped on the bakery door and let herself in. The building didn't so much as groan.

She brandished a stack of papers triumphantly and plunked herself onto a bar stool with a satisfied sigh. I poured chocolate chunks into a bowl and covered them with the cream that had been on the verge of bubbling on the stove.

"Did you find anything?"

"Did I ever!" Her bright smile darkened for a second before flaring back to life as she fanned out the papers she'd brought. "So, as the photo indicates, your great grandparents did have three children. George, your grandfather, William, his younger brother by three years, and Beatrice, the baby, who was born almost two years after William. They all lived here in Portney until the start of World War II.

"When the US entered the war, William would have only been sixteen, pushing seventeen, but it looks like he enlisted with the first wave of Portney boys who went off to fight. There's a list of them in an article of the local rag. It doesn't look like George enlisted. At least not at the same time."

"How on earth did a sixteen-year-old enlist?" That seemed insanely young to go off to war. At sixteen, I'd been more preoccupied with the state of my bangs than the world around me.

"Apparently, it was possible with a parent's permission." Juliette turned down the corners of her mouth. "I guess people were really excited about doing their patriotic duty back then. Hard to fathom anyone would have been in favor of sending their child off to war though."

"Seriously." I shuddered. I'd seen enough World War II documentaries to know how horrible things had been. Sending a child into that would have given me nightmares for years.

"Anyway, it seems George stayed in Portney, as did Bea, obviously since she wasn't quite sixteen yet. I'm guessing George stayed to work in the bakery. Apparently, Blackwells have run the Portney bakery since the start of the town."

"Did William survive the war?"

"From what I found, it looks like he did survive for a while, but he didn't make it in the end. The local paper ran lists of the boys lost to the war and his name shows up at the end of August 1945. He would have been close to twenty."

"Ugh, that is so sad."

"Yeah," Juliette agreed. "Such a waste."

"What happened to the family then?"

"Ah, well, that's when it gets interesting. The local paper ran a gossip column, and I found a small snippet that reads..." She paused long enough to grab a page out of her stack of photocopies.

> *'Which well-loved Portney bachelor had a huge falling out with his family and was seen hopping the south-bound train last Tuesday at the crack of dawn? Let's just say that*

*now the young
ladies of marriable
age are going to
be a whole lot
less motivated to go
buy bread for their
families.'*

"Huh. I guess that's when George moved down to Georgia," I mused, dipping the first biscotti into the silky ganache that I'd finished mixing.

"Guess so."

"And the column doesn't hint at why he split?"

Juliette shrugged. "I couldn't find anything else about that. Your great grandparents both passed away the following year, leaving the bakery to Bea, who, as you know, passed away last year at the ripe old age of ninety-six."

"Well, that's interesting and all, but I'm not sure it answers the question about why the building let someone other than me get their hands on the grimoire."

Juliette's eyes flared slightly before she shrugged again, letting my comment about the building slide. "No clue."

I was about to call out her reaction when my mind snagged on something she'd said. "Wait." I rewound our conversation while I laid down the dipped biscotti on a small cooling rack. "William was twenty when he died. Could he have fathered a child?"

Juliette stilled for a second. Her eyes flashed dark again before turning pensive. "I dunno. Other than the notices about him enlisting and about his death the paper didn't have much to say about William. The librarian might know. She seems old enough to have been here at the time. She was busy today, so I wasn't able to ask her any questions."

"I'll have to find time tomorrow," I said with a groan before grabbing a bag of milk chocolate chips to make more ganache.

"I can go for you!" There was something strange about how quickly she offered, but I was too tired to do more than take her offer at face value.

"You sure?" I asked, looking up at her. "I feel bad already for making you do all this work today."

"It's no trouble. I need to go back for something else anyway."

"I'd really appreciate it," I said with a smile. "I'll make you a little package of biscotti to share with her."

"Better make it some oatmeal raisin cookies. I'm not sure her teeth can handle biscotti."

TWENTY FOUR

I t didn't take long to realize I wanted to visit the librarian myself. Juliette did her best to convince me it was no trouble for her to go in my place, but I managed to send her home with a packet of biscotti and a quick hug. Even though there was a bit of a desperate edge to it I didn't understand, her insistence warmed my heart. It was so nice to have met people who genuinely seemed to want to help me.

The sun hit me square in the face as soon as I stepped outside. I paused for a moment with my eyes closed and my face turned to the sky, letting the warmth and light of the late afternoon sun cascade over me until I felt my shoulder muscles unclench. I had enjoyed every moment of my first official day in the bakery, but between the break in, the full workday, my walk to the park and then to Juliette's followed by more baking, my body had taken a beating and I was feeling it.

"Nice, isn't it?" The voice startled me out of my moment and my eyes sprung open. I had to blink a few times to dispel the sunspots enough to be able to see who was talking to me.

"It sure is," I said to Hattie with a smile. She was leaning against the door of her store grinning at me. "Is my kid driving you crazy yet?"

"Nah, she's a godsend," she replied. "Don't you worry about her at all. She's currently reorganizing my stockroom, something that badly needed to be done."

"Aurie? Reorganizing?" I raised my eyebrow and stared at her. Aurie was many things, but neat and organized wasn't one of them.

"Oh, yes! She's doing a fantastic job." Hattie's eyes shone with barely suppressed laughter. "I told her there was a box of puppy toys in the way back."

"I guess she just needed the right incentive." I laughed.

"Where are you off to?" Her voice was so nonchalant that I couldn't tell if she was being polite or if she was truly curious, but the way her eyes narrowed as she awaited my answer made my stomach clench. Why would Hattie care about where I was going?

"Just down to the library for a moment." At the last second, I felt the urge to fudge the truth a little. "I need something to read. Figured it might be nice to bring the librarian a little treat." I held up my package of cookies as proof of my errand.

"Oh, Miss Bitsy will love that, I'm sure." Somehow my statement had relaxed Hattie and any trace of the weirdness I'd glimpsed was gone. I shrugged it off. The events of the last few days clearly had me on edge. "Be sure to tell her I said hello!"

The late afternoon sun put a bounce in my steps, and I took my time as I made my way to the picturesque library. It was so quaint and perfect it made the little girl inside me do cartwheels of joy. I had a soul-deep fondness for libraries. They felt like portals to unexplored worlds. Quaint, old-timey libraries had always seemed especially magical to me.

The door was painted white and felt warm and inviting under my hand. A few more tight muscles relaxed. This place emitted good vibes. The interior of the library was as welcoming and perfect as the outside. Short shelves dotted the space, creating small nooks from which overstuffed armchairs beckoned.

One day soon, I'd find the time to come back, grab a thick book, and snuggle down into one, but today, I barely had time for the task at hand. I gave one of the armchairs a longing pat as I walked by and went off in search of the librarian. I found her sitting at a desk, squinting at an ancient computer screen.

"Darn thing. Why don't you ever do what I want you to?" She mumbled some choice curse words under her breath, and I couldn't keep myself from laughing.

Miss Bitsy looked up and broke into a thousand-watt smile when she saw me. "Why hello! You must be Cassie Blackwell!"

"I must? I mean, yes technically, but it's Cassie Berry actually."

"Of course, dear. I knew that, I'm sorry." She waved at the package I was clasping in my hand, "You come bearing treats! That makes you doubly welcome." She clasped her hands with glee.

"A little bird told me you might be partial to fresh oatmeal raisin cookies," I replied with a smile.

"You'll have to thank the little birdy for me! Was her name maybe Juliette?" Her grin turned cheeky. "I'm sorry I wasn't able to help her earlier. Did she find anything useful? Wait! Don't answer yet!" She held up her hand and got up from her seat with a groan. "I'll put the kettle on, and we can have a nice little chat over those cookies."

"A cup of tea sounds lovely, thank you," I said, following her into the library staff kitchen.

We sat down in the cozy kitchen, and I felt the rest of the tension in my shoulders seep away. I couldn't believe I hadn't made a beeline for the library as soon as we arrived in town. It was such a sign of how far off-kilter the divorce, move, and discovery of my witchy nature had pushed me. Books were usually my go-to haven and, by extension, libraries my home away from home.

"This is such a welcoming and warm space," I remarked to the librarian. "I need to bring my daughter in. She's going to love this place."

"Aurora?" Miss Bitsy looked surprised. "She's already been here."

"She has?" I replied, surprise sending my own eyebrows up my forehead.

"Oh, yes. She was here just yesterday. Looking for books about puppy training. Hattie sent her. Such a sweet, polite child. She does you proud."

"Oh." I didn't know what else to say. We'd lived in a relatively small city known for its friendliness, but it hadn't been the kind of place a preteen could run around on her own. And I hadn't thought Aurie would run around town without telling me.

My heart sank. It was my own damn fault. I'd been so wrapped up in the bakery opening I hadn't paid her the kind of attention she was used to getting. Time to clear a space on the mantel for the Mother-of-the Year award that was sure to arrive any day now.

At dinner last night, Aurie had been bursting with self-confidence and stories about puppies and the pet shop. I'd assumed it meant she was starting to get used to the thought of living here. It had certainly never crossed my mind it was because she was spreading her wings and exploring her independence.

"It's alright, sweetheart." Miss Bitsy was looking at me, a small, concerned frown creasing her face. "This is a good town. We watch out for each other. Aurora is perfectly safe here."

I forced my lips into a smile. Even if it was true, it was going to take me time to accept that we now lived somewhere Aurie could have a taste of freedom and the kind of childhood I'd always dreamed of having.

"Of course, I couldn't give her a library card without an adult present, but she pored over the books for a long while."

Aurie? Poring over books for a long while? My kid who couldn't sit still for more than four seconds at a time? Hard to fathom. Maybe we were more alike than I'd thought.

"Now, why don't you tell me what I owe the pleasure of this visit to," Miss Bitsy said with a twinkle in her eye. "I'm assuming it has something to do with what Juliette was researching earlier. I'm sorry I was unable to assist her personally."

"Actually, it does," I replied. "I know very little about my family, and I'm trying to piece together what I can. Juliette was able to find a few basic facts, but I was wondering if maybe you knew them personally or might know someone who did. I'm especially curious about my great uncle William and the events that led my grandfather to leave Portney."

A look crossed Miss Bitsy's face I found hard to interpret, but it vanished almost as quickly as it had appeared. She tapped her chin and thought, her eyes trained on the ceiling.

"Let's see. I'm just a few years younger than your great aunt Beatrice. Well, I guess I mean I *was* younger." A lone tear beaded up in her right eye and she swiped away at it distractedly. "That Bea, she was something else, you know. The town isn't the same without her here." She was quiet for a moment, then she shook her head and gave me a small smile.

"I'm sorry, I got off track. As I was saying, I was a few years younger than Bea, which made me even younger than William, so I was never in his social circle, but I do remember some things about him. He was such a dashing young man." A little smile tugged at the corners of her mouth. It seemed young Bitsy might have been a little infatuated with my great uncle.

"Do you remember when he went off to war?" I prompted.

"Oh, yes. He was so very young. It was such a shame." Her eyes met mine and she looked embarrassed for a moment. "Not that he went off to war. That was the patriotic thing to do. The right thing! We all thought he was a hero. Everyone was supportive of his decision. Well, most everyone."

"Most everyone?"

"His parents were upset." Miss Bitsy looked embarrassed again. Like she'd said too much. She hurried to continue, waving her hands in the air as though to brush away what she'd said. "But all that is in the ancient past. It's of no consequence now."

I ignored her protest. "They weren't happy he enlisted?"

"Livid." Her hand flew in front of her mouth like she was surprised she'd spoken.

"It's okay, Miss Bitsy. I promise I won't tell anyone." I winked at her, and she giggled. "You're really helping me. I'm so curious about my family."

"Well, you are family, so maybe it's okay." She still looked a little worried, but it didn't stop her from leaning forward, eyes gleaming to whisper. "People say he lied on the enlistment paperwork. Didn't tell his folks until he was ready to ship out. They went to the recruitment office and told them how old he actually was, but the army didn't believe a word they were saying. So many parents were worried about their boys, you know." She nodded knowingly. I nodded back. "Not that any of us knew how bad things were going to get at that time." Grief tightened her eyes for a moment.

"They say that's why George never enlisted. His parents were beside themselves and they made sure their only other son couldn't go fight with his brother. No one knows exactly what they did to keep him home, but people sure talked." Her eyebrows rose alarmingly, making me wonder exactly what was whispered in dark corners. "In any case, they were forgiven in the end seeing as William never came home."

"Never? Not even once on leave?"

"Oh, you know how it was. The war moved fast, and the army was strapped for cash. They didn't have the means to send the boys home for any length of time."

"Oh, that's so sad. I mean, it makes sense, but I guess I never thought about it. That's a long time to be away from home."

"It was. Very sad. But there were letters!" She perked up a little. "We even have some here in the library! People have donated them over the years."

"You have letters from William? Here?" Hope bloomed in my chest. I didn't know what I was expecting to find in the letters, but part of me yearned to see his handwriting.

Miss Bitsy's face fell. "Oh no, I'm sorry. Nothing from William. Other boys. In any case, Bea sometimes told her friends what he said in his letters. The news trickled out to the rest of us. William met a girl while fighting in France. In his last letter he said he was planning on bringing her home with him. His parents were in an uproar, but then they got the telegram, and well, no one said anything else about the girl."

"Oh. I can't even imagine getting that telegram." My heart hurt for Bea's parents. I'd read enough war stories to picture it, but it wasn't the same. Knowing it had happened to my family made it all so much more real and even more heartbreaking.

"There were just so many of them in the end." Miss Bitsy said, sadness etched into every line of her face. "So many boys who never came home."

We sat silently for a moment, thinking about all those young soldiers whose lives had been cut too short. I was still thinking about it when Bitsy started talking again, and I missed what she said at first.

"... why George left."

"I'm sorry, I didn't catch the first part of your sentence. What did William dying have to do with George leaving?"

"I'm not sure exactly. No one was. The telegram arrived and days later, George was taking a train south. Some people speculated that he left in anger because his parents had let William go to war, others that it had to do with his guilt over not going himself. He was the older sibling; I presume he felt responsible for his brother's death. There were whispers it had something to do with William's girl, but those were never confirmed." This time frustration twisted her features and I almost laughed. Like me, Bitsy wasn't a fan of being cut out of the loop. "In any case, Bea never said. Never even mentioned her brothers again, at least not to me. She inherited the entire Blackwell estate when her parents passed, and no one batted an eye."

"Huh." I had never stopped to wonder why my grandfather hadn't inherited part of the Blackwell estate. Actually, I had never even stopped to wonder if he had or hadn't. The library door jangled as someone opened it, startling me out of my musings. I glanced at the clock and realized Bitsy had been bending my ear for well over an hour. "Oh my goodness, Miss Bitsy, I'm so sorry. I've taken up so much of your time!" I hopped out of my chair and waited as the librarian stood up more slowly.

"Don't you worry for a moment about it, sweetheart," she said, patting me on the arm. "I enjoyed our little talk. You be sure to come back with that girl of yours so we can get her all set up with her library card, you hear?"

She escorted me out of the kitchen and waved goodbye as I hurried out the door. It was well past Aurie's dinner time, and I needed to focus on the present for a few hours. Whether or not my conversation with Miss Bitsy had shed pertinent light on the mystery remained to be seen, but at least I felt a little more connected to the town and to my family, something I hadn't realized I'd been craving so intently.

TWENTY FIVE

B y the time the sun peeked over the horizon the next morning, I'd already been in the kitchen for two hours. The last batches of pastries were in the oven, and all I had left to do was clean up. I filled the sink with hot water and let my mind drift as I tackled the teetering pile of bowls and baking sheets.

If the building was only attuned to the desires of Blackwell family members, it should only be listening to Aurie and me. But someone else had been able to get in and grab the grimoire. The bakery itself had been packed, but I didn't think the building would let just anyone back into the kitchen.

Did I have a cousin? *Or a sibling?* My heart stuttered. It was possible. My dad hadn't exactly kept in touch after he'd left us. He might well have fathered another child I'd never heard of. By the same token, William had been away from home for a few years before he'd died. Anything could have happened while he was in the army.

It still seemed like a stretch, and not information I was going to stumble upon as I went about my day. A timer beeped and pulled me out of my spiraling thoughts.

I slammed down the baking sheet of croissants I'd just pulled from the oven and growled. The whole thing was so frustrating. I'd been handed my greatest dream and it was being ruined by this infuriating situation. I just wanted to bake delicious things, not hunt down a missing book or worry about someone waltzing into my home whenever they got the urge.

The thought of turning my back on the situation and focusing on the bakery was a tempting one, but I couldn't deny my curiosity had been piqued. What about the grimoire had made it worth stealing? And maybe it contained information about my elusive family. It was odd knowing I was connected to these complete strangers. Maybe the grimoire contained information about who had equal claim on the building.

As an only child with no extended family and whose father had skipped out before she could even string together three words, I'd craved family like other kids crave sugar. There's nothing more depressing than a two-person Christmas dinner.

Knowing it could have been different poked at a wound I'd long thought healed.

I grabbed the croissants that had bounced off the baking sheet and hissed when they burned the tips of my fingers. Served me right for having a tantrum. I was still shaking my hand and grumbling when Crystal arrived for her morning shift.

"Well, aren't we a ray of sunshine this morning?" Her eyes narrowed. "Did someone else break in?"

"No. No. I think I just woke up on the wrong side of the bed." I forced a smile past my scowl. "Burning my fingers did nothing to improve the situation."

"Ouch. Anything I can do to help?"

"Coffee. Coffee would definitely help." My hands came together in supplication to give my request extra weight. I needed to shake off my cranky mood before the bakery opened or I was going to ruin everyone's day.

"One piping hot latte with extra whip coming right up!" Crystal whistled a cheery tune as she turned on her toes and headed back into the bakery. I glanced at my prep list to confirm I was almost done. The croissants had been the last thing to come out of the oven, and, other than stocking the display case, I was ready to open. The free sample for the day was coffee cake—*sans* magic. I hoped.

I glanced at the pretty tray and felt cold fingers trail down my back. *Please, please, please, please.*

The silent prayer looped through my mind as I mentally raced through my morning. Thoughts about my mysterious family members had been running through my head all morning, but had I been thinking of a specific question when making the cake?

Crystal walked in with my steaming latte, took one look at my face, and stopped. "What did you do?"

I glanced at the tray of coffee cake morsels and froze. "I'm not sure. I don't know." I grimaced. "Want to be my guinea pig?"

"Uh," she looked at the plate warily. "I'm not sure. What do you think you might have done to it?"

"Worst case scenario, I imbued it with magic to get people to tell me what they know about my family. Best case scenario, it's harmless coffee cake." I dragged my bottom lip through my teeth. "I honestly have no idea."

"Okay. I mean, I barely know anything about your family, so I'm not sure I'm a useful benchmark, but I guess I can try." She picked up a piece of cake and eyed it dubiously before popping it in her mouth with a shrug. "Mmm. That's good!"

I resisted the urge to make a hurry-up gesture. I wasn't looking for a taste tester; I knew the cake was good. I was more worried about how it would affect her. "Feel any different? Anything you urgently need to tell me?"

Crystal smiled, then she let out a little giggle, before finally bursting out with a loud guffaw of a laugh. "Did you know your great aunt had a secret addiction to cozy mysteries? Oh, and she really loved a good romance. The cheesier the better."

"Actually, I did know that. I found quite a few on her bookshelf." I giggled. "Well, at least I knew about the cozies. I didn't find any romances among her books."

"Ha! No, she kept those really well hidden." Crystal put her hand in front of her mouth, but another giggle escaped. "There's something else." She bit her knuckle and looked at me, eyes brimming over with glee. "Bea also liked to sunbathe," she paused and continued in a hissed whisper, "in the nude." Her giggles morphed into loud laughs, and I couldn't stop myself from joining in.

"She did not!" I had a hard time imagining a ninety-something-year-old woman sunbathing naked.

"She did! Right out there in the yard! I caught her once!" Crystal said, mischievous grin plastered across her face. "She was so matter of fact about it I started to question if I was more of a prude than I thought! Couldn't get the image out of my head for days."

"I bet!" I replied.

"I mean, every self-respecting witch I know bathes naked under the moon, not the sun!" The way my jaw swung open made her laugh even harder. "Just kidding! Or am I?" Her eyebrows wiggled suggestively. Perfect. Naked witches in the night. Adding that to my list of things to figure out. Later. Way later.

"Okay then, anything else you want to tell me about my great aunt?" I asked, shooting her what I hoped wasn't too exasperated a look. "Because I clearly spelled the cake."

Crystal looked up at the ceiling and thought for a moment. "Nope. I mean, I can think of a couple other random facts like that, but I no longer feel compelled to tell you any of them. Guess the spell has a limited effect."

"I guess. Maybe I was wishing people would share a few things about my family while I was making the cake. Set an unintentional cap, which I suppose is a good thing. How horrible would it be if you couldn't stop telling me things about Bea?" I shuddered then, imagining a room filled with witches spouting random facts about my great aunt. I grabbed the tray and set it by the sink. "No samples for today, I guess."

"Wait? Why not?" I glanced over, but she wasn't joking.

"Uh." I gestured in her direction. "Because this?"

"Oh, don't be absurd." She dismissed my reaction with a wave of her hand. "So, you learn a couple silly things about Bea." I felt the blush start at my cheeks and rapidly progress to my hairline. "You might also find out some useful things about your grandfather and William." I'd caught her up on my quest via text the night before to see if she knew anything that might help, but she hadn't had anything to offer beyond what I'd already discovered.

I paused. It was true I wanted to know more about them, and I'd exhausted all of my research options, but was it ethical to compel people like that? It took only a moment for me to realize the desire to discover all there was to know about my family trumped the morality of the situation.

"If you think it's okay... Is it overstepping? Is there a rule against compelling people for personal gain?"

"I'd say it's a bit of a gray area. Information doesn't really fall under personal gain, plus, it's not like you're asking for more than a couple anecdotes. Even if there's a little magical blowback, it'll be so mild you probably won't even notice." Her wide-eyed, innocent look should have worried me more than it did.

TWENTY SIX

"Is it over? Please tell me it's over," I groaned as I watched the door close after the last of the customers left the bakery.

Crystal snickered. "I think so."

"Oh, thank the Universe." I let my pounding head fall onto the cool marble counter.

"Come on, that wasn't so bad!" Even without looking up, I could tell a shit-eating grin was plastered across her face.

All she got in reply was a glare. The magical blowback had erupted fast and hard. From the moment the first customer had popped a bite of coffee cake in her mouth, the words hadn't stopped coming at me. The deluge might have been stemmed if I could have removed the plate from the counter, but customers kept grabbing it to hand samples out to their friends.

Luckily the cake had run out shortly after ten, but somehow word had gotten out that I wanted to know about my family and—as we said in the South, *bless their hearts*—the witches in this town didn't need cake to loosen their tongues.

Over a dozen people had shared my great aunt's predilection for nude sunbathing, and another dozen told me about her nude moon bathing. I was starting to wonder if Bea spent any time wearing any clothing at all. I learned she was a fan of all sorts of genre novels, had a sweet tooth bigger than the state of Massachusetts, and had a fake tooth she enjoyed popping out of her mouth to torment the neighborhood kids. She delighted in meddling in people's love lives and lives in general, was a world class baker (some of the ladies did make a point of telling me they liked my pastries better, but it didn't feel entirely sincere). She also made gorgeous quilts many of the women promised to show me, had a green thumb and grew the prettiest peonies in town (much to Margie's dismay), and she'd been resolutely single her whole life. That last tidbit was shared by a few of the women along with knowing winks, which certainly explained why she'd never gotten married.

No one brought up William—either because they knew nothing, or they were used to avoiding the subject—and I had a sneaking suspicion none of them had shared anything about George out of respect for me. If I had any doubts the entire town was gossiping about me, they were well and truly quashed. Juliette had clearly let it slip my father was a bit of a sore subject since she was the only person I'd told about the jerk who left when I was still in diapers.

"You wanted to know about Bea's brother William, didn't you?" The statement startled me into lifting my head from the counter.

The unexpected sight of Margie looming over the counter sent my heart into overdrive. Not only could I have sworn the place was empty of customers a moment ago, but she was also glaring at me with an intensity that threatened to burn me. She stood in front of me, fists on her hips, and kept right on glaring as I wrangled my racing heart into submission and figured out how to make my mouth form words again.

"I wanted to know about everyone, actually. Unfortunately, no one had much to say about the men of the family."

She scowled at me. "Well, next time, instead of spelling people to talk—"

I interrupted her with a groan. "That was an accident. It'll never happen again, I swear."

She huffed out a sound that sounded a lot like an I'll-believe-it-when-I-see-it harumph.

"As I was saying," I winced at the snap in her tone, "next time, instead of spelling people to talk, you should just ask. For one, it's the polite thing to do. Second, as I'm sure you noticed, none of these witches have the ability to bite their tongue."

I groaned again and shook my head. "Yes, I noticed."

"Ladies, would either of you like a cup of coffee before I clean the machine?" Crystal asked.

"Yes, please," I begged. Margie looked down her nose at Crystal and demanded a cup of tea. Crystal waited to turn around to roll her eyes.

"Coming right up."

Margie moved away from the counter and sat down at a nearby table. She gestured imperiously at me to join her. Suppressing my own eye roll, I headed in her direction, grabbing a couple left-over pastries on the way.

The groan that escaped as I sat down earned me a judgmental look, which I chose to ignore. We eyed each other warily until Crystal brought us our drinks. Or, rather, I eyed Margie warily while she shot daggers at me like I'd personally ruined her day and was intent on ruining what remained of her life.

"So? William?" I prompted, desperate to get the conversation started so it could eventually end. I took a swig of the hot latte Crystal brought and waited.

Margie glared at me and didn't say a word until she'd prepared the tea to her liking. I tamped down my irritation. The longer I sat here, the more things I could think of that I would rather be doing. If I hadn't had a hunch she had something worthwhile to share, I would have gladly walked away.

The deep breath she took as she set down her spoon caught my attention and allowed me to glimpse the flash of sadness that transformed her scowl for a second. It came and went so quickly I wasn't sure I hadn't imagined it. Margie pursed her lips and narrowed her eyes.

"It's really none of your business, but I suppose you have a right to know since he *was* family to you. No one else in this town knew him like I did." She huffed and shook her head. "William was..." She looked off over my shoulder and her eyes lost their focus. Her voice softened minutely as she continued. "He was a special boy. When he walked into a room, it was like he brought the sun in with him. He had a way of making you feel like you were the most important person he'd ever talked to and being with you was the highlight of his day."

A realization struck me. "You loved him," I whispered.

"Everyone loved him," she snapped back.

"No, you *love* loved him," I insisted in a louder voice.

Margie looked away and shrugged. "So what if I did? Didn't stop him from leaving."

Not a single appropriate response came to mind. And I wasn't clear on why she'd felt the need to tell me this. There was no tactful way to ask so I just stared at her until she started talking again.

"In any case, that's neither here nor there." Her acerbic tone was back, sharper than ever. Her next words were crisp and emotionless. "As I was saying, everyone loved William. It broke his mother's heart when he enlisted. She never recovered. I don't think any of them ever recovered."

"That's so sad." I murmured. Margie, lips pursed and hands clasped tightly on her lap, ignored me.

"George pretended he didn't care that William had gone off to war, but it was obvious it upset him. I badgered Bea for details, but she only ever hinted that William had enlisted because of George and that it had caused a rift. Either she didn't know, or she'd been sworn to secrecy because I could never get her to tell me more."

"I wonder..." I let my voice drift, loath to interrupt Margie's detached recounting of the past. So far she hadn't said anything surprising, but maybe if I let her keep talking, she'd let something slip.

No such luck. Her head snapped up and she pinned me with laser-focused eyes. "You wonder?"

"Bea's grimoire," I said.

Something flickered in Margie's eyes, but when she blinked, they were once again cold and intently focused on me as she snapped, "What about it? Did you read something of interest in it?"

The skin on the back of my neck prickled and I squirmed under her intense gaze. As far as she knew, I'd inherited the grimoire along with everything else and had it safely in my possession. A wave of shame washed over me as the magnitude of the loss hit me. I'd had a priceless piece of my family's history in my hands, and I'd been careless enough to lose it. This woman already thought little of me, last thing I wanted was for her to know I no longer had the grimoire.

"Sadly, no. You know," I waved my hand around me vaguely, "busy. Haven't had time to sit down with it and give it the full attention it deserves." The intensity in her gaze eased up and her whole demeanor softened.

Her eyes narrowed on me as I tried to figure out how to ask why she found that reassuring, and she tensed up again.

With a glare, she continued, "Then what about it?" I hadn't thought her voice could get any colder or sharper. "If you don't have anything helpful to contribute, don't say anything." My mouth snapped shut and my eyes widened. A little noise over by the coffee machine caught my attention. Crystal was leaning against the counter staring at Margie with a similarly horrified look.

At one point in my life, I might have let her push me around, but it had been a long morning and I was tired of bossy old ladies who thought they could belittle me. I forced my body to relax and, with one eyebrow raised, acted like everything was fine.

"As I was trying to say, I wonder if the grimoire contains any information from that time."

Margie's icy stare made me quickly reconsider my combative stance. Her eyes took on a mean quality and her lips turned up into a smug smile. She lifted her tea to her lips and sipped, never letting her eyes drift from mine.

"Well, you be sure to let me know if you find anything." With no warning, her tone had turned almost sickly sweet.

I stretched my lips into a semblance of a smile. I had no clue why she'd suddenly changed gears, but I'd grown up in the South; I knew how to play the game.

"But of course, you'll be the first I call," I drawled sweetly.

She tittered again and her transformation into a doddering old lady would have been flawless if her eyes hadn't remained as sharp and focused as an eagle on the hunt. She turned her attention to the pastries on the table. "Oh, what are these? Something delectable, I'm sure." The continued sweetness of her tone set my teeth on edge.

I blinked a few times and glanced over at Crystal whose eyes were equally wide with confusion. When I turned my attention back to Margie, she was taking a bite of an apple turnover. If the corner of her lip hadn't been twitching with contempt, I might have fallen for the old lady act and wondered if maybe she was suffering from dementia.

I was still trying to process the way our conversation had shifted when she put down the apple turnover and clapped her hands together before standing up. "Well, I think I must be going now. I hope I made it clear you won't find anything sordid in your great uncle's past. He was a good man." Her lips twitched up in a pained smile and, without saying another word, she turned and let herself out.

"That was weird, right?" I glanced over at Crystal, still huddled by the coffee machine.

"So weird." She shook her head and rubbed her eyes, like maybe she'd been imagining the whole thing. "So. Freaking. Weird. And why would she say that? Were you looking for dirt on William?"

"I didn't realize I should be."

TWENTY SEVEN

T he next day's prep called to me, but the thought of jumping right back into work made my lower back twinge, so I decided to treat myself to a mid-afternoon lobster roll on the beach. I had most definitely earned myself a break.

Aurie was elbow deep in a pile of puppies and even the thought of hot, buttery lobster couldn't lure her away. Their little squeals and bumbling walks almost convinced me to stay and play, but the need to put my toes in the sand and smell the ocean trumped their nearly irresistible cuteness.

I stepped out of the pet shop with a last longing look back and spotted Crystal and Juliette hurrying up the street, heads tilted toward each other, deep in conversation.

My cheery hello barely slowed them down. They waved, but they didn't stop walking or talking.

"Where are you guys off to in such a hurry?" I cringed as I called after them, feeling as needy as I most likely sounded.

This time they stopped and glanced back at me.

"Sorry! Gotta go! We're late!" Crystal pointed to her watch and shrugged.

"Sorry! Talk to you later!" Juliette looked anxiously up the road and back at me, her smile little more than a twisted grimace. Crystal grabbed her arm and, with another quick smile in my direction, started pulling Juliette up the street again.

Fine, be that way. The bitterness that gripped me was unexpected. These women were barely more than acquaintances. We were friendly, and in time, I was sure we'd be actual friends, but it wasn't all that surprising they would have plans together that didn't include me. Yet my gut still twisted painfully as I watched them duck around the next street corner.

I tried to shrug off the heaviness that had settled on my shoulders as I got in the car. I was on my way to the beach to eat a fresh lobster roll. There was nothing to be down about.

I almost succeeded in convincing myself Crystal and Juliette hadn't been mean intentionally when my phone pinged with a text from Crystal.

> Sorry, didn't mean to run off like that.
> Had to be somewhere that was about to close!
> I'll swing by the bakery in a little bit to help with prep.

I hesitated before hitting reply, still a little hurt by their snub.

Cassandra Berry, you do not have enough friends in this world to start jeopardizing new friendships willy-nilly because you're getting your panties in a twist over nothing. My little mental talking-to did the trick, and, feeling sheepish, I typed back a quick response.

> Please don't worry about it.
> Heading to the beach. Back in a bit.

Crystal's reply ping came surprisingly fast.

> You're going to the beach?

A sudden flood of shame made me squirm in my seat. I certainly had plenty to keep me busy in the kitchen. I had a bakery to run now. I didn't have time to go galivanting to the shore in the middle of the day. My need for a quick break warred with the certainty I was already letting everyone down and the bakery would undoubtedly fail if I didn't give it my all, all the time. I had almost talked myself back into the store when my phone pinged again.

What time are you coming back?

A second text came in hot on the heels of the first one.

Just asking so I know when to come by.
Hope you have a nice time at the beach!

See, Cassie, she didn't mean anything by her text. You're being overly sensitive again.

I growled at my mother's patronizing voice inside my head and fired back a reply letting Crystal know I'd only be gone an hour or so. Then, still feeling a little shameful about going, I started the car.

The appeal of a lobster roll on the beach had waned, and guilt over the work waiting for me had quadrupled, but I did my best to shake off my morose mood and put the car in gear. An hour at the beach wasn't going to destroy my fledgling business and would give me a much needed mental break.

The rest of my bad mood didn't stand a chance against the warm sun, the tasty lobster roll, and the crashing ocean. It felt almost decadent to be sitting on the sand by myself. No one needing to be entertained or cared for. It had been a very long time since I'd been on my own like this without feeling like I was a bad mom for letting someone else watch Aurie. For the first time since her birth, I didn't feel like I was imposing on whoever was watching her.

Aurie had spent nearly as much time at Hattie's as she had in our apartment, and not once had Hattie made me feel like she was doing me a huge favor. Instead, she'd made me feel like Aurie was already part of her family and would always be welcome by her side.

How sad was it that a brand-new friend could make me feel that way when my actual family never had? Thinking about Hattie led me to think about Crystal, who had stepped up so selflessly to help me in the bakery, and Juliette who'd been so excited to make a friend who also adored books. So what if they'd acted a little distant earlier? In every way that mattered they'd shown up for me and made room for me in their lives.

A burst of gratitude for Great Aunt Bea warmed my heart. She couldn't possibly have known what it would mean for us to find the perfect home in a town of people thrilled to welcome us into their hearts. *Could she?*

I closed my eyes and let myself bask in the warmth of the sun and the feeling of contentment.

My thoughts didn't turn back to the bakery or my endless to-do list until I spotted a farm stand overflowing with a wild array of fresh berries on my way back to the car. I gave in to the lure of a bushel of plump elderberries. The small purple berries were relatively uncommon in the South, so I didn't have a lot of experience baking with them. The moment I tasted a sample of the jam the farmer had on display, a recipe for elderberry slab pie started taking shape in my mind.

The recipe was fully formed by the time I got back to the bakery, berries in hand, and the compulsion to make the pie made me ignore everything, even my frantic bladder, until it was ready to go into the oven. It wasn't until the pie was happily bubbling away that I was finally able to turn my attention to the next day's prep.

Between the scent of warm berries, the dried salt making my skin tingle happily, and the profound sense of belonging that had settled over me while at the beach, I felt at peace in a way I couldn't remember ever feeling before.

TWENTY EIGHT

The oven timer dinged at the same time as the bakery door bell jingled. I ignored the door in favor of the oven. The humans could take care of themselves. The pie could not.

"That is gorgeous." Crystal's smile widened as she eyed the sheet pan still in my hands.

I glanced down at the purple and gold masterpiece.

"It is pretty, isn't it?" I'd let my creative side loose and decorated the pie with an assortment of lattice and little flowers cut out of leftover dough. The result was a gorgeous golden crust sitting on a gleaming dark purple filling. The smell made my mouth water. "Wanna give it a try?" I asked her with a mischievous wink.

Almost before she was done nodding yes, Crystal was pushing two plates in my direction and had perched herself on a tall stool.

The pie filling held up well, and the whole thing looked exactly how I'd pictured. I paused a moment to breathe it in. Crystal paused, eyes slightly narrowed, her fork almost in her mouth.

"Uh, is it, *special*?" She looked torn between suspicion and the desire to put the pie in her mouth. I laughed.

"No. I made 100% sure to only think about berries and pie while I made it. Promise. I wanted..." I hesitated.

"What?" Her fork stopped right in front of her mouth.

"Nothing. It's dumb."

When she didn't reply or move her fork, I continued.

"I wanted to prove I could make yummy things without using my magic."

Crystal rolled her eyes and held up a finger. She put the fork in her mouth and closed her eyes as she savored the bite.

If I'd had any doubts about my abilities, the look of pure joy that crossed her face made them all vanish.

"That good?" I asked, hesitating before putting my own bite into my mouth. Crystal wasn't wrong; the pie was excellent. The sugar complemented the tart berries to perfection and there was just enough cornstarch to make the filling firm. But the crust was the thing that took the pie to magical heights. It was flakey and buttery and robust enough to give the pie a solid base.

"Mmmmmmm." Was all the reply I got.

Crystal lowered her finger and ate her whole slice without saying another word. Her eyes roved over the berry juice smeared on her plate as if she was seriously considering licking it clean. Instead, she put down her fork with a sad look on her face.

"You know, I can cut you another piece," I teased.

She gave the pie a longing look before turning down my offer. "I'd better not. You need to sell that tomorrow. It's going to put your name on the map. Anyway, I was going to say, there is no baking without magic for you. You are a kitchen witch. It's who you are. It's in your blood. You can't turn it off any more than you could change your blood type on a whim."

"No."

"No?" Amusement danced in her eyes.

"No. I don't buy that. I'm a good baker. I was one before all this magic stuff happened."

Crystal gave me a curious look before shaking her head.

"Are you almost done with tomorrow's prep?"

"I actually am," I said. "I think I've figured out a good system."

"That's great! On both counts."

"Why?"

"Oh, no real reason. It's a gorgeous afternoon for a walk. I, uh, feel bad for rushing off earlier, wanted to make it up to you." Her tone didn't quite match her words and the way she was doing her best not to catch my eye made me leery. I waited for her to tell me more, but she was intently focused on placing our dishes in the dishwasher. "What do you think?"

I hadn't lied to her; I was pretty much done for the day. I did, however, feel a little guilty I hadn't checked in on Aurie since I'd gone to the beach.

"I really need to check on Aurie," I said with an apologetic look. "I haven't seen her all day. I'm not sure a walk is a great idea." *Plus, my gut is telling me it's a bad idea for reasons I don't quite understand.* I didn't say the last bit out loud, and I did my best to keep it off my face.

"Oh, Aurie's fine. I ran into Hattie and her on my way here. They were heading to get some ice cream." The words coming out of her mouth sounded plausible, but the way she still wouldn't meet my eyes as she said it made the hairs on the back of my neck prickle.

I pretended her behavior wasn't weirding me out and shrugged. "Then I guess a walk sounds lovely."

"Sweet." Crystal pushed open the door for me, ushering me out with her other hand. If she hadn't been acting so weird, it would have seemed like a friendly gesture. Instead, it made the rest of my back prickle.

I shied away from her hand and doubled back to the desk. "Hold up. Let me leave Aurie a note telling her where we went."

Crystal's forced smile made me glad I'd thought to leave a note.

"Where are you thinking of walking?" I asked, as nonchalantly as possible.

I had never felt a bad vibe from Crystal before, but something about her behavior was setting off all sorts of warning bells in my gut. It was baffling. A minute ago we'd been joking about licking berry juice off our plates and now I was leaving a note in case I vanished.

"Oh," she waved her hand vaguely. "Just around. Wherever." Another warning bell jangled.

"Uh-huh." I nodded, scribbling a short note saying I'd gone out with Crystal, and I'd be back in less than an hour. Other than my skin crawling and my gut jangling all over the place, I had no real reason to worry, but if I didn't make it back when I said I would, at least there would be a trace of where I was supposed to be.

The pen cap clicked into place, and I hoped my smile didn't convey how nervous she was making me. Her frozen grin did nothing to dispel my concerns.

"What is up with you?" Crystal asked with a forced chuckle, slipping her arm through mine. "You're acting like I'm kidnapping you or something."

I managed to laugh in reply, but I couldn't help noticing that her arm tightened around mine when I tried to slip it back out.

Was it possible I had completely misread her from the start? I'd been so grateful she'd shown up out of the blue, knowing how to work the espresso machine that I hadn't questioned her credentials or asked for references. Suddenly that felt like a glaring oversight. What if she hadn't actually worked for Bea?

"Have I mentioned recently how glad I am you moved here? We are so very lucky to have you. Of course, we all miss Bea," her voice cracked, "but you're a breath of fresh air this town sorely needed. Plus, that pie." She sighed wistfully as if remembering something she'd tasted years before and not something we'd literally just finished eating.

"That good, eh?" I asked again, laughing. Now that we were walking down the street, some of the tension had left her body and I relaxed slightly. I tried slipping my arm out of hers, but she clamped down again.

"Oh, yeah. Seriously. People are going to lose their minds. You really have a way with food, you know?"

"So I've been told," I brushed off the compliment, uncomfortable with the praise.

As if she heard what I didn't say, Crystal glanced over at me.

"Listen. I meant what I said earlier. You are a witch. It's part of your genetic makeup. You need to let go of this weird hang-up about your food not being worthy of praise because you have magic running through your veins."

I shrugged uncomfortably. I couldn't help it. Knowing that magic enhanced my baking abilities felt like cheating, like getting a great job because your dad was tight with the CEO of the company or getting into the college of your dreams because your uncle played golf with the dean of admissions.

"Cass, we aren't like other people," Crystal said quietly. "I'm not going to say whether that makes us better or worse, but it certainly makes us unique. You shouldn't be ashamed of what makes you special."

Was it shame I was feeling? And, if so, where was it coming from? A vague memory of my mother making a disgusted face was starting to take form when Crystal stopped in front of a large, white house with a bright red door. The yard, enclosed in a cute picket fence, was bursting with colorful plants and flowers. The whole scene would have been right at home in *Better Homes and Gardens* magazine.

I glanced around and realized I'd been so caught up in our conversation I'd forgotten to look at where we were going. *Great job, Cassie. If you ever do get kidnapped, you're toast.*

"Whose house is this?"

"Margie's," she replied. "Isn't it pretty?"

"Margie's? Bitter, angry Margie lives here?" I frowned and looked closer at the garden, expecting to see thorns and brambles amongst the pretty flowers, but I only saw bright blooms. "How?" I waved my hand vaguely around the yard.

"Magic," Crystal replied with a laugh. "She's an earth witch. I think she funnels any positive feeling right into the ground." She laughed again at the face I was making. "I told you, magic is nothing to be ashamed about. Look at this," she gestured with her chin, "think Margie feels an ounce of shame over using magic to make her garden look this good?"

I couldn't stop myself from chuckling. This was not the garden of someone ashamed of their abilities. If anything, this garden screamed, "Look what I can do!" Properly chastised, I glanced back at Crystal. If there was such a thing as magic-privilege shame, I was mired deep in it, but I could see what she meant.

"I guess it all depends on how you use your magic, right?"

"It does. Like everything else, if you have something and you choose to use it selfishly, then yes, you should feel shame." She shrugged with one shoulder. "But I honestly don't know too many witches who aren't generous with their magic. The threefold rule pushes us all in that direction, but for the most part, it seems to be the natural tendency."

Another part of me that had been struggling relaxed. Financial privilege had never sat well with me while I was married to Max, but that had been because of the way the people in our circle wielded their wealth. They used it like a mallet to open doors and clear obstacles in their path. None of them had been generous with their money. In fact, it had been the opposite. The more money they had, the less they gave away—unless it was for tax purposes—and the more they lorded their wealth over everyone who had less. It had made me sick to my stomach. It was a relief to hear that wasn't the case with magic here.

"Point made. Thank you." I smiled and tugged Crystal away from Margie's yard. Her left shoulder inched up and she scrunched her nose up in an apologetic grimace before pushing open the gate.

TWENTY NINE

"Stop! Have you lost your mind?" I hissed, trying fruitlessly to extricate my arm from the death grip she had on it. "I'm not going in there."

"I'm sorry. You have to." She still looked apologetic and maybe even a little ashamed.

"I swear, if this is your idea of a prank...," I glared at her and tried to free my arm again, "we are going to have a serious talk about what I think is funny."

"It's really not. I promise." She pulled me up the stairs and rapped three times on the door. I stifled a groan. The last thing I needed was more of Margie's negative energy.

As I was bracing myself and forcing a smile onto my face, the door flew open to reveal a mass of excited women. Someone inside shouted a muffled 'Surprise!' that the rest of the crowd echoed.

If Crystal hadn't still been holding on to my arm, I would have fallen off the stoop as I stumbled back.

"Crystal!" I yanked on the arm that was holding mine. "What is going on?" I hissed at her through my teeth, keeping a smile plastered on my face. The crowd was still ogling me from beyond the open door. Some of the faces I recognized from the bakery, but the rest belonged to complete strangers.

The smile that had bloomed on her face when the door burst open faded as she took in the horror on my face.

"Oh no! You're upset! Margie insisted on throwing you a little surprise 'welcome to town' party. Said something about how it was the matriarch's job or something. I didn't think it would upset you!"

I took a deep breath and schooled the scowl on my face. Before I could say anything, a hand reached out from the crowd and snagged mine, pulling me into the fray.

Greetings came at me from all sides, and I stared wide-eyed at the teeming crowd, panic brewing deep in my chest. I'd never felt safe in a crowd and even though this wasn't a busy public space, it still took all my willpower not to turn tail and run.

"Give the girl some air!" A voice I almost recognized boomed out, putting a momentary halt to the cacophony. "If you don't let her catch her breath, you'll have her running for the hills and, I, for one, would like to not go back to being deprived of good bread!" Miss Sadie cackled at her own joke as she elbowed her way through the throng. "Don't mind them." She waved vaguely around us. "Everyone is just excited you're here. And we embrace any excuse for a good party!" She cackled again. "Stick with me. I'll protect you."

The notion that the diminutive woman could protect me made me laugh, and just like that, the panic dissipated. Miss Sadie tucked her arm into mine and pulled me into the fray. The crowd parted and, to my surprise, I spied Aurie next to the incredible spread of food accepting a bright pink drink from a woman who was beaming at her. The ridiculous sight of Persimmon's massive body draped across her small shoulders made me feel instantly better.

Aurie felt me looking at her as the cat wrapped his tail around her possessively. The smile she sent my way was a little shaky. I knew exactly how she felt. I smiled back at her and watched as the woman who'd handed her the drink patted her shoulder affectionately and pointed out the gaggle of kids making a beeline for her.

Aurie's eyes widened almost comically, and she threw me a terrified look, but before I could swoop in and rescue her, she was surrounded by children all talking at once. I braced, ready to go intervene, but as I watched, a tiny girl pushed her way through the fray and came to stand next to Aurie. She

259

crossed her arms in front her, jutted out her chin, and stared the kids down until they were all quiet.

I laughed and turned my attention to the rest of the room.

Miss Sadie walked me around, introducing me to friendly-looking women. One handed me a drink, another a plate of cheese and crackers. A third simply welcomed me, and suddenly I had met over a dozen women. It didn't take long for all of their faces to start to blend together. I was going to sorely regret not remembering everyone when they eventually stopped by the bakery, which, of course, they all promised to do as soon as possible. Everyone gushed at me and said all sorts of nice things I couldn't even begin to take in.

"How are you doing? Are they letting you at least drink your wine?" Hattie teased, sidling up to me as one of the ladies moved away.

I chuckled. "Some." To prove my point, I took a sip. "No puppy today, eh?" I asked, nodding at the corner of the room overrun by children. Aurie and her rescuer sat in the middle with Persimmon happily stretched out between their knees. The rest of the kids lounged in a heap next to them.

The pet store owner laughed. "Not for lack of begging on Aurie's part, but the puppy is too little to be away from her mama for very long. Persimmon offered to come instead."

"Of course, he did," I said, nodding as if it were totally normal for a cat to offer to go to a party. Hattie saw right through my bluff and chuckled before patting me on the arm and moving away. Another witch waylaid me as I was about to follow her to the buffet.

"And how are you getting settled, dear?" The witch talking to me didn't look familiar, but I'd seen so many people since the store had opened I couldn't be quite sure. When I opened my mouth to greet her and came up blank, she came to my rescue with a smile.

"Millie. Millie Barnsworth. Old friend of Bea's."

"Wasn't everyone?" I replied with a laugh.

She gave me a knowing look. "Eh, you know how it is. Small towns. Big personalities." She shrugged and pointedly looked at Margie before turning back to me, an eyebrow raised suggestively. Huh, Margie had hinted like she and Bea had been tight. Maybe that hadn't been entirely truthful.

"So, how are you liking Portney?" Millie asked as if she hadn't thrown some serious shade at the hostess. I dragged my attention back to the party.

"Uh. It's nice. We're still getting settled, I think," I replied honestly. "But so far, it's been lovely. Everyone has been so incredibly welcoming."

"And how're you adjusting to the notion of being a witch?" The side of her mouth quirked up in a half smile.

"That's a whole other story," I laughed.

She nodded knowingly, patting my arm. "Take it one day at a time and you'll be just fine."

We stood in companionable silence for a moment, watching the party, until my bladder suddenly reminded me I'd worked a full morning, gone to the beach, spent a few hours baking, had been mingling for at least an hour, and hadn't once visited a restroom in that whole time. I tried to hide my squirming, but Millie pointed to the hallway off to the right with a knowing smile.

"Second door on the left."

Before anyone else could come chat me up, I headed in the direction she'd pointed. I'd just rested my hand on the door when a voice stopped me.

"Cassandra! There you are! I've been trying to get a moment alone with you, but it's been quite the challenge." My heart sinking and my bladder threatening to burst, I turned with a smile plastered on my face to greet the small, intense woman storming down the hallway. The scowl on her elderly face caught me by surprise and I took an awkward step back, upending the cheese plate precariously balanced on my glass so I could open the bathroom door.

Cheese cubes flew everywhere, and I felt a genuine pang of sadness as two pieces rolled through the door of the library situated across from the bathroom. That cheese had looked super tasty. An annoyed harumph from the older woman reminded me I had some manners squirreled away somewhere.

"I am so sorry," I said to the older woman, dropping into a squat to gather up my spilled food.

She huffed in reply and stalked away. Great, another old lady in this town who'd be happier if I left. I wanted to shrug it off, but it was starting to bother me. Hopefully, the other elders of the town would turn out more like Bitsy and Miss Sadie.

I had almost made it to my feet without peeing my pants or dropping more cheese when I wobbled. I grabbed the nearest doorjamb to keep myself from faceplanting onto the carpet and into further embarrassment. The last thing I wanted was to give the people of Portney another story to share about me.

The room beyond the doorway was dark, and I might not have peeked in if something hadn't caught my eye. An ancient ornate desk dominated the room. Sitting on it in plain sight was a large, faintly glowing, leather bound book. An even more subtle thrumming confirmed what I was seeing.

Margie had my grimoire sitting on her desk.

No, that couldn't be my grimoire. Could it? Nah, there was no way it was my grimoire. Maybe all magical books glowed. Margie was probably not above stealing it, but how had she done it? And was she arrogant enough to leave it out pretty much in plain sight? *Maybe. Okay, probably.*

Without going in and actually touching the book, there was no way for me to tell if the book was mine. Peeking into a room was one thing, but blatantly going into a room probably off limits to guests was another. It was the opposite of how I'd been raised, and I could almost hear my mother's horrified intake of breath as I considered it.

THIRTY

G uilt hammered at me as I darted from the bathroom and into the room I'd just spent five minutes telling myself I should not, under any circumstance, check out before going back to the party. Snooping was rude and beneath me. If I suspected Margie of stealing my grimoire, I should just march up to her and demand she give it back.

Which I would never do in a million years. She intimidated me too much. Plus, if she was willing to stoop to theft, there was no doubt she'd also quite happily lie about it. Which left me with no other option. I slipped into the room and pushed the door almost all the way closed, leaving it open just enough to hear if someone was coming.

I'd always dreamed of having a library in my house. This was not the library of my dreams.

The floor to ceiling bookshelves would have been at home in a gothic novel. The desk I'd glimpsed from the hallway was massive and looked like it had born witness to countless shady dealings in its lifetime. The antique wooden globe undoubtedly hiding fancy bottles of booze belonged on a pirate ship.

For a moment I felt like I was back in Georgia, visiting with some of the country club people Max loved to pretend were his peers, all of whom had pretentious decorators with zero taste. But a quick glance at the shelves revealed books none of those people would have been caught dead owning. One particularly gorgeous volume bound in green leather caught my eye. I had almost deciphered the title when footsteps echoed in the hallway.

Shit!

My eyes darted around, looking for a place to hide. *Under the ornately carved desk or behind the plush armchair by the bookshelf?* The footsteps came closer, and I made a snap decision. I threw myself behind the desk and held my breath.

The grimoire was only a foot away and its increasingly intense thrumming beat in tune with my pounding heart. It was so close, but there was no way to grab it without leaving my hiding place.

I poked my head out from my hiding place. The footsteps had stopped a few feet away from the door and I could hear quiet murmurs. If I was super quiet, maybe I could pop out, grab the book, and be back in my hiding place before the person came any closer.

My hand was inches away from the grimoire when the footsteps suddenly sounded as if they were right outside the door. Startled, I miscalculated my reach and my hand brushed against the antique globe. For something so old, it spun surprisingly well, but sadly, not quietly. I glanced at the grimoire still out of my reach as I threw myself back under the desk and held my breath. There was no way whoever had been outside hadn't heard the commotion.

The footsteps stopped in the hallway and Margie called out, "Hello? Is anyone in the bathroom? Cassie? Is that you?"

She knocked politely on the bathroom door, and then louder when no one replied. I took advantage of the noise to take a deep breath. I was debating whether I also had time to scoot myself into the space under the desk when I noticed the bookshelf behind me had swung open a crack.

My heart stopped. That bookshelf had been flush against the wall a moment ago. I'd looked at all the books and I would have noticed something that obvious.

It could only mean one thing.

A secret passage behind a bookshelf. A genuine secret passage behind a bookshelf! My distaste for

Margie's gothic décor gave way to my excitement about what else this room might be hiding.

Margie was now pounding on the bathroom door and demanding to be let in, so I changed direction and crawl-scootched myself toward the small opening. As I'd hoped, the bookshelf made no noise when I pulled it open wide enough to crawl behind it.

The effort to stifle my squeal of delight left me breathless.

Oh my god. Oh my god. Oh my god. My heart was beating a mile a minute from the combined fear of being discovered and the thrill of having found a secret passageway. Stacey was never going to believe me.

Margie pushed open the library door with an annoyed sniff as I pulled the secret door closed.

"No one had better be snooping in here. This door was supposed to be closed." I froze and placed my hands over my pounding heart. She took a few steps and sniffed again, then her footsteps receded, and the door snicked shut.

I let out the breath I'd been holding, then my heart sank. I hadn't had time to grab the grimoire before throwing myself behind the bookshelf.

THIRTY ONE

I pushed at the back of the bookshelf. Nothing happened. It stayed in place, exactly how I would expect a bookshelf to behave. Except this was no ordinary bookshelf and I was on the wrong side of it. Frantically, I ran my hands over the panel that made up the back of the secret door. All I found was smooth wall. No hidden lever, switch, or button anywhere. It would have been easier if it hadn't been pitch-black, but other than a faint glow from the bottom of the bookshelf door, I was surrounded by darkness. My heart sped up and I felt a cold sweat break out on the back of my neck. Terror was quickly eclipsing my delight over the secret passageway.

Okay, Cassie, focus on your breathing. In. Out. In. Out. Panicking isn't going to help.

Not that there wasn't any air back here, but if I held my breath any longer, I'd pass out. And if

I breathed too fast, maybe I'd run out of air. My breaths sped up.

What if there's a limited amount of air in here? What if I've already used up more than half. Am I going to die here?

I leaned my head against the door and focused on breathing slowly. I was not going to die back here, in this secret passageway Margie probably never used. That would be just wrong. And so unfair.

Breathe, Cassie. Breathe.

In any other situation, I would have used the flashlight on my phone to help me see, but I'd left my phone in my jacket which was sitting on a bed in Margie's guestroom. It also meant I couldn't call anyone for help or moral support.

I'm going to die alone. I'm going to die alone in the coolest secret passage I've ever found. Okay, maybe the only secret passage, but that doesn't change the fact that it's the coolest.

I don't want to die here! The breaths I'd managed to slow started to speed up again, and I forced myself to count as I breathed in and out.

"Oh, how quickly the turn tables, eh? From excited about a secret passageway to dying alone in under 60 seconds," Stacey's voice quipped deep inside my head. Great. Now I was hearing voices. Fantastic. At least it was Stacey's voice. It was

almost like not being alone in the dark in a secret part of a stranger's house. Almost.

The urge to sit down and cry overwhelmed me. It had been a ridiculously long and stressful day. All I wanted to do was crawl under my comforter with a glass of sweet tea—Southern-style, thank you very much—and lose myself in a book until life started to feel normal again. Whatever that meant these days.

Never in all my years of reading about witches and houses with secret passageways had any protagonist gotten stuck in one. No, they used their fancy magic and got themselves out of situations like these.

The snort that came out of me was more cynical than amused.

Figures you'd manage to get yourself utterly useless magic. The voice in my head now sounded more like Max's mother than Stacey. She had always been quick to assume the worst of me, no doubt she would manage to be disappointed in me in this as well. But for once, I agreed with her a tiny bit.

What good is discovering you're a witch if all your magic does is make your already pretty damn good baking taste a little better? Oh, sorry, and allows you to influence people's actions, but only toward what they were going to do anyway.

Pathetic. This time, the voice was all Max, but, again, I didn't disagree.

I forced down a sob threatening to cut off my air supply and leaned my head against the wall.

If only I'd been able to grab my grimoire before I'd gotten stuck. Not that I would have known what to do with it, but maybe it would have been able to guide me or something.

The sob I'd suppressed worked its way free.

A faint whimpering sound froze my blood until I realized I was the one making the pathetic noise. When my sorry attempt to laugh at myself resulted in another strangled sob, I gave up, letting myself slide to the ground and dropping my head onto my knees.

Nothing I'd tried had opened the bookshelf, so if I was ever going to hug Aurie again, I was going to have to find another way out somehow. I was pondering how hard you had to punch wood for it to splinter and if there was any way I had that kind of strength in me when the hairs on my arms tingled. I froze. They tingled again, like they were being teased by a draft.

Draft.

Moving air.

If my arms were being caressed by a breeze, that meant air was circulating. If air was circulating, then I wasn't trapped in a sealed box.

I lifted my head from my knees and found my eyes had adjusted to the dark just enough for me to make out a steep flight of stairs facing the door.

Duh, Cassie, of course there are stairs. Who would build a secret passageway to nowhere? This time the snark was all me.

The fact that there were steps should have been reassuring, but I couldn't see past the first one and had no clue where they led. And there was the issue of the slight scrabbling I could hear coming from their depths.

Terror started to overwhelm me, and I squashed it angrily.

No, absolutely no. This is not you, Cassie. Not anymore. You are not going to sit in this stupid secret passageway and feel sorry for yourself while you wait for whatever that is to come up the stairs and eat your face. Just. No.

I was so done having zero control over my life. None of this was supposed to happen. Not the witch stuff, not the new town, not even the divorce! I had done everything right. I had been the perfect wife. Max had made endless, ridiculous demands of me, and I had bowed to all of them.

I had hosted dinner parties for people I loathed and gone to countless boring and stupid events. I'd been supportive and kind and I had given him the child he'd insisted he wanted, and still, he'd thrown me away like none of it mattered. He'd thrown both of us away!

And then, out of the blue, a mysterious great aunt? What kind of bullshit was that? I'd needed family while I was growing up! Why couldn't she have contacted me when she could have been helpful? Instead, I was in this bizarre town, surrounded by people I wasn't sure I trusted, dealing with magical powers of all things!

Something snapped deep inside me, and the tantrum of the century, fueled by anger and not a little bit of hunger, started to bubble up from deep in my gut. Emotions roiled inside me, hot and intense, and as I was about to let loose with a screech of pure rage, a tiny little squeak stopped me in my tracks.

"What was that?" My shaky whisper echoed around the empty space.

In reply, all I got was another little squeak.

With my heart in my throat, I tilted my head down to see if I could hear the noise better.

Please don't be a mouse. Please don't be a mouse. Please don't be a mouse.

Something soft and furry scrambled across my shoe and I leapt to my feet, my heart thudding in my chest.

It was a mouse. I had a mouse on my body. A strangled shriek tried to force its way out, but I was holding my breath too hard for it to get anywhere. The urge to shake it off my foot warred with the absolute certainty that if I did it would hold on and then run up my pant leg. And that would be a thousand times worse than having it on my foot. If I didn't move a muscle, maybe it wouldn't move a muscle.

I took a few deep breaths to quell the mounting panic and awarded myself major points for not screaming bloody murder when the mouse dug its little claws into my ankle.

"Mouse! Mouse! Mouse!" I whispered hoarsely to no one. "There's a mouse on my foot." My rational brain knew I was bigger and stronger than a little rodent. The rest of it was hopping around inside my head screaming, "Ew! Ew! Ew! Mouse! Ew! Ew! There's a mouse on my foot."

Completely unimpressed with my histrionics, the mouse sat up and started washing its face. At least that's what it looked like it was doing. I could barely make out its shape in the dark. Every so often it would stop and poke my leg with its tiny little hand. Eventually the poking grew annoying enough that it drowned out the hysteria unfolding in my brain.

"Stop poking me, stupid mouse." Holding my breath, I twitched my foot in the hopes it might jump off and run away. *I was talking to a mouse.*

In reply, the mouse stopped grooming itself for a second, looked up at me with little beady eyes glinting despite the dark, then very slowly and deliberately, reached out and poked me again.

"Stop doing that!" I hissed.

Again, the mouse stared at me intently and intentionally poked me. Then, still keeping its eyes on me, grasped the thin fabric of my pants and yanked. My jaw dropped.

Even in the zillion Disney movies Aurie had forced me to watch over and over again, I'd never seen a mouse act like this. Except maybe in that one about the terrible chef. But that was a rat. This was a mouse. My train of thought slowed. Rat that cooks. By controlling a human. Disney movies. Aurie. *Aurie!*

"Hold up. Are you one of Aurie's friends?" I hissed at the mouse, leaning forward cautiously so I wouldn't startle or unseat the thing. Even if it was a friend of Aurie's, I still didn't want it running up my pants. Like it knew what I was thinking, the mouse tilted its head and leapt onto my pants and scurried up my leg. It took every ounce of self-control I had left not to jump up and down screeching. Instead, I stayed rock still, even when the mouse kept running up to my shoulder, down my arm, and pausing on my cuff as if it were waiting for me to open up my hand.

Suppressing my gag reflex, I turned my palm up and the mouse scurried onto it. With an annoyed little *whiff,* the mouse turned to look at me.

"Okay then," I said, pretending I wasn't talking to a tiny rodent looking up at me from its perch on my hand. "I'm not entirely clear on how you knew to come find me, but if you're one of Aurie's little guys—and boy do I hope you are and I'm not holding a random mouse in my hand—I'm hoping you can help me get out of here."

I moved closer to the light seeping through the bottom of the door and raised my hand to my face until the mouse and I were nose to nose. It looked at me intently and twitched its whiskers. It was either cuter than the average mouse or I had never given much thought to rodent aesthetics. Either way, its pointy little face was oddly endearing.

"Alright little guy, how about this, nod once if you know Aurie." I held my breath. If it didn't respond and I had to face the fact that I was talking to a run of the mill mouse, I was going to utterly lose it.

The mouse bobbed up and down quickly on my hand.

"Okay, now we're getting somewhere," I said. "I think. Unless that wasn't a nod."

The mouse did its unimpressed staring thing.

"How about this," I continued. "Nod twice if that was a nod."

The mouse bobbed up and down twice, looking smug when it was done.

"Okay little dude, nod once for no and two for yes, okay?" The mouse tilted its head and looked me square in the eye. It was a little unsettling to be honest. Its eyes were two tiny black beads, but they still made me feel like it was looking deep into my soul. I shivered a little. "Can you help me get back into that room?"

The mouse bobbed once, slowly, whiskers and ears drooping. My heart sank. Part of me had hoped I could somehow get back into the library and grab the grimoire without anyone noticing.

"Bummer. Moving on. Can you help me get out of this passageway?"

The mouse bobbed twice, whiskers twitching with excitement. It wrung its little hands and glanced into the darkness shrouding the staircase. I groaned.

"It's really dark. How am I going to be able to follow you?" I asked the mouse, the utter absurdity of the situation not easing up in the least. The mouse squeaked then lifted a hand to its ear and rubbed it a couple times. "You'll make noise and I follow the noise?" I asked. It bobbed twice in reply, its whole body quivering with excitement. "Right then. No time like the present."

I placed the mouse back on the ground gently and took a deep breath. It chittered up at me as if to make sure I could hear it. "Coming in loud and clear," I replied. Taking the first tentative step took more courage than I'll ever admit.

THIRTY TWO

I f I felt silly following a mouse chittering its way down the stairs, it was nothing compared to how ridiculous I felt when I realized the staircase that had made my knees shake with fear was a short, straight flight of stairs that ended in front of a small door. Rolling my eyes at my wild overreaction, I peered through the thick layer of dust coating the small window embedded in the door.

"Wait, what? How the heck are we at the other end of town? I can see the bakery from here!"

The mouse had nothing helpful to contribute other than a bored look.

"Well, forgive me for not being up to speed on secret passageway magic!" I hissed at it.

The mouse squeaked once sharply, looking exasperated.

"How exactly am I supposed to get back to the party now? I've already been gone forever. Even if I drive, I have no idea how to get to Margie's. I don't even know her address. And how am I going to explain that I went to the bathroom and now I'm coming back in through the front door?"

It was utterly irrational for me to be angry at the mouse. It hadn't gotten itself stuck in a passageway it couldn't escape, with or without magic, but that's still where my frustration directed itself.

The mouse watched me rail with zero reaction beyond rapidly twitching whiskers. Part of me suspected it was laughing at my antics, which did nothing to cool my irritation.

"You are no help at all!" I growled. At that, the mouse's ears dropped, instantly making me feel like a real jerk. "Aw, little guy. I'm sorry. I didn't mean that. I'm just frustrated I'm in this situation in the first place." The mouse's ears perked up a tiny bit, and he looked hopefully in my direction. I sank to the bottom stair and rested my face on my knees.

Assuming I could find my way to Margie's house, maybe I could sneak in undetected. There were dozens of people in there; they would never notice me slip through the front door, right? Then again, Margie had somehow stolen my grimoire. What did I care if she thought me rude or strange? The mouse chittered unhelpfully. It bugged me that I did care. Other than Margie and that old lady in the hallway, everyone had been so kind and welcoming, and this was pretty much an ideal place to raise Aurie.

Unless everyone was being kind because they felt sorry for me for having such pathetic magical powers. They'd probably been expecting someone special like Aunt Bea and the instant they realized I couldn't fill her shoes they'd make it clear we weren't welcome in their witch town. Plus, did I want to raise Aurie in a place where magical books got stolen out of people's homes by old ladies?

The mouse jumped onto my foot and poked my ankle surprisingly hard.

"Ow! Cut that out! I thought we were done with the poking." It glared at me from its perch on the tip of my shoe and chittered angrily. Had it been talking to me the whole time I'd been lost in thought? I grimaced. "Sorry, little dude. Didn't realize I was ignoring you."

The mouse huffed and let out a string of squeaks, furiously pointing to the left. I groaned sheepishly when I turned and peered into the darkness.

"This isn't the end of the passageway, is it." The mouse bobbed twice in quick succession.

"I was overreacting again?" The mouse bobbed twice again, the rodent equivalent of a smirk on its face.

"And I should follow you that way?" The mouse bobbed twice more and jumped off my foot, chittering back at me as it darted into the shadows.

"Whoa! Slow down! I don't move as fast as you." I heaved myself to my feet and dusted off the back of my pants. From the amount of dust that had collected on the stairs, it was clear no one had used this secret passageway in a good long time. The mouse squeaked at me from a few feet away. I felt for the wall and used it to guide me to where it was waiting for me.

I swear, first thing I do when I get out of here is buy one of those tiny flashlights, and I'm never leaving home without it again. Or, you know, never leaving my phone in my jacket again.

A few feet from the staircase, a second door appeared, making me once again feel like an idiot for flying off the handle. The mouse kindly refrained from commenting. I peered through the tiny window and sighed with relief. I could see Margie's front door from this one.

"I'm not even going to try to figure out the physics involved here," I muttered to myself.

"Hey, mouse! Any suggestions for how I get back into the house unnoticed?"

The mouse let out a long string of squeaks and chirrups that made absolutely no sense. In response to my apologetic shrug, it let out an annoyed huff and squirmed its way through a tiny hole at the bottom of the door.

"So much for that," I muttered.

I had my hand on the front door and was about to turn the handle when chaos erupted inside. Screams coming from every direction allowed me to slip in and close the door behind me without being noticed.

At first glance, it was hard to tell what had triggered mayhem, but a crash drew my attention to the trashed buffet table and my little mouse friend perched on the windowsill with a massive piece of fried chicken clutched in its tiny hands. It winked at me and jumped out the window, narrowly missing being clubbed by a witch armed with an oversized ladle.

Aurie yanked on my sleeve. "Mom? Was Mighty helpful?" Her eyes shone with a mix of excitement and pride.

"Mighty?" I asked. "That's its name? Really?"

"Don't be so judgy, Mom." She rolled her eyes. "He came to tell me you were stuck. I told him to help. Did he?"

"He totally did, babe. Thank you," I said. Aurie beamed with pride. "You did good."

"Anyway. Where were you stuck? Were you really in a secret passageway? Can I see it?"

"Yes, I was. No, you can't," I replied, knowing full well if I gave her any more information than that, she'd wheedle a different answer out of me. "Maybe later," I hurried to say when her face fell. "Can you tell Mighty I said thanks? He really saved my bacon back there."

"Mom. No one says that anymore," Aurie said. "Hey, can I have another brownie? They're not as good as yours, but still, chocolate."

"Sure, get me one too, would you?" I replied with a laugh before I sighed with relief. I'd made it back in and as far as I knew, no one had noticed a thing.

As Aurie wove her way to the dessert table, I let my eyes drift to the hallway. I hadn't noticed it much in the passageway, maybe because of the panic and disorientation, but now I was back in the house, the grimoire was once again calling to me. It made my skin itch to know it was so close but still out of reach. But the chair Margie had placed in front of the door to the library made it clear that the only way I was getting my hands back on my grimoire was to make a scene or come back another time.

THIRTY THREE

"What was I supposed to do? Stand up and tell everyone there that she's a conniving thief and demand she return my book? Come on, she's the matriarch. They would have tarred and feathered me before marching us out of town."

Stacey snorted a laugh.

"That's quite a visual."

"Plus, if I'd done that, I would have had to admit I'd been snooping. No one likes a snoop, Stacey."

Stacey rolled her eyes at me from the other side of the phone screen. She'd never pretended she didn't love to snoop around bathrooms in other people's homes. "Come on! She stole it from you! That's way worse than snooping."

"I dunno. She's not the type to see it that way." Angry Margie was probably only one step removed from her usual crankiness, but I wasn't anxious to find out.

"Fine. If you won't confront her, then you need a way to get her to confess." She pursed her lips and nodded her head thoughtfully. "Any ideas?"

"Torture is out. I hate even the thought of blood. What am I going to do? Withhold baked goods until she caves?" I snickered. "Unless..." It wasn't the most ethical idea, but it had potential.

"Unless?" Stacey prodded.

"But what if she's not the one who stole it? What if someone else took it and gave it to her?"

"Even so, it's not like she doesn't know who did. The thing didn't suddenly show up in her house."

Our eyes widened at the same time.

"You don't think...?" Stacey whispered.

"No." I shook my head. "Books don't teleport. That's crazy."

"Right. Right. Of course, you're right." Stacey shook her head.

"Anyway, anyone could have stolen it for her. There's a whole town of witches I don't know yet!" *And a few I know I probably shouldn't trust blindly.* I threw up my hands. "This sucks."

Anyone could be a suspect, really. Crystal had been my rock since day one, but for all I knew she'd only been hanging around to get her hands on the grimoire. Juliette was sweet, but she'd been oddly drawn to the bookshelf in the kitchen. And what if Hattie had only taken Aurie under her wing to get insider access to our things? Margie, well, that was an easy one, but there had to be a reason she was so well-respected. My heart hurt.

My phone wobbled alarmingly when I thunked my head on the table.

"I don't even think I was this sad when Max told me our marriage was over," I moaned. "I wanted everything here to be perfect." I lifted my head and wailed. "Is that too much to ask?"

Stacey twisted her face into an exaggerated pout and managed to make a few soothing sounds before her compassion ran out.

"Go back to that 'unless' you said earlier. Unless what?" Her voice made it clear she was over the pity party.

I sighed and slumped down in my seat. "Unless I use magic," I mumbled.

"Yes! I love it when magic is the answer!" Stacey pumped her fist in the air.

"Yeah, yeah," I replied, dread pooling in my gut. The thought of using magic I barely understood and definitely didn't trust wasn't sitting right, but I couldn't think of a mundane solution that wouldn't turn the whole town against me.

"So, what are you thinking? Something to make her so violently ill she begs for an antidote you refuse to give her until she confesses?" Stacey asked, eyes sparkling. I shot her a horrified look in reply.

"No! I..." I paused and took a deep breath. "I was thinking I could bake a truth-telling cake."

"A whole cake? Just for Margie?"

I squirmed in my seat, mortified at what I was about to suggest.

"No. For Juliette, Crystal, Hattie, *and* Margie. I'll invite them all over to say thank you for being so welcoming." My stomach churned at the thought of doing something so deceitful under the guise of doing something nice. "Then I'll serve them the truth cake and ask a few pointed questions. Hopefully, I'll get all the answers I need." *And maybe find out who's a friend and who's pretending.*

My heart ached. I'd be crushed if any of my friends weren't who they were pretending to be. I couldn't even wrap my brain around how Aurie would feel if Hattie turned out to be using her to get to me.

"You are so devious!" Stacey said, her voice perfectly matching the delight evident in her eyes.

I couldn't bring myself to mimic the smile on her face.

THIRTY FOUR

Shockingly, acting cool and collected when inviting people over for coffee and magical cake so I could force them to talk didn't come naturally to me.

I stammered my way through asking Crystal, blushing all the way, and completely lost my cool when she started looking at me like I had lost my mind. She agreed, if a little hesitantly. After that, I chickened out and sent the other three guests texted invitations. For a moment, I wondered if texting might be too techy for someone as old as Margie, but her acceptance came through first, effectively erasing my concerns.

Well, not *all* my concerns. There was still the very real chance they would hate me for tricking them, but I knew this was the only way I could be around them without constantly wondering who was lying to me. Still, my stomach was in knots as

I imagined the disappointment on their faces when my subterfuge was revealed.

I wasted no time in scheduling the little get together, so I wouldn't have time to overthink things. As it was, clearing my head enough to infuse the cinnamon coffee cake with only a tell-all hex was hard enough. It's not impossible I inadvertently added a little "please don't hate me too much" into the mix.

By the time the ladies were scheduled to arrive, I'd stress cleaned the bakery from top to bottom and everything gleamed. The frantic cleaning helped keep my mind off the cake which smelled so good I was almost drooling as I scrubbed. It wasn't clear if I was immune to my own magic, but I wasn't all that anxious to test it.

Margie let herself in as I was about to start wiping down the counters a fourth time.

"Of course, everyone is late. Young people these days have no sense of courtesy." Margie scowled at me as she settled herself into one of the chairs at the table I'd set. I didn't bother pointing out she was ten minutes early. As usual, her bright, flowery outfit was in direct opposition to the dour look on her face. A little pang of guilt pinched my heart as I watched her eyeball the cake.

Juliette and Crystal arrived together a moment later. They held the door open as Hattie meandered over from the pet shop, shouting instructions to Aurie as she walked away.

"Are you leaving her there on her own?" I blurted out. My anxiety over the cake was suddenly eclipsed by the thought of Aurie in charge of a store filled with animals.

"Hardly!" Hattie replied with a laugh.

Relieved, my breath hissed out of me with a faint wheeze.

"Picasso is with her." She sat down at the table with a deep groan of pleasure.

"Picasso?" The name only rang a faint bell, which was weird, because I wouldn't have easily forgotten a person named after my favorite artist.

"Hattie's familiar," Juliette said with a smile, pulling out her chair. "Fat, chatty parrot. I'm sure you've seen him around the pet store."

"Ha!" Hattie chortled. "Don't let him hear you call him fat. You'll never hear the end of it!"

"I'm sorry. You left my child in charge of a pet shop, and she's only being supervised by a parrot?" I blinked at Hattie, hoping the look on my face would convey how horrified I was at the thought.

"Don't worry so much, Cassie," Hattie replied with a gentle pat on my arm. "It's all good. Picky pretty much raised me. They're going to be fine. Now, is this a self-serve situation here?" she asked, eyeing the table, "because that cake looks amazing!"

"Uh," I replied, drawing a blank. Hattie's gaze narrowed as she really looked at me for the first time since she'd walked in. Three other heads turned in my direction and I felt their collective gaze settle on my face. I squirmed under the scrutiny.

"Cassie, is there something you want to tell us?" Crystal joked as she slid a tray of coffee drinks onto the table. "Did you hex our cake?"

Everything about her tone made it clear she was teasing, but I couldn't stop myself from twitching a little in response.

"Ha ha ha!" My laugh was a titch too loud and a little too forced, but no one seemed to notice. "Of course not. Here look, I'll prove it." I grabbed a plate, plonked a piece of coffee cake on it and jabbed it aggressively with a fork. I shoved the bite into my mouth and smiled around the fork. "Sheee, noh hect."

Crystal looked at me like I'd grown a second head before reaching over to pat me on the shoulder. "I know, sweetie, I was only teasing. Maybe I should make you a decaf latte instead." She reached for my cup, and I jerked again, grabbing it before she could take it away.

"No, no, I'm fine. I swear!" I clutched the mug to my chest and yelped when the hot liquid sloshed onto my shirt. "Oh, shit!" I jumped up and plonked the cup on the table. "I'm sorry, I'll be right back."

On my way to the kitchen, I quickly video called Stacey.

She watched me hyperventilate as I dabbed at the coffee with a dishtowel and helpfully informed me it was time to get a grip.

"I know!" I wailed in the phone's general direction. "I'm just so nervous. They're going to hate me. They're going to tell everyone I'm a horrible human being who hexes people right and left and no one will ever shop here again. And I'll have no friends. And then what will Aurie and I do? Go back to Georgia?"

"That is not going to happen," Stacey said, with a shake of her head and a roll of her eyes. "No one in their right mind could ever hate you."

"Max does," I mumbled.

"Well, Max is an ass who doesn't count. No one else could possibly hate you. And even if they do, I'll always be your friend."

"See?" I wailed again. "You think they'll hate me too."

"Tits up, doll face. It's too late to back down. I'd bet my bottom dollar they polished off the cake and licked the plate clean already. Time to go reap what you sowed. The damage is done. Might as well get something out of it." She waved me away with her hands and ended the call, leaving me with no choice but to head back into the bakery to face the music on my own.

"Margie, you're so brave to wear such bright colors. My mother would never have been caught dead in an outfit like yours. It's like someone ate a rainbow and threw it up again." I felt my lips moving before I knew words were going to come out. By the time I'd slapped my hand over my mouth, it was too late. "Crystal, did I ever tell you that your hair makes me think of corkscrews? Whenever I see you, I crave a large glass of wine. Also, I'd kill for hips like yours." To my mounting horror, the words kept pouring out of me. The women at the table looked at me with huge eyes and wide-open mouths.

"You *should* wish you had hips like hers. You have curves in all the wrong places." Hattie instantly looked horrified. "Uh, I mean, how did you ever push out a child?" She slapped a hand over her own mouth. Her eyes spun around widely, unsure where to land.

Juliette laughed quietly to herself, staring down at the table.

"What exactly is funny, young lady?" Margie demanded, looking beyond offended.

"She's right. Why do you always dress like a rainbow threw up all over you?" Juliette asked, a grin splitting her usually serene face.

"Well, at least I don't dress like an aging spinster!" Margie snapped back. Juliette's smile vanished and she looked down at her somber gray shift.

"I like my dress. It's practical," she whispered.

"And ugly." Crystal chirped from her seat. This time it was her turn to slap a hand over her mouth. She eyed the cake plate warily. "Cassie, what did you do?" she yelped through her fingers.

"It's not my fault! I had to!" I wailed, throwing myself in my seat and burying my face in my hands. *Note to self, not immune to my own magic. Good to know.*

"Had to what?" Juliette asked, a hint of betrayal in her voice.

"Had to find out who was guilty." Even if I'd wanted to, there was no way to keep the truth from spewing out of my mouth. "Someone stole Aunt Bea's grimoire and I saw it at Margie's when I was snooping around."

"I knew it!" Margie threw me a piercing look. "Did you use my secret passageway to get out?"

"Yes." I mumbled. Shame heated up my face. I could feel my ears burning.

"What does the grimoire have to do with this cake and what the heck does it have to do with me?"

Crystal asked, her face contorted with disgust. Of all the women at the table, she looked the most betrayed and my heart sank at the hurt in her eyes. This stupidity was going to cost me a good friend.

"I needed to know who had taken it and why."

"And you couldn't have asked?" Her voice was so cold, I was amazed little icicles didn't fly out with her words.

"I'm sorry. I just, why are you so nice to me if it isn't to get something from me?" By now I was almost whispering and wishing I could crawl into a deep hole and never ever climb out, but I couldn't stop myself from speaking.

"Uh, maybe because I'm a nice person and because I liked your great aunt and maybe because I promised her I'd make sure you got off on the right foot so her family name would be honored properly?" She slammed her mouth shut and stood up stiffly. "And maybe because I always wanted to be made partner, but Bea wouldn't hear of it, and I thought I could make it happen if I befriended you from the get-go." The anger that had coated her face was rapidly giving way to embarrassment.

"Please don't go!" I begged her, grabbing for her arm. "I'm so sorry. What can I do to make it up to you?" She stared down at me and I held my breath as anger flashed in her eyes.

"Make me a partner."

"Done. 30% yours. Because baking is way harder than making coffee." Damn this truth cake.

Crystal snorted. "Fair enough. But I bet you won't be saying that when I refuse to make you a cup tomorrow morning."

"You wouldn't!" I gasped, hand flying to my chest in horror.

"Maybe I will, maybe I won't," she responded with an unreadable smirk.

"Ahem," Margie coughed not all that gently. "Could we get back to the matter at hand?"

"Yes!" I nearly shouted. "Why is *my* grimoire in *your* house?"

"It's not," she replied, looking smug. I paused and thought about how I had worded my question.

"Fine, why *was* my grimoire in your house?"

Annoyance crossed her face and she sighed. "Because I wanted it."

"I'm sorry, what? That's not exactly an excuse to go around stealing things. I want..." In that moment I couldn't think of a single thing I wanted that I didn't already have, so my sentence lost steam. I took a breath and refocused. "Why exactly did you want it so badly that you'd resort to stealing?"

"I didn't steal it." Margie said, shooting me another smug look. Either the effects of the truth spell were wearing off or the woman was somehow able to fight the compulsion.

"Listen you old witch, I don't care that you're the town matriarch. You're ruining what should be an awesome thing for me and I'm seriously over it. I just want to bake. I want to run my bakery and take care of my child and live a peaceful life. I don't care about magic; it's more of a bother than anything. And I don't care about the grimoire. I don't see why it's such a big deal and I honestly wish I'd never ever heard of it. I. DON'T. CARE! I. JUST. WANT. TO. BAKE."

The way they were all staring at me with big, rounded eyes might have been funny if I hadn't been on the verge of bursting into tears. Apparently, the truth spell wasn't wearing off on *me*. No one said a word or moved a finger as if even breathing a little too hard in my direction might make me explode. The thought made me want to both laugh and scream.

My whole life, one way or another, I hadn't been allowed to be myself, to speak my truth, to be as loud or as colorful as I wanted. I'd been told to be a good little girl who didn't make too much noise and then a good little wife who didn't make waves. I'd been told what to do and when to do it and then, despite everything I had sacrificed for him, Max had ripped my life to shreds, without a thought about how it would devastate me. For the first time ever, I was doing what *I* loved, what *I* wanted to be doing.

I was in charge of my own life and my own fate, and I'd be damned if I was going to let this old hag take that from me.

"Here's what's going to happen," I said, forcing myself to lower my voice, "you're going to tell me why you needed my grimoire so badly. And then you're going to give it back. And that's going to be the end of it. Because I have better things to do than deal with this bullshit." Margie reared back at the tone of my voice and pursed her lips. "As for the rest of you, you're all going to tell me why you've all been so weirdly helpful and kind and what you have to do with this particular situation so we can put it behind us and get on with our blessed lives."

"Hey, I just like you and your kid. I have no horse in this race." Hattie said, throwing up her hands at the same time as Juliette said, "I'm the one who stole the grimoire. But only because *she* blackmailed me," with a glare in Margie's direction.

I held up a finger in Juliette's direction and rounded on Hattie. "You just *like* us? You've been letting my kid spend hours in your shop every day because you just *like* us?" If my voice didn't express my disbelief properly, I'm sure the baffled look on my face did a great job of conveying how little I believed Hattie.

"What can I say? It's not every day a talented witchling like yours shows up on my doorstep.

Watching her explore her powers is a trip." Hattie quirked her left shoulder and held open her hands. "Plus, she's doing every dirty job I can throw her way."

"We can discuss how you're exploiting my kid later. And we should probably talk about Aurie's powers then, too." I glared at her and turned my attention to Juliette. "And you. What the hell, Juliette? So, this whole time, you really were just being friendly so you could scare me half to death by breaking in to rob me?" I fought the tears that threatened to overflow. I wasn't shocked Margie was a conniving old woman, but I really liked Juliette and I thought we were on our way to being good friends. The betrayal hurt more than I expected.

"No! That's not how it is at all! Our friendship is real, I promise!" The fear on her face made me check myself, and I tried hard to tone down my intensity. The truth spell was making it hard to temper my emotions.

"Friends don't steal from friends, Juliette! That's part of the friend code, or haven't you heard?"

"I know." Her voice was low, and she wasn't meeting my eyes. "I didn't know you when I agreed to Margie's terms. If I'd known how much I was going to like you, I would never have let her bully me into it. She said you were going to be a sniveling entitled brat who hadn't earned the right to her family grimoire. I should have known better than to trust her." Her eyes cut to Margie with a glare.

The pinch in my heart eased up a little. I hadn't completely misread the situation. The winds whooshed out of my sails, and I sat down heavily in my chair, but not before I threw a glare at Margie that she ignored completely.

"Can someone please tell me what's going on?" I asked quietly. The exhaustion that had been piling on for the last week was settling on my shoulders, and I had to fight the urge to put my head down on the table and weep. I side-eyed Margie. "Not you. For some reason, this truth spell isn't working right on you."

A smug expression settled on her face as she leaned back in her chair, crossing her arms defensively across her chest. "You don't get to be a witch my age without learning a few tricks." She turned her attention to Juliette and growled, "You best remember your place, child."

Juliette audibly gulped and turned an ashen gray that made me actively worry about her immediate wellbeing. To my shock, instead of fainting dead away, Juliette sat up straighter, pulled her shoulders back, and after shooting another glare at Margie, started speaking in a firm voice. "It's probably best if I start at the beginning."

"Oh, here we go!" Margie said, throwing her arms up dramatically.

"Hush you," I growled at her. "Juliette, please go ahead. Tell us everything." I paused, "Wait. Not *everything*, everything. Just everything about this." I waved my hand around.

She took a deep breath, bracing herself. "It all started before I was born." Margie rolled her eyes, and I shot her a warning look. Then I smiled gratefully at Crystal who was making her way to the coffee machine.

"Go on," I said as encouragingly as possible, sitting back in my chair and giving her my full attention.

"Way back in the day, Margie and your great uncle William had a *thing*," Juliette said, her voice gathering strength as it went. Margie growled under her breath.

"Last warning, Margie. Next time you're out," I said without even looking at her. She scowled at me and twisted up her lips, but she stopped making menacing sounds.

Juliette continued as if she hadn't been interrupted. "They were an item before he enlisted. That relationship resulted in a child, my mother, Emeline." My jaw dropped. Hattie and Crystal's eyes widened like saucers. No wonder Margie was acting all sorts of defensive.

"Because Margie was barely fifteen, her parents sent her away to a town deep in the heart of Nova Scotia where they knew a few witches. Once the baby was born, Margie was to leave her in the care of the witches there and then go home, claim she'd had a wonderful stay at the coast, and pick up her life where she'd left off. But, before Emeline was born, Margie's parents were killed in a tragic accident, leaving Margie on her own. With William off at war and her parents gone, Margie could easily have stayed in Nova Scotia and made a life for herself and the baby, but she stuck to the plan and, to my knowledge, never looked back." Margie didn't react to the condemning tone or look that went with it.

"My mother was always a bit odd, a little quiet, a little slow. She lived with her head in the clouds, a little like she wasn't entirely connected to the earth. As it sometimes goes," anger flashed in Juliette's eyes, "certain men took advantage of that. One of the fishermen got her pregnant. I've never been sure why he married her, I doubt he loved her, but maybe he wanted to do what he thought was the right thing. Either way, they were married shortly before I was born. He was lost at sea just a few months later."

Sympathetic noises echoed around the table, but Juliette ignored all of us.

"Long story short, we got by. People let my mother do odd jobs for them and one neighbor educated me along with her own children. It wasn't a bad life, just not an easy one. My mother only told me about her mother when she was dying last year. Once she passed away, I reached out to Margie. It felt like the right thing to do." Juliette looked like she regretted doing so. If the tightening of Margie's mouth was any indication, she wasn't thrilled about it either.

"Oh, give me a break." Margie rolled her eyes. "I've been nothing but nice. I set you up with that store and gave you money to run it, didn't I?"

Juliette shrank away from Margie's—her grandmother's—sharp words. I reached out and placed my hand on her arm. "And the grimoire? How did she bully you into taking it?"

"Bullied? Poppycock!" Margie scoffed. "I asked her, nicely, to get me what was rightfully mine."

"Rightfully yours?" I asked, my eyebrows flying up. At the same time, Juliette spoke again.

"Telling someone you'll take away everything you gave them and ruin their reputation if they don't do what you say isn't asking nicely!" Juliette's hand flew to her mouth in shock. I barked out a laugh. Apparently my spell wasn't quite done making people speak their truths.

305

"It's the Blackwell family grimoire! It goes to the oldest family member! As William's wife, it should have come to me!"

"William's wife?" I asked, my eyebrows crawling even higher up my forehead. "You were fifteen! How did we go from a teen fling to you being his wife? Didn't someone say William had a sweetheart in France?"

At that, Margie almost snarled. "It wasn't a fling! We had an agreement. He was going to marry me when he got home."

I sidestepped that loaded comment, thinking of all the shotgun weddings that had taken place moments before soldiers had boarded boats taking them to the front. Those guys hadn't wanted to risk waiting. It spoke volumes that William had. Though, to be fair, he'd been little more than a child himself. "So, no girl in France?" I asked instead, genuinely curious.

"I took care of her," Margie said in an ominous tone.

"You what? How?" I both wanted to know and didn't.

"It's why she wants the grimoire, I'd wager." Hattie nodded, her lips pursed, startling everyone who had forgotten she was sitting at the table, which is to say all of us. She sat back with an impish grin and took a sip of the steaming mug of coffee she held in one hand. In her other hand, she was clasping a pastry she had taken from who knows where. The delight on her face at the drama unfolding right in front of her would have been hilarious if I hadn't been at the heart of it.

"Exactly," Juliette replied, totally ignoring how awkward it was that Hattie was enjoying herself so much. "I think I explained this the other day, but grimoires are more than just spell books. They're more like family diaries. Witches use them to journal life events that feel noteworthy as well as keeping track of spells and the like."

"Wait, so..."

"Margie thinks Bea might have written secret stuff about her in the grimoire." Hattie's eyes sparkled with glee.

"What kinds of stuff?" I asked, but Juliette just shrugged.

I carefully worded my next question, so Margie wouldn't be able to give me a half answer.

"Margie, what were you concerned—wait, no—what do you think Bea might have written in the grimoire about you?" I pinned her with my best mom glare and waited for her to answer. She visibly struggled, pinching her lips together and clenching her jaw, but I'd worded my question perfectly.

"Stuff," she ground out.

"I'm gonna need you to be more specific," I replied, forcing myself to be calm. "And preferably before I completely lose my cool."

Margie glared at me and then caved.

"Fine," she huffed. "I'll tell you. Not that it'll make a lick of difference. There's nothing in the grimoire after all." She straightened up and threw her chin up. "Dark magic. That's what I thought Bea had written about. The dark magic I used to put an end to William's dalliance with that French tart."

The collective gasp of horror from everyone in the room made me jump.

"You didn't!" Hattie gasped, all traces of delight replaced with shock.

"I did, and I'd do it again. Did he think he could knock me up and run off to war like that and there would be no consequences? Why should I be the only one to suffer? I gave up my baby! People talked! They had no proof, but they still considered me spoiled goods and kept their precious sons from marrying me. Did I deserve that? What did that girl ever do to deserve him? He. Was. MINE!" Her shout surprised even her, but not as much as the shimmer of tears in her eyes.

We stared, unblinking, but she met our stares head on, daring us to condemn her actions. I certainly wasn't going to throw the first stone. Who knows what I would have done to Jimmy Krantz if

I'd had magical powers back in middle school when he pretended to like me just to make his buddies laugh?

"Don't you dare pity me, child!" Margie barked at me, jarring me out of my empathetic moment. "I neither want nor need it." She glowered at me as if daring me to feel another ounce of compassion for what she'd gone through.

"Fine," I said, leaning away from her and crossing my arms protectively across my chest. "Have it your way."

"Did you really attempt dark magic?" Hattie asked, a hint of the earlier delight back in her eyes. The rest of us were clearly a little shaken by Margie's outburst, but Hattie was like a kid in a front row seat at the circus minus the giant bag of popcorn.

"I did," Margie said, straightening up a little and shooting Hattie a smug smile.

"Wait, I'm confused again. Surely something called dark magic is a bad thing, no?" I asked, looking around the group at the more experienced witches.

Juliette looked grim. "It is. It's a very bad thing. Dark magic taints your soul. The more you practice it, the darker your soul gets until eventually all the good in you is smothered."

"Well, that sounds peachy," I deadpanned while eyeing Margie. It explained so much.

"Oh, stop looking at me like I eat baby souls for supper," Margie sneered, rolling her eyes. "It was the one time. I never did it again." As she spoke her eyes darted right. Unfortunately, I couldn't remember if that was an indication of lying or truth telling. The skeptical look on Hattie's face made me lean more toward lie.

"They say that it's a little like heroin, one hit and you're addicted for life," Juliette whispered, carefully not looking at her grandmother.

"Pish posh," Margie said, with a dismissive wave of her hand. "If you're a strong enough witch to practice the dark arts," a glimmer of pride shone out of her face, "you're strong enough to resist its call. Which I have, ever since I sent that one spell." Shame and something that might have been pain briefly overshadowed the pride in her face, but she shook both off and stared us all down, once again daring us to condemn her.

I narrowed my gaze on her. "What are you not telling us about your spell?" I didn't think about the question or how it would affect the hex, but the sudden fear that pooled in Margie's face told me I'd worded it exactly right. There was something she didn't want us to know, and my spell wouldn't allow her to keep it from us.

She fought the words for a moment before visibly giving in.

"It was a clumsy attempt to break them up, but it ended up keeping them apart for all eternity." Other than the way she was biting her bottom lip, it was impossible to tell how she felt about botching the spell. Juliette saw right through the façade and let out a sad sigh. The look she sent her grandmother was a mixture of compassion and horror. Margie's head snapped in her direction as I tried hard to keep up with the unspoken communication.

"Maybe." She shrugged. "Part of me has always wondered."

"I'm sorry, what?" I asked, feeling beyond dumb for not understanding. Juliette and Crystal stared me down until the pieces collided in my head. "Oh, you... the spell... William..." No wonder she'd never tried her hand at practicing dark magic again.

"There's no way to be sure. All I know is that I sent that spell and a month later he was gone forever." Her eyes got glassy, but she steeled herself and no tears spilled over. "I told Bea about it late one night after we had consumed enough wine to fell an elephant. William was her brother. She deserved to know. And I needed to get it off my chest. We never spoke of it again, but she never looked at me the same."

"Just... wow," Crystal said from the counter where she'd perched herself after making everyone's coffee.

Margie kept her gaze laser focused on Juliette.

"So you see why I needed the grimoire." A mere hint of vulnerability leaked through in her voice.

Emotions warred on Juliette's face. It was clear she was fighting her way through the deluge of information.

I jumped in to give her a moment to process. "So, you thought Bea might have written down your confession in the grimoire? Still doesn't explain why you couldn't simply ask to see it."

"Oh, yeah, asking, what a novel idea," Crystal quipped sarcastically from the sideline. I scowled at her.

Margie turned her gaze on me and snorted. "Sure, like you would have let me look at the book and tear out a few pages without asking any questions."

I gaped at her. A part of my brain snickered at the fact that I was more horrified at the thought of her ripping pages from a book (a book!) than the thought that she might have murdered my great uncle, or at the very least, caused his death.

"It was all so long in the past, why would it matter anyway?" I asked, a little baffled by the conversation.

"Oh! There's no statute of limitation on the use of dark magic in the witching community," Hattie cut in gleefully. "As Juliette said, it's rumored you get addicted for life after only one hit. Or at least, your soul is marked for life. There's no telling when you'll be lured in again. A witch who has successfully practiced dark magic can never be trusted again." The twinkle of delight in her eyes belied her grim tone.

"It has taken me a painfully long time to become the town matriarch," Margie said with a glare in my direction as though I had any hand in how long my great aunt had lived. "I couldn't let anything get in the way of finally taking my rightful place in our community."

Understanding dawned again. "Not even, say, an illegitimate granddaughter?" I asked, pointedly.

Margie had the grace to squirm a little and shoot Juliette a sideways glance.

"I would have told people eventually," she said defensively. "I wanted my position to be a little more secure before people found out."

"So, you had me steal a book. And then you told me that if I ever said anything about our relationship, you'd tell everyone I was a thief?" Juliette asked, her voice getting increasingly shrill. "Again, you could have just told me! You're my grandmother! I would have been more than happy to do as you asked! It's hardly the 1940s anymore. No one cares that you had an illegitimate child!"

"Your legitimacy aside, you would have helped me keep the secret that I might have killed your grandfather?" Margie asked sarcastically.

"We'll never know, will we!" Juliette threw her hands up.

"Every single day since William left and my parents died, I've had to fight for my place in this community." Margie's voice had taken on a steely quality that sent shivers up my arms. "No one helped. No one stood with me. I had to become a different person. Someone others would respect despite my past, despite my marital and familial status. Someone strong and self-sufficient. I don't know you. I had no reason to trust you. I still don't."

Juliette blinked back tears Margie didn't notice.

"I don't believe it anyway," Hattie said matter-of-factly, taking a bite of her pastry, totally oblivious to the heart breaking in front of her.

"Don't believe what?" I asked, turning my focus on her.

"Don't believe the spell in that letter did any harm to that boy." She shrugged.

Margie's look would have made a weaker woman wither. "Are you saying I'm such a terrible witch that I couldn't manage a simple dark spell?"

"Oh, please," Hattie said with a dismissive wave of her hand, "put that misguided pride away. First of all, there's no such thing as a *simple* dark spell. Second of all, are you, a seasoned witch, going to tell me you truly believe that a spell, dark or otherwise, sent overseas in a shipping container, could have arrived in good enough condition to cause any real harm? I doubt you sent it airmail."

Her words visibly stunned Margie. The old witch stared straight ahead for a long moment, then she blinked once, twice, and a third time, before realization dawned on her face. "Well, I'll be." Shock made her jaw slack. "Salt water."

"Salt water," Hattie echoed with a knowing and definitive nod of her head.

"I ...," Margie voice trailed away as she placed her forehead in her hand with a tiny mirthless laugh.

"You were young and in love and it made you forget one of the most basic laws of magic." Hattie waved her hand dismissively.

"Which is?" I asked, once again feeling like the dummy in the room.

"Salt disrupts magic," Crystal said quietly. "If you ever have a spell go wrong, drop it in a bucket of salt water. It dissolves the magic."

"But the letter didn't go into the ocean, did it?" I asked. "And I bake with salt. And clearly that doesn't affect the spells."

"It's a quantity issue." Margie said quietly. "It wouldn't matter if the letter got wet or not, being surrounded by that much salt water would have nullified the magic. A teaspoon or two of salt in a cake dampens the magic a bit, but a whole ocean is a different story. I can't believe I never thought of that in all these years." For a moment she looked almost angry, then her face softened. "I didn't kill him." She looked down at Juliette and for the first time, something that might well have been affection softened her face. "I didn't kill William."

THIRTY FIVE

"That did not go how I expected." I said with a wry smile in Crystal's direction as I closed the door behind Hattie, Juliette, and Margie.

"Oh, really? And how did you think feeding everyone cake that forced them to be truthful would go?" I wasn't exactly surprised to see real anger sparking in her eyes.

I stopped tidying up and took a seat at the table where she'd sat down.

"Crystal." I grabbed her hands and forced her to look me in the eye. "I am so very, very, deeply sorry for what I did. There is no excusing my actions. I can only promise never to do it again. It was wrong and uncalled for. I was out of line, and I hope you can forgive me."

Crystal looked deep into my eyes and burst out laughing. "Did you read a book on how to apologize? Or are you still feeling the effects of your cake?"

"It was a podcast," I protested. "A good one too. I learned a lot. And maybe I'm still being a little influenced by the cake. But I really am sorry. I shouldn't have doubted you."

"Of course, you should have! We met, like, three weeks ago!" She rolled her eyes at me. "Just because we are clearly kindred spirits united in our eternal love for the holy java doesn't mean you were wrong to assume I was only being nice to you so I could steal your great aunt's grimoire. Could you maybe have asked me instead of spelling me? Well, yes. But, wait, no. I have no but." Her voice dropped. "You should have asked, Cassie. Heck, you should have asked the four of us instead of assuming we'd lie to you. Though, I guess I wouldn't trust Margie to tell the truth even if her life depended on it, so you weren't entirely off base with that one."

Shame flooded me from the top of my head to the tips of my toes. She was right.

"I should have asked. You're right. And I'm not sure what it says about my past that I didn't trust any of you to tell me the truth if I asked, but it's probably not good." I shook my head. "I doubt Margie would have shared her whole sordid tale, but she might have at least told me about the grimoire."

"Eh, probably not." Crystal said with a little shrug. "Listen, I don't know why it's been hard to trust people before, but Margie aside, I hope that now you know the rest of us are on Team Cassie, right? You can count on us to have your back." She smiled and squeezed my hand. "Now are we going to talk about what went down this afternoon, because whoa. Am I right?" She rounded her eyes in mock surprise.

"Whoa is definitely right," I chuckled. "But seriously, are we okay?"

"Are you still giving me thirty percent of the business?"

"Are you still going to make my morning coffee?"

"Like I could ever deprive you. I just wanted to torture you a little." Crystal smirked.

"Then can I please have a cup, *partner*. I have a ton more pastries to make, and I won't get through it all without caffeine."

"You know," Crystal said, sliding off her stool and heading back into the bakery. "I may not be as gifted as you, but I *can* cook. You don't *have* to do everything yourself."

"Slow your roll there, friend," I replied with a laugh. "Asking me to trust *and* lean on someone all in one day? You might be pushing your luck." I took a deep breath. The truth cake ordeal had taken a lot out of me, and the prep list was long. A little help in the kitchen wouldn't be unwelcome, but more than that, it was the companionship I'd been craving that kept me talking. "That said, how do you feel about shaping and cutting scones?"

"You're in luck, I think my kitchen abilities stretch just about that far." Crystal laughed and got up to help me collect the dirty dishes. "You know, I really don't think this afternoon was the disaster you think it was."

I turned a dubious eye in her direction. "Uh, you don't? I forced a woman to reveal a secret she was clearly intending to take to her grave."

"Yeah, and in the process, you helped her start to heal a trauma that has been eating her alive that whole time."

Maybe I hadn't imagined that Margie's steps had been a fraction lighter as she'd left the bakery.

"You seriously think so?"

"I do actually." Crystal tilted her head and pursed her lips. "I'm not saying that you should make a habit of forcing people to reveal their deepest and darkest secrets, but I think that in this instance, it was warranted. And maybe..." She glanced at me and let her voice trail away.

"Maybe what?"

"It doesn't matter. You're not going to believe me anyway."

"No. What? Tell me!"

"Fine. Maybe your magic guided you in the right direction. It provided the solution when you were at a loss for what to do, right?"

I hesitated, but it was impossible to deny that it had. "Yeah."

Crystal shrugged. "Your magic knew how to get you the answers you needed."

The thought sent shivers down my back. "It's... *sentient*?" I whispered.

Crystal barked out a laugh. "No, you goofball. It's part of you. It gives your subconscious mind an added layer of intuition, if you will. You might not yet believe in your magical abilities, but that doesn't make them any less real or any less potent."

My first instinct was to brush off her words like the nonsense I wanted them to be, but they struck a chord I couldn't ignore.

"Your magic works differently than your great aunt's did. Her strength was potions. She somehow always knew what people needed. It was entertaining to see her hand vials to people before they even asked for anything. But I think your magic is going to prove equally impactful and beneficial to the community."

The sincerity of her words and the affection in her gaze as she spoke them eased something deep inside me. For the first time since we'd arrived in Portney, I was starting to believe this wasn't just a place I wanted to be, but it was where I was meant to be. The thought that my magic might be needed stunned me to my core.

"You really think people need what I have to offer?"

"Yes, and not just to improve their mornings."

THIRTY SIX

T he scones I slid into the display case the next
day weren't as perfectly shaped as they would
have been if I'd cut them, but I had to admit that
letting Crystal help me get everything ready had
made the morning a heck of a lot more pleasant.
Everything was ready earlier than planned and we'd
even had a moment to share another cup of coffee
and hammer out the details of our partnership.

We were wrapping things up when the door to the
upstairs apartment hit the wall with a loud bang.

"Sorry, Mom!" Aurie shouted in my direction as
she raced through the bakery, weaving around the
tables like a seasoned rodeo barrel racer.

"Whoa, whoa, whoa!" I cried, making a slow
down gesture with my hands. Aurie reluctantly
came to a stop a few inches from the front door and
turned to scowl at me. "Where are you going in such
a hurry? It's still early."

"Mom," Aurie whined. "I have to go. I have to go see Willow."

"Willow?" I asked, digging deep to try to place the name. A vague memory of her telling me something about a Willow at dinner a few days ago hovered at the edge of my mind.

"Willow? My puppy? Remember?" Aurie asked, rolling her eyes so hard I half worried they might get stuck in the back of her head.

"Yes. Right, Willow the puppy." I resisted the urge to roll my eyes back at her. Someone in our relationship needed to be the adult and paperwork somewhere indicated that it might be me. "What about Willow? Weren't you just over there?" I squinted my eyes and stared Aurie down. The way she was holding her hands behind her back was triggering my mom senses.

Aurie twitched visibly and jumped a little. A panicked look crossed her face and she pleaded with me with her eyes. "Mom, please, I really gotta go."

"Uh-uh." I shook my head at her and crossed my arms. "Not until you tell me what's going on and possibly not until you've eaten some breakfast."

A flash of anger crossed her face, immediately followed by a spark of light behind it. She flinched.

"Aurie, what is going on?" My heart leaped into my throat as I inched my way toward her. I hesitated as she shrunk away from me. Aurie had never shied away from me. Even when she'd thrown tantrums as a baby, she tended to throw them while burying her face in my lap. "Baby, come here."

"No," she snapped. "I've got this. I don't need your help. I can do this on my own."

Hearing my words thrown back at me hurt almost as much as her rejection.

"You know," I aimed for nonchalant and probably missed by a mile. "It has recently been pointed out to me it's okay to ask for help. I know that you're a tough cookie and that you're super smart, but you don't have to deal with whatever this is," I waved a hand in her direction, "by yourself. I'm here for you, honey bunch."

"No, you're not. You're busy. You have the store to open." Her words hit me like a physical blow. Teen scorn twisted her face. "Don't call me honey bunch. I'm not a baby anymore."

"Hold up, kiddo..." I stopped myself. My mother would have punished me for talking to her like that. I knew better. I took a deep breath and focused on the issue at hand. "I'm not sure what's going on with you or why you need the puppy, but if you fill me in, maybe I can help."

Another spark flared behind her, and Aurie's eyes widened with terror as she brought her hands out from behind her. Tiny lightning bolts shot out of her fingertips.

"Holy shit!" I jumped back and momentarily lost control of whatever mom cool I was striving for. "Uh," I started, but no plan came to mind. "Let's stay calm." I kicked myself when my words had the opposite effect, and the lightning started shooting out faster. "Crystal? Any advice here?"

Crystal shrugged helplessly. "Sorry, I have no experience with fire witchlings."

"I thought you guys said she was an animal witch!" I glared at her. Why couldn't anything about magic be simple?

"She is, but clearly she's got a strong affinity for the fire element."

I resisted the urge to groan out loud. This was neither the place nor time for my frustration with magic to rear its head. Aurie looked at me, eyes wide with imminent panic. The lightning coming out of her fingers was beginning to shoot tiny sparks. One landed on the floor and flared brightly before extinguishing itself.

"How about we go talk about this outside where nothing can catch on fire."

"That's where I was trying to go. You're the one who stopped me." The teen snark was back, but with a little less fire. Probably because it was shooting from her fingers.

"Watch it, kid, you're in enough trouble for keeping this from me."

"I knew you would be mad. That's why I didn't tell you." She glared as she stomped past me and tried to shake the sparks from her hands. One landed next to her foot and set a leaf on fire. She growled, stomping out the tiny flame. "This sucks."

I reached for her, and she shied away. "Don't. If you touch me, it'll hurt you. I shocked someone at the pet store yesterday. She said it really hurt."

I looked at her and blinked. How had I not known my baby was suddenly a human sparkler? Shame flooded me. I'd been so wrapped up in the bakery and my own magical debacle it hadn't even occurred to me she might be going through some of the same.

"I'm not mad at you. You are 100% right. I have been preoccupied with the bakery and I am so sorry. I hate that you didn't think you could come to me with all this."

"It's okay, Mom." Aurie sighed like she was resigned to my absence. "You've been busy." She focused on the ground. "I get it. And I'm fine."

Another gut punch. My mother had been too busy for me, and I had sworn I would never put my work or my passions ahead of my child's needs. I'd lasted less than a month. I pushed aside the feelings tumbling around in my heart and raised my eyebrow

327

in the direction of her pyrotechnic hands in my patented 'you're not convincing me' look.

"Okay, maybe not fine, fine, but if you'd just let me go see Willow, it'll be okay."

"Willow? The puppy? What does she have to do with anything?"

Aurie rolled her eyes again and started moving toward the pet shop. "Can I please just show you?"

It was early enough that *A Familiar Place* was still locked up tight, and Hattie was most likely fast asleep in her apartment above the store. The jaunty "Closed" sign didn't faze Aurie for a moment.

"There's a key in the dog bone." She gestured at a wooden dog holding a massive bone in his mouth next to the entrance. "Can you get it?" She held up her sparkling hands and shrugged.

When I hesitated, she rolled her eyes and sighed. "It's okay, Mom. Hattie said I can use the key whenever I need it."

"Hold up. *Hattie* knows about this?" I waved at the electricity shooting from her hands.

"Duh," Aurie said, shaking her head. "Key? Please?" She added when I raised both eyebrows.

There was no obvious place for a key on the front of the dog bone, so I slipped my hand around to the back and found a little opening hidden out of sight. I wiggled my fingers into it, praying I wasn't waking up a spider or two and heaved a quiet internal sigh of relief when all my fingers encountered was a key. I pulled it out triumphantly and showed it to Aurie.

"Good job, Mom. You found a key exactly where I told you it would be."

"Hey!" I protested. "You and I are going to have to have a little talk about this new attitude, young lady."

"Sure, whatever, but maybe we can do it later?" She waved her hands in front of her and I scurried away from the sparks that jumped out at me.

"Yep, sure thing." I turned the key in the lock and paused. The instant I opened my mouth to ask whether there was an alarm to worry about, the puppies started barking, the birds started screaming and the parrot started yelling "Intruder! Intruder! Intruder!" So much for that thought.

"Shut it, Picasso!" Aurie yelled back at him. "It's only me, you're safe."

The parrot mumbled "only me, you're safe" a few times before he fell silent and watched us make our way to the mosh pit of puppies in the middle of the room. They'd grown in the last week since I'd seen them. Their eyes were open, and they looked more like puppies than little naked mole rats. One of them made a beeline for Aurie and stood up against the pen, squealing and wriggling with excitement.

Before I could grab her arm to stop her, Aurie held her hands out to the puppy. To my complete shock, instead of shying away from the sparks, the puppy reached out its little tongue and started lapping at the lightning. My jaw dropped as it sucked down the electricity pouring from her fingers.

Once the sparks were fully extinguished, she nuzzled her head into Aurie's hand and let out the sweetest little burp possible. Aurie lifted the puppy into her arms and sank to her knees in front of the pen. She curled herself around the puppy and heaved a sigh of relief.

I hesitated, unsure how she would take it, then gave in to the need to pull her shaking body onto my lap. With a sob, Aurie sank into my arms as tears poured out of her. The puppy snuggled deeper into her lap.

Aurie held the puppy and I held her as she cried herself out. After a while, the puppy squirmed and popped her head up, giving us a look that made us both giggle.

"So, that's new, eh?"

"Yeah." Aurie let out a laugh that ended in a sob.

I reached out a finger and rubbed the soft spot on the puppy's forehead. "We're going to figure it out, okay?" I said, feigning confidence I didn't feel. "But, maybe, in the meantime, Hattie will let us bring this little one home earlier than planned."

"I think we can work something out," Hattie said from the other side of the room, startling me. "Good morning, Aurie. Good morning, Cassie. And how are things with the both of you today?" The slight twist to her smile told me she knew exactly how our morning had gone. I smiled wryly back at her.

"Just peachy," I replied. "You?"

"Can't complain, really," she said. "Aurie? Sweetheart? How are you feeling?"

Aurie lifted her tear-streaked face toward the pet shop owner and gave her a tremulous smile. "Willow saved the day again."

"Told you she would," Hattie said with pursed lips and a nod. "She's a good girl that one." It wasn't clear if she meant Aurie or the puppy, but the way she was gazing at the pair, a tender smile on her lips, she might have meant both of them.

The puppy squirmed under all the attention and almost leapt out of Aurie's arms to get back to her siblings. Reluctantly, Aurie placed her gently inside the pen and giggled when the other puppies mobbed her. The longing look she threw Hattie almost broke my heart.

"I can't take her away from her siblings. She's too little, but..." She waved her hands helplessly.

"Yep, it's a conundrum," Hattie said, pursing her lips and nodding again before turning her gaze on me, one eyebrow raised questioningly.

"No. Absolutely not. No way, no how," I said, shaking my head firmly.

Hattie shrugged. "Have it your way. Aurie, sweetheart, has your mom showed you how to use a fire extinguisher?"

I sputtered. My mouth opened and closed again when words refused to come.

"You look like a fish, mom." Aurie giggled and imitated me. I slammed my mouth shut and scowled at Hattie.

"Sometimes magic is a little *erratic* when it first manifests in a young witch."

"Erratic?"

She shrugged again. "A little electricity never hurt anyone."

"Yes, yes it has!" I protested. "What can we do about it? How do I keep her safe? And when exactly were you going to come tell me my kid is a human sparkler?"

"It's really okay, Cassie. I promise. Aurie isn't the first witchling to spark a little. There are people here to help her learn to control her magic. As for telling you, I was leaving that up to Aurie, but maybe I should have said something yesterday."

"Ya think?" I raised both eyebrows and shook my head. "What do we do in the meantime? Do I order a case of fire extinguishers?"

"In the meantime, keep Aurie calm and things will be fine. If things get out of control..." Hattie's voice trailed away as she gestured to the roiling pile of puppies.

Sure, because pre-teen emotions were so easy to calm. Hattie snickered at the exasperated look on my face.

"You can always..." She looked pointedly at the puppies, and I groaned. She was right, if we couldn't take Willow away from her family quite yet and Aurie was likely to set fire to the house without Willow to...eat?...her fire...I gulped. There was only one valid solution.

"Fine, but you're in charge, Aurie. You keep their bed clean, and you make sure they're safe and happy. I won't be able to run upstairs every five minutes to check on them."

Aurie clapped her hands and bounced on her knees. "Really? Seriously? They can come home with us?"

"It's only for a few weeks," Hattie murmured reassuringly. "We can separate them from their mom in three weeks or so. And Aurie can bring them here during the day, so they're not constantly underfoot."

"Right. The mom has to come too." Both Hattie and Aurie raised their eyebrows at me. I threw my hands up. "Sorry! Sorry! I forgot about her for a moment."

They both chuckled and I sighed. Exactly what my life needed, more complication.

"How do we get them all to the apartment?"

It took two trips, but the puppies and their mother were happily settled in a corner of Aurie's room moments before the bakery door jangled from the morning's first customer. I washed my hands carefully and made my way downstairs. Crystal's look was full of questions, but I shook my head slightly and busied myself with helping the next customer in line. If I told her, everyone standing in line would hear, and I just couldn't bear to be the talk of the town again.

My silent plea went unanswered. The woman standing at the cash register had caught the tail end of the puppy parade. She gave me a knowing smile and patted my hand gently.

"It'll all be okay. You'll see. My little one was a sparker and she turned out just fine."

The next person in line told me it had taken their child the better part of six months to gain control of their magic. The person after that had a baby who kept making things fly around the room. All morning, customers told me stories about how their children's magic had emerged and the only common thread to their stories was how the community had pulled together to help.

From the moment Aurie had shown me the fire coming from her fingers, I had felt like the worst mother in the world. Who didn't notice their child was on fire? Back in Georgia, I would have hidden all of it like my life depended on it. Every mother's move had been scrutinized and judged by the other mothers like they were handing out prizes at the end of the year. Something this big would have had me ostracized for the rest of Aurie's childhood.

But I didn't see a single condemning look in any of the customers' eyes, only compassion and support. It was hard to comprehend.

"Get used to it, friend," Crystal said, nudging me with her elbow and nodding at the retreating back of a customer. "One witch's business is every witch's business, and we take supporting each other rather seriously around here."

Her statement should have filled me with horror, but all I felt was gratitude that I wouldn't have to parent Aurie on my own after all.

THIRTY SEVEN

A blissful quiet settled over the bakery after the last of the patrons had collected their belongings and given cheery reminders to hang in there. Between the emotional whirlpool of the truth-cake party, the fiery morning, and a full day of manning the bakery and talking to countless people, I was completely burned out. No pun intended.

I'd sent Crystal home, promising I could handle the clean up and get started on the next day's prep. She'd taken one look at my face and, recognizing my need for a little quiet, promised to be back a little later in the day to help me in the kitchen. I was tired enough to be moved almost to tears with gratitude.

It took all of ten minutes for the silence to become oppressive. My thoughts kept turning to the debacle of the day before and how much worse it could have gone. Stacey picked up on the first ring, her face so close to the camera I could only see the top half of it.

"OMG! I thought you were never going to call! What happened? Why didn't you call me yesterday? Tell me everything!"

"Sorry, I meant to call, but things got crazy, and it slipped my mind. Next time I'm keeping you on the line so you can hear it for yourself." I slumped down at a table and closed my eyes. "It was something."

"Oh! Did someone spill a deep dark secret?"

"That's one way to put it." My tired chuckle made her eyes narrow.

Stacey laughed. "Missing the country club life right about now?"

"God, no." I shuddered again. "I'll reenact that scene a thousand times a day if it means I never again have to set foot in that place wearing an uncomfortable dress and shoes designed to torture."

"Well, good. Because you'd be awfully lonely here by yourself."

"What are you talking about? I was never lonely in Georgia. I always had you."

Stacey shrugged and her eyes darted away. "I wasn't kidding the other day. I really am done with Dylan. I'm working on a fresh start for Shane and me. Not sure what that'll look like, but I have some ideas."

JESSICA ROSENBERG

"Well, you know, I know of this quaint little town near Boston where the people are nice..." She laughed at my wide-eyed, innocent expression.

"You think? I hear the people are a little on the woo-woo side." She cocked her head.

"Eh, most of the locals are cool. Plus, I have it on good authority that there's an amazing bakery in this town."

She giggled. "Oh, yeah? I do love a good croissant. But is the coffee any good?"

"So good," I said, with a laugh. "Goes really well with the pastries. The baker's business partner makes it, and she has a way with the machine."

"Business partner? What exactly happened yesterday? Are you going to tell me, or do I have to live with this unbearable suspense forever?"

Before I could even figure out where to start, the jingle of the door interrupted us. To my absolute shock, Margie was standing in the doorway looking suspiciously contrite.

"Hold on," I murmured to Stacey. "Hello, Margie. I wasn't expecting to see you today." *Or anytime soon*, I murmured to myself. "Did you forget something yesterday?" I glanced around the bakery knowing full well I'd already cleaned the place twice since the end of our "party" and she hadn't left anything behind.

"No, the opposite." She hesitated in the doorway. I glanced at my phone and raised my eyebrows. Stacey frowned at me and shook her head violently, so I left the video call on and propped the phone up against my mug.

Wariness made my voice shake. "Please, come in," I said, as welcomingly as I could, ignoring the little flutter of anxiety in my belly. She was the most powerful woman in town, and she had spilled a secret she had intended to take to her grave because I had slipped her a magical Mickey. Being nervous that we were now facing off, alone in my bakery, wasn't paranoia.

"Uh, can I get you anything? Coffee?" I couldn't help myself.

Margie waved off my offer with a scowl. "You won't catch me putting anything from here in my mouth ever again." She threw a disgusted look at the empty display case and sniffed.

"Suit yourself! What can I do for you?"

Margie slipped a bright patchwork tote bag off her shoulder and reached into it. My heart stuttered. Could it be? With no fanfare, she pulled out the grimoire and shoved it at me. The instant it touched my hands, something deep inside me shifted and settled. The worn leather was warmer than I'd expected, and I could feel the pulsing I'd felt in the kitchen and in her library. It echoed the beating of my heart.

I cradled the grimoire against my chest and sighed. To my rational brain, feeling like the book was finally home was utterly absurd. It was a book. A nice one. Covered in ornately molded leather, but it was still just a book. Yet in my soul, I knew it was so much more than a bunch of paper bound in leather.

All this time, I'd told myself I was looking for Bea's grimoire because it was wrong for something so important to her to be lost. Now, I realized I'd been looking for it for myself. It was going to help me connect to my roots, but most importantly, it was going to help me figure out what I was and where I fit into the magical world.

EPILOGUE

I walked into my room, a hot mug of chamomile tea in my hand, intent on sitting down in the armchair the house had gifted me to finally enjoy a hard-earned moment of peace and quiet.

After setting the tea carefully on the side table, I wandered to the bookshelf, running my hands over the books I had stashed there, waiting for something to catch my attention. My eyes glided over a well-loved series and kept right on gliding when none of my old friends called to me. They came to rest on a stack of baking magazines I kept meaning to read, but even the thought of pouring myself a bubble bath and reading about brioche and puff pastry didn't hold the usual appeal.

I stopped ignoring the tug deep in my heart and finally turned my attention to the grimoire sitting on the same table as my tea. I'd put it on the shelf a few times, but whenever I came back into the room, I found it on the table, basking in the sun. If that's where it wanted to be, far be it for me to try to dissuade it. Why hadn't it transported itself back from Margie's? Food for thought for another day.

The ancient leather, intricately decorated with swirls and whorls that shifted when I tried to focus on them, looked right at home on the little table despite being a relic far out of time and place. My World's Best Baker mug didn't even look out of place next to it.

I settled myself in the armchair and forced myself to take a calming swig of tea before pulling the book to me. A little pulse of heat warmed my hand when my fingers touched the leather, making my heart lurch. I left my hand there for a moment before lifting the cover of the grimoire.

A handwritten list of names with dates next to them ran down the first page, giving the book an old-school family Bible feel. I ran my finger down the list and tried to decipher some of the older names. The first one astoundingly only contained three numbers in the year. I skipped past the harder to read names and let my eyes drift over the more recent ones.

Before I reached the end of the list, a bright light pulsed near the bottom of the page. As I watched, my name appeared, then Aurie's, one letter at a time, in flowing script as though someone invisible was writing it. The letters flashed once and settled onto the page. I ran my finger over the letters, but they felt exactly like the letters of all the other names on the page. If I hadn't seen it happen, I would have assumed our names had been there the whole time.

I took a tremulous breath and blinked. I'd seen magic performed, but this was a whole new ball game.

Hands shaking, I turned the page and started reading. The first few pages were covered in a script I could barely decipher. The spelling seemed more phonetic than anything else and I struggled to find words I even recognized. I skipped to the next section and then past a few others that were equally hard to read.

As I flipped through the book, the ink started to look less faded and the words more recognizable, but I could still only make out a few things here and there. Some made me laugh out loud, like the recommendation to suck on a rusty nail to ease a sore throat, because ew, and just no. Others made me nod in agreement, like the note about how a steady diet of raw carrots could help improve night vision.

I started flipping through the thick velum pages. A few entries looked intriguing, and I was about to read one that started "*This morning Mistress Grady came by to teach me the art of picking herbs at the right time of day,"* when suddenly the pages of the grimoire started flipping forward on their own, faster and faster, becoming a blur of black and white until they stopped, falling open to a page near the end.

My name leapt out at me from the top of the page and my breath caught in my throat.

My dearest Cassandra,

Welcome to your life as a Blackwell witch. I'd tell you how upsetting it is to me that I cannot deliver these words in person or be there to guide you as you come into your powers, but that would do neither of us any good. What's done is done and there's nothing to be gained from lamenting the past.

As I am sure the lawyers have informed you, the house and bakery are yours to do with as you will, but it is my deepest hope that you will choose to stay here and make a life for yourself and your child. Portney is a wonderful place to live, as I'm sure you will discover.

If I had my druthers, you would already be an accomplished witch safely ensconced in our community, but a promise is a promise, and I swore to your father that as long as I lived, I would not intervene in your life. Silly boy never could think things through to their logical conclusions and never made me promise that I wouldn't meddle after I passed. His loss, your gain, my child. Ours is a rich legacy; it would have been a shame for it to end with me.

Welcome home, Cassandra. This place has been waiting for you for a long time.

May the light guide you and keep you whole,

Yours Always,

A Note from the Author

Dear Reader,

I hope that you enjoyed getting to know Cassie, Aurie, Crystal, Hattie, Juliette and everyone else as much as I enjoyed writing their tale. They're waiting for you in book 2, <u>Bread, Coffee, Magic</u> and book 3, <u>Bitter, Sweet, Magic</u>.

This story was born during the dark days of 2020 when reading wasn't offering as much escape from reality as I craved. At that time, Paranormal Women's Fiction was a genre on the verge of exploding and, as I blew through the original series written by the PWF Fab 13*, I realized I wanted to be writing my own stories about gutsy women on the cusp of the second half of their lives.

The rest, as they say, is history. I wrote this book, then a book about a woman who accidentally becomes a wolf shifter, then the second and third books in this series. Somewhere along the way, I became determined to share this book with other Paranormal Women's Fiction lovers like you.

This is the part where I throw myself on your mercy and beg for your help.

An indie author's success rests heavily on reviews. It will only take you a few minutes to give this book a star rating and/or write a short review and you will make a world of difference in the success of this series.

Thank you in advance for your support.
With endless gratitude and appreciation,

Jessica Rosenberg

P.S. Did Cassie's baking make you hungry? Get a small sampling of her recipes by **signing up for my newsletter** by visiting blueoctopuspress.com or using your smart phone camera to scan the QR code and following the link. As a bonus, signing up means you'll never miss updates about upcoming releases!

* Paranormal Women's Fiction is a genre started by 13 fabulous paranormal fiction authors who were tired of reading and writing about 20 something heroines facing down magical creatures and wanted to write characters a little closer to home. Read more about the original series and authors at paranormalwomensfiction.com.

About The Author

Jessica Rosenberg is an emerging author of cozy paranormal and fantasy fiction. She writes the books she wishes were already written from her home office on the Central Coast of California where she's closely supervised by Axl, the office cat, and Dottie and Sorella, the family dogs. When she's not at her desk, she can be found on the beach looking for sea glass and other treasures.

Made in the USA
Monee, IL
25 April 2024

57502918R00208